PRIEST

SIERRA SIMONE

Cover by Date Book Designs 2015
Interior formatting by Caitlin Greer

To the Dirty Laundry girls and the Literary Gossip posse—
I can't tell which one of us is the bad influence on the other. Let's never change.

And to Laurelin, for all those late-night theology sessions and the Sunday morning sermon trading. We're in sync. Jinx again.

Content Note

This book contains mentions of systemic sex abuse and a sister's death by suicide.

AUTHOR'S NOTE:

I spent the majority of my life in the Catholic faith, and while I'm no longer Catholic, I still have the utmost affection and respect for the Catholic Church. While the town of Weston is real (and delightful), St. Margaret's and Father Bell are inventions of my imagination and entirely fictional. That being said, this novel is about a Catholic priest falling in love. There is sex, more sex, and definitely some blasphemy. (The fun kind.)

You've been warned.

PROLOGUE

There are many rules a priest can't break.

A priest cannot marry. A priest cannot abandon his flock. A priest cannot harm the sacred trust his parish has put in him.

Rules that seem obvious. Rules that I remember as I knot my cincture. Rules that I vow to live by as I pull on my chasuble and adjust my stole.

I've always been good at following rules.

Until she came.

My name is Tyler Anselm Bell. I'm twenty-nine years old. I have a bachelor's degree in classical languages and a Master of Divinity degree. I've been at my parish since I was ordained three years back, and I love it here.

Several months ago, I broke my vow of celibacy on the altar of my own church, and God help me, I would do it again.

I am a priest and this is my confession.

CHAPTER ONE

It's no secret that reconciliation is the least popular sacrament. I had many theories as to why: pride, inconvenience, loss of spiritual autonomy. But my prevailing theory at the moment was this fucking booth.

I hated it from the moment I saw it, something old-fashioned and hulking from the dark days before Vatican II. Growing up, my church in Kansas City had a reconciliation *room*, clean and bright and tasteful, with comfortable chairs and a tall window overlooking the parish garden.

This booth was the antithesis to that room—constrained and formal, made of dark wood and unnecessarily ornate molding. I'm not a claustrophobic man, but this booth could turn me into one. I folded my hands and thanked God for the success of our latest fundraiser. Ten thousand more dollars, and we would be able to renovate St. Margaret's of Weston, Missouri into something resembling a modern church. No more fake wood paneling in the foyer. No more red carpet—admittedly good for hiding wine stains—but terrible for the atmosphere. There would be windows and light and modernity. I'd been assigned to this parish because of its painful past…and my own. Moving past that would take more than a facelift for the building, but I wanted to show my parishioners that the church was able to change. To grow. To move into the future.

"Do I have any penance, Father?"

I had drifted. One of my flaws, I'll admit. One I prayed daily to change (when I remembered to).

"I don't think that's necessary," I said. Though I couldn't see much through the decorative screen, I had known my penitent the moment he stepped in the booth. Rowan Murphy, middle-aged math teacher and police scanner enthusiast. He was my only reliable penitent throughout the month, and his sins ranged from envy (the principal gave the other math teacher tenure) to impure thoughts (the receptionist at the gym in Platte City). While I knew some clergy still followed the old rules for penance, I wasn't the "say two Hail Marys and call me in the morning" type. Rowan's sins came from his restlessness, his stagnation, and no amount of Rosary-clutching would change anything if he didn't address the root cause.

I know, because I've been there.

And aside from that, I really liked Rowan. He was

funny, in a sly, unexpected way, and he was the type of guy who would invite hitchhikers to sleep on his couch and then make sure they left the next morning with a backpack full of food and a new blanket. I wanted to see him happy and settled. I wanted to see him funnel all those great things into building a more fulfilling life.

"No penance, but I do have a small assignment," I said. "It's to think about your life. You have strong faith but no direction. Other than the Church, what gives you passion in life? Why do you get out of bed in the morning? What gives your daily activities and thoughts meaning?"

Rowan didn't answer, but I could hear him breathing. Thinking.

Final prayers and a final blessing, and Rowan was gone, heading back to the school for the rest of his afternoon. And if his lunch break was almost over, then so were my reconciliation hours. I checked my phone to be sure, then pushed against the door, dropping my hand when I heard the booth open next to me. Someone settled in, and I sat back, masking my sigh. I had a rare free afternoon today, and I had been looking forward to it. No one besides Rowan ever came to reconciliation. No one. And the one day I had been looking forward to skating out early, to taking advantage of the perfect weather...

Focus, I ordered myself.

Someone cleared their throat. A woman.

"I, uh. I've never done this before." Her voice was low

and beguiling, the aural rendering of moonlight.

"Ah." I smiled. "A newbie."

That earned me a small laugh. "Yes, I guess I am. I've only ever seen this in the movies. Is this where I say, 'Forgive me Father, for I have sinned'?"

"Close. First, we make the sign of the cross. *In the name of the Father, the Son, and the Holy Spirit...*" I could hear her echoing the words with me. "Now you tell me how long it's been since your last confession, which was—"

"Never," she finished for me. She sounded young, but not too young. My age, if not a little younger. And her voice carried the accent-less rush of the city, not the leisurely twang I sometimes heard out here in rural Missouri. "I, um. I saw the church while I was at the winery across the street. And I wanted to—well, I have some things that are bothering me. I've never been particularly religious, but I thought maybe..." She trailed off for a minute and then abruptly inhaled. "This was stupid. I should go." I heard her stand.

"Stop," I said and then was shocked at myself. I never gave orders like that. Well, not anymore.

Focus.

She sat, and I could hear her fidgeting with her purse.

"You aren't stupid," I said, my voice gentler. "This isn't a contract. This isn't you promising to come to Mass every week for the rest of your life. This is a moment that you can be heard. By me...by God...maybe even by yourself. You came in here because you were looking for that moment, and I can give it to you. So please. Stay."

She let out a long breath. "I just…the things that are weighing on me, I don't know if I should tell them to anyone. Much less to you."

"Because I'm a man? Would you feel more comfortable talking to a female lay minister before you talked to me?"

"No, not because you're a man." I heard the smile in her voice. "Because you're a priest."

I decided to guess. "Are the things weighing on you of a carnal nature?"

"Carnal." She laughed, and it was breathy, rich music. I suddenly found myself wondering what she looked like—whether she was fair or tanned, whether she was curvy or slender, whether her lips were delicate or full.

No. I needed to focus. And not on the way her voice made me suddenly feel much more man than priest.

"Carnal," she repeated. "That sounds like such a euphemism."

"You can be as general as you would like to be. This is not meant to make you uncomfortable."

"The screen helps," she admitted. "It's easier to not see you, with, you know, the robes and stuff while I'm talking."

Now I laughed. "We don't wear the robes all the time, you know."

"Oh. Well, there goes my mental image. What are you wearing, then?"

"A long-sleeved black shirt with a white collar. You know the kind. The kind you see on TV. And jeans."

"*Jeans*?"

"Is that so shocking?"

I heard her lean against the side of the booth. "A little. It's like you're a real person."

"Only on weekdays, between the hours of nine and five."

"Good. I'm glad they don't put you in a crisper between Sundays or something."

"They tried that. Too much condensation." I paused. "And if it helps, I normally wear slacks."

"That seems significantly more priest-like." There was a long silence. "What if…do you ever have people who have done really bad things?"

I considered my answer carefully. "We're all sinners in the eyes of God. Even me. The point is not to make you feel guilt or categorize the magnitude of your sin, but to—"

"Don't give me that seminary horseshit," she said sharply. "I'm asking you a real question. I did something bad. Really bad. And I don't know what happens next."

Her voice cracked on the last word, and for the first time since I'd been ordained, I felt the urge to go to the other side of the booth and pull the penitent into my arms. Which would have been possible in a more modern reconciliation room but would have probably been alarming and awkward in the Ancient Booth of Death.

But in her voice—there was real pain and uncertainty and confusion. And I wanted to make it better for her.

"I need to know that everything will be okay," she continued quietly. "That I will be able to live with myself."

A sharp tug in my chest. How often had I whispered those same words to the ceiling in the rectory, lying awake in bed, consumed with thoughts of what my life could have been? *I need to know that everything will be okay.*

Didn't we all? Wasn't that the unspoken cry of our broken souls?

When I spoke again, I didn't bother with any of the normal reassurances or spiritual platitudes. Instead I said honestly, "I don't know if everything will be okay. It may not be. You may think you are at the lowest point now and then look up one day and see that it's gotten so much worse." I looked down at my hands, the hands that had pulled my oldest sister from a rope after she hung herself in my parents' garage. "You may not ever be able to get out of bed in the morning with that security. That moment of okay may never come. All you can do is try to find a new balance, a new starting point. Find whatever love is left in your life and hold on to it tightly. And one day, things will have gotten less gray, less dull. One day, you might find that you have a life again. A life that makes you happy."

I could hear her breathing, short and deep, like she was trying not to cry.

"I—thank you," she said. "Thank you."

There was no doubt that she was crying now. I could hear her pulling the Kleenexes from the box put inside the booth for just that purpose. I could catch only the faintest suggestions of movement through the screen, what looked like glossy dark hair and what could have been the pale white of her face.

A really base and awful part of me wanted to hear her confession still, not so I could give her more specific counseling and assurance, but so that I could know exactly what carnal things this girl had to apologize for. I wanted to hear her whisper those things in her breathy voice, I wanted to take her into my arms and kiss away every single tear.

God, I wanted to touch her.

What the fuck was wrong with me? I hadn't wanted a woman with this kind of intensity for three years. And I hadn't even seen her face. I didn't even know her name.

"I should go now," she said, echoing her earlier words. "Thank you for what you said. It was…it was unnervingly accurate. Thank you."

"Wait—" I said, but the door to the booth swung open and she was gone.

I thought about my mystery penitent all day. I thought about her as I prepared my homily for Sunday's Mass. I thought about her as I ran the men's Bible study and as I prayed my nightly prayers. I thought about that glimpse of dark hair, that throaty voice. Something about her…what was it? It's not like I'd been a corpse since taking the robe—I was still very much a man. A man who'd liked fucking a lot before he'd heard the call.

And I still noticed women, certainly, but I had become quite adept at steering my thoughts away from the sexual. Celibacy had become a controversial tenant of the priesthood these last few years, but I still abided carefully by it. Especially in light of what had happened to my sister. And what had happened to this parish before I came.

It was paramount that I was the apex of restraint. That I be the kind of priest who inspired trust. And that involved me being incredibly circumspect both publicly and privately when it came to sexuality.

So even though her husky laugh echoed in my ears the rest of the day, I firmly and deliberately tamped down the memory of her voice and went on with my duties, the only exception being that I prayed an extra rosary or two for that woman, thinking of her plea. *I need to know that everything will be okay.*

I hoped that wherever she was, God was with her, comforting her, just as he'd comforted me so many times.

I fell asleep with the rosary beads clenched in my fist, as if they were an amulet to ward off unwanted thoughts.

In my small, aging parish, there are usually one or two

funerals a month, four or five weddings a year, Mass almost every day, and on Sundays more than once. Three days a week, I lead Bible studies, one night a week I assist with the youth group, and every day save for Thursday, I hold office hours for parishioners to visit. I also run several miles each morning and force myself to read fifty pages of something not related to the church or religion whatsoever.

Oh, and I spend a lot of time on *The Walking Dead* Reddit. Too much time. Last night I stayed up until two a.m. arguing with some neckbeard about whether or not you could kill a zombie with another zombie's spinal column.

Which you can't, obviously, given the rate of bone decay among the walkers.

The point is, for being a holy man in a sleepy bed-and-breakfast town in the Midwest, I am fairly busy, so I can be forgiven for being surprised that next week when the woman returned to my confessional.

Rowan had just left, and I was also getting ready to stand and leave when I heard the other door open and someone slide into the booth. I thought maybe it was Rowan again—it wouldn't have been the first time he'd doubled back because he'd remembered some new menial sin that he'd forgotten to tell me about.

But no. It was that husky, knowing voice, the voice that had inspired my extra rosaries last week.

"It's me again," the woman said, with a nervous laugh. "Um, the non-Catholic?"

My words came out deeper than I'd meant them to, more clipped. A tone I hadn't taken with a woman in a long time. "I remember you."

"Oh," she said. She sounded a little surprised, as if she hadn't actually expected me to remember her. "Good. I guess."

She shifted a bit, and through the screen I saw hints of the woman behind—dark hair, white skin, a flash of red lipstick.

I shifted a bit too, unconsciously, my body suddenly aware of everything. The custom-tailored slacks (a gift from my businessmen brothers), the hard wood of the bench, the collar that all of a sudden was too tight, much too tight.

"You're Father Bell, right?" she asked.

"That's me."

"I saw your picture on the website. After last week, I thought maybe it would be easier if I knew what your name was and what you looked like. You know, more like I was talking to a person and not to a wall."

"And is it easier?"

She hesitated. "Not really." But she didn't elaborate and I didn't press, mostly because I was trying to coach myself away from the host of implausible desires that crowded my mind.

No, you can't ask her name.

No, you can't go open the door to see what she looks like.

No, you can't request that she only tell you about her carnal sins.

"Are you ready to begin?" I asked, trying to redirect my thoughts back to the matter at hand, the confession.

Follow the script, Tyler.

"Yes," she whispered. "Yes, I'm ready."

CHAPTER TWO

POPPY

So I have this job. Had this job, I should say, because I do something different now, but up until a month ago, I worked in a place that could be considered...sinful. I think that's the right word, although I never felt sinful working there. You'd think that would be why I'm here—and in a way it is—but it's more that I feel like I should be confessing it to someone because I *don't* feel like I should confess it. Does that make any sense? Like I *should* feel awful about what I've done and how I've earned my money, but I don't feel awful in the least, and I know that's wrong somehow.

Also, I'm not a prostitute, if that's what you're wondering.

You know what else I should feel guilty about?

The fact that I've wasted everyone's time and money. My parents in particular, but even you, this person I don't know, I'm detaining you and making you listen to all of my fucked-up-ery and thereby wasting your time and your church's money. See? I'm a wreck, wherever I go.

Part of the problem is that there's this slice of myself that has always been there with me, or maybe it's not a slice, but a layer, like a ring of a tree. And wherever I go and whatever I do, it's there. And it didn't fit into my old life in Newport, and then it didn't fit into my new life in Kansas City, and now I realize it doesn't fit anywhere, so what does that mean? Does that mean that I don't fit in anywhere? That I'm destined to be alone and detestable because I carry this demon on my back?

The funny thing is that I feel like there's this other life, this shadow life I've been offered, where that demon can run free and I can let that ring, that layer, consume me. But the price is the rest of me. It's like the universe–or God–is saying that I can have it my way, but at the cost of my self-respect and my independence and this vision of the person I want to be. But then what's the cost of this way? I run away to a small town and spend my days working a job I don't care about and then spend my nights alone? I have my self-respect, I have good deeds, but let me tell you, Father, good deeds don't warm your bed at night, and I'm filled with this awful kind of despair because I can't have both and I *want* both.

I want a good life, *and* I want passion and romance. But I was raised to see one as a waste and the other as distasteful, and no matter how hard I try, I can't stop feeling like "Poppy Danforth" has become synonymous with waste and distaste, even though I've done everything I possibly can to escape that feeling…

"Maybe we should continue this next week."

She'd been quiet for a long time after her last sentence, her breathing shaky. I didn't need to see inside her booth to know that she was barely holding it together, and if we were in a *modern* reconciliation room, I would have been able to take her hand or touch her shoulder or *something*. But here, I could extend no comfort other than my words, and I sensed that she was past absorbing words right now.

"Oh. Okay. Did I—did I take up too much time? I'm sorry, I'm not really used to the rules."

"Not at all," I said softly. "But I think it's good to start small, don't you?"

"Yes," she murmured. I could hear her gathering her things and opening the door as she spoke. "Yes, I suppose you're right. So…there's no penance or anything that I should do? When I googled *confession* last week, it said that sometimes there is penance, like saying a Hail Mary or something."

Debating with myself, I also stepped out of the booth, thinking it would be easier to explain penance and contrition to her face rather than through that stupid screen, and then I froze.

Her voice was sexy. Her laugh was even sexier. But neither held a candle to *her*.

She had long dark hair, almost black, and pale, pale skin, highlighted by the bright red lipstick she wore. Her face was delicate, fine cheekbones and large eyes, the kind of face that peered out of fashion magazine covers. But it was her mouth that drew me in, lush lips that were slightly parted, letting me see that her two front teeth were ever so slightly larger than the rest, an imperfection that for some reason made her all the sexier.

And before I could stop myself, I thought, *I want my dick in that mouth.*

I want that mouth crying my name.

I want—

I looked toward the front of the church, toward the crucifix.

Help me, I prayed silently. *Is this some sort of test?*

"Father Bell?" she prompted.

I drew in a breath and sent another quick prayer that she wouldn't notice that I was transfixed by her mouth…or that the flat-fronted wool slacks I wore were suddenly growing a little too tight.

"There's no need for penance right now. In fact, I think coming back here to talk is a small act of contrition in and of itself, don't you?"

A small smile quirked her mouth, and I wanted to kiss that smile until she was pressing herself against me and begging me to take her.

Holy shit, Tyler. What the fuck?

I said a mental Hail Mary of my own while she adjusted the strap of her purse on her shoulder. "So maybe I'll see you next week?"

Crap. Could I actually do this again in seven days? But then I thought of her words, so full of pain and bleak confusion, and I once again felt the urge to comfort her. Give her some kind of peace, a flame of hope and vibrancy that she could take with her and nourish into a new, full life for herself.

"Of course. I'm looking forward to it, Poppy." I hadn't meant to say her name, but there it was and when I said it, I said it in *that* voice, the one I didn't use anymore, the one that used to have women dropping to their knees and reaching for my belt without me having to do so much as say *please*.

And her reaction sent a jolt straight to my dick. Her eyes widened, pupils dilating, and her pulse leapt in her throat. Not only was my body having an insanely unprecedented response to hers, but she was just as affected by me as I was by her.

And somehow that made everything so much worse, because now it was only the thin line of my self-control that kept me from bending her over a pew and spanking that creamy white ass for making me hard when I didn't want to be, for making me think about her naughty mouth when I should be thinking about her eternal soul.

I cleared my throat, three years of unflagging discipline the only thing that kept my voice even. "And just so you know…"

"Y-yes?" she asked, biting into that full lower lip.

"You don't have to drive up from Kansas City just to come here for confession. I'm sure any priest there would be happy to hear you. My own confessor, Father Brady, is really good, and he's based in downtown Kansas City."

She tilted her head ever so slightly, like a bird. "But I don't live in Kansas City anymore. I live here, in Weston."

Well, shit.

Tuesdays. Fuck Tuesdays.

I said early morning Mass to a mostly empty sanctuary—two hat-wearing grandmothers and Rowan—and then I went for my run, mentally cataloging all the things I wanted to get done today, including putting together an informational packet for our youth group trip next spring and writing my homily for this week.

Weston is a town of river bluffs, a topography of fields sloping towards the Missouri River, punctuated with punishingly steep hills. Runs here are brutal and vicious and clarifying. After the first six miles, I was covered in sweat and breathing hard, turning up my music so that Britney's voice drowned out everything else.

I rounded the corner onto the main drag through town, the sidewalks mostly clear of people browsing antiques and art shops since it was a weekday. I only had to dodge one elderly-looking couple as I forced myself up the steep road, my thigh and calf muscles screaming. Sweat dripped down my neck and shoulders and back, my hair was soaked, each breath felt like punishment, and the morning sun made sure that I was greeted by waves of August heat rolling off the asphalt.

I loved it.

Everything else bled away—the upcoming renovation to the church, the homilies I needed to write, Poppy Danforth.

Especially Poppy Danforth. Especially her and the knowledge that the mere act of thinking about her made me stiff.

I hated myself a little for what had happened yesterday. She was clearly a well-educated, intelligent, and interesting woman, and she had come to me, despite not being Catholic, for words of help. And instead of seeing her as a lamb in need of guidance, I had been unable to fixate on anything other than her mouth while we were talking.

I was a priest. I was sworn to God not to know another's body while I lived—not even to know my own body, if we were getting technical about it. It wasn't okay to think the kind of thoughts I had about Poppy.

I was supposed to be a shepherd of the flock, not the wolf.

Not the wolf who had woken up this morning grinding his hips into the mattress because he'd had a very intense dream with Poppy and her carnal sins in a starring role.

Guilt wormed through me at the memory.

I'm going to hell, I thought. *There's no way I'm not going to hell.*

Because as guilty as I felt, I didn't know if I could control myself if I saw her again.

No, that wasn't quite right. I knew that I could—but I didn't want to. I didn't even want to give up the right to carry her voice and body and stories in my mind.

Which was a problem. As I came up on the final mile of my run, I wondered what I would tell a parishioner who was in the same situation. What I would offer as my honest insight into what God would want.

Guilt is a sign from your conscience that you've strayed from the Lord.

Confess your sin to God openly and sincerely. Ask for forgiveness and the strength to overcome the temptation should it arise again.

And lastly, remove yourself from the temptation altogether.

I could see the church and the rectory, only a short distance away. I knew now what I would do. I would shower and then I would spend a long hour praying and asking for forgiveness.

And for strength. Yes, I would ask for that too.

And the next time Poppy came in, I would have to find a way to tell her that I couldn't be her confessor again. The thought made me depressed for some reason, but I'd been a priest long enough to know that sometimes the best decisions were the ones with the most short-term unhappiness.

I stopped at an intersection, waiting for the light to change, feeling lighter now that I had a plan to follow. This would be so much better; everything was going to be fine.

"Britney Spears, huh?"

That voice. Even though I'd only heard it twice, it had been seared onto my memory.

It was a mistake, but I turned anyway as I pulled out my earbuds.

She was running too, and by the looks of it, she'd run just as far as I had. She wore a sports bra and very, very short running shorts, that only *just* covered her perfect ass. Sweat dripped from her too, and she was absent the red lipstick, but her mouth looked even more amazing without it, and the only thing that saved me from staring hungrily at it was the fact that her toned thighs and flat stomach and perky tits were on such ready display.

Blood rushed to my groin.

She was still smiling at me, and I remembered that she had said something.

"Sorry, what?" My words came out harsh, breathless. I winced, but she didn't seem to care.

"I just didn't peg you for a Britney Spears fan," she said, pointing to where my iPhone was strapped to my bicep and clearly displaying the cover of *Oops…I Did It Again*. "Retro Britney too."

If I weren't already roasting from the run and the heat, I would have flushed. I reached for my phone and tried to subtly change the song.

She laughed. "It's okay. I'll just pretend I saw you listening to—what is it that men of God listen to when they run? Hymns? No, don't tell me. Chanting monks."

I took a step closer, and her eyes flicked across my shirtless torso, sweeping down to where my shorts hung low on my hips. When she met my eyes again, her smile had faded a little bit. And her nipples were hard little points in her running bra.

I closed my eyes for a minute, willing my swelling dick to settle down.

"Or maybe it's totally opposite, like Swedish death metal or something. No? Estonian death metal? Filipino death metal?"

I tried to think unsexy thoughts as I opened my eyes. I thought about my grandma, the threadbare carpet by the altar, the taste of boxed communion wine.

"You don't like me very much, do you?" she asked, and that brought me crashing back to the present. Was she insane? Did she think that my uncontrollable hard-ons around her were a sign of dislike?

"You were so nice the first time I came in. But I feel like I made you mad somehow." She glanced down at her feet, a move that only highlighted how long and thick her eyelashes were.

Her *eyelashes* made me hard. That was a new benchmark for me, I had to admit.

"You didn't make me mad," I said, relieved to hear that my voice sounded more like normal, in control and kind. "I'm so grateful that you found enough value in your experience to come back to the church." I was about to follow that up with my request that she find a new place to say her confessions, but she spoke before I could.

"I did find value in it, surprisingly. Actually, I'm glad I ran into you. I saw on the church's website that you have office hours just to talk, and I was wondering if I could visit sometime? Not for a confession necessarily—"

Thank God for that.

"—but, I don't know, I guess to talk about other things. I'm trying to start a new phase in my life, but I keep feeling like something is missing. Like the world I'm living in is flattened somehow, desaturated. And after I spoke to you both times, I felt...lighter. I wonder if religion is what I need—but I honestly don't know if it's something I want."

Her admission awakened the priestly instinct in me. I took a deep breath, telling her something I had told many people, but I still meant it every bit as much as the first time I'd said it. "I believe in God, Poppy, but I also believe that spirituality isn't for everybody. You may find what you're looking for in a profession you're passionate about, or in travel, or in a family, or in any other number of things. Or you may find that another religion fits you better. I don't want you to feel pressured to explore the Catholic Church for any reason other than genuine interest or curiosity."

"And what about a crazy hot priest? Is that a sound reason for exploring the Church?"

I must have looked horrified—mostly because her words were nipping at my strained self-control—and she laughed. The sound was almost stupidly bright and pleasant, the kind of laugh bred to echo across ballrooms or next to a pool in the Hamptons.

"Relax," she said. "I was joking. I mean, you *are* crazy hot, but it's not the reason I'm interested. At least"—she gave me another up and down look that made my skin feel like it was covered in flames—"it's not the only reason." And then the light changed, and she jogged away with a small wave.

I was so fucked.

CHAPTER THREE

I went straight home and took the coldest shower I could stand, staying under the water until my thoughts were clear and my erection finally, finally relented. Although, if recent events were any indication, it would return the moment I saw Poppy again.

Okay, so maybe I couldn't expunge this desire from myself, but I could exercise more self-control. No more fantasies. No more waking up to find that I'd fucked my mattress dreaming of her. And maybe talking to her would be exactly the thing I needed—I would see her as a person, a lost lamb seeking her God, and not just as sex on legs.

Perfect legs.

I pulled a pair of slacks over my boxer briefs and put on a fresh black shirt, rolling the long sleeves up to the elbows as I usually did. I didn't hesitate before I reached for the collar. It would be a much-needed reminder. A reminder to practice self-denial and also a reminder of *why* I practice self-denial in the first place.

I do it for my God.

I do it for my parish.

I do it for my sister.

And that was why Poppy Danforth was so upsetting. I wanted to be the epitome of sexual purity for my congregation. I wanted them to trust the Church again; I wanted to erase the marks made on God's name by awful men.

And I wanted some way to remember Lizzy without my heart shredding apart with guilt and regret and powerlessness.

You know what? I was making a big deal out of nothing. It was all going to be fine. I ran a hand through my hair, taking a deep breath. One woman, no matter how hot, was not going to unravel everything I held sacred about the priesthood. She was not going to destroy everything I'd worked so hard to create.

I don't always go home on my Thursdays off, even though my parents live less than an hour away, but I did this week, mentally and physically strained from avoiding Poppy during my morning runs and also from taking approximately twenty cold showers over the space of two days.

I just wanted to go someplace—without the collar—and play some video games and eat food that my mom had made. I wanted to have a beer (or six or seven) with Dad and listen to my teenage brother mope about whatever girl he was being "friend-zoned" by this month. Someplace where the Church and Poppy and the rest of my life was muffled and I could just relax.

Mom and Dad's didn't disappoint. My other two brothers were there as well—even though they all had places and lives of their own—drawn by Mom's cooking and that unquantifiable comfort that comes with being at home.

After dinner, Sean and Aiden whipped my ass at the latest *Call of Duty* while Ryan texted the latest girl on his phone, and the house still smelled like lasagna and garlic bread. A picture of Lizzy watched us all from above the television, a pretty girl forever memorialized in 2003 with side bangs and dyed-blonde hair and a wide smile that hid all the things we didn't know until it was too late.

I stared at that picture for a long time while Sean and Aiden chattered about their jobs—they're both in investments—and while Mom and Dad played Candy Crush in their side-by-side recliners.

I'm sorry, Lizzy. I'm sorry for everything.

Logically, I knew there's nothing I could have done back then, but logic didn't erase the memory of her pale, bluish lips or the blood vessels that had exploded in her eyes.

Of walking into the garage looking for flashlight

batteries and instead finding the cold body of my only sister.

Sean's low voice seeped into my grim reverie, and I gradually came back to the moment, listening to the squeaking of Dad's recliner and Sean's words.

"...invitation only," he said. "I've heard rumors of it for years, but it wasn't until I got the letter that I thought it was actually real."

"Are you going to go?" Aiden was speaking quietly too.

"Fuck yes, I'm going."

"Going where?" I asked.

"You wouldn't care, priest boy."

"Is it the invitation-only Chuck E. Cheese? I'm so proud of you."

Sean rolled his eyes, but Aiden leaned in. "Maybe Tyler should know about it. He probably needs to work off a little excess...energy."

"It's *invitation only*, dickhole," Sean said. "Which means he can't go."

"It's supposed to be like the world's best strip club," Aiden continued, unfazed by Sean's insult. "But no one knows what it's called or where it is, not until you're personally invited. Word is that they don't let you come until your annual clears a million a year."

"Then why is Sean getting invited?" I asked. Sean, although three years older than me, was still working his way up through his firm. He made a very healthy salary (fucking incredible, from my standpoint) but he was nowhere near a million dollars a year. Not yet.

"Because—douchenozzle—I know people. Being connected is a more reliable form of currency than a salary."

Aiden's voice was a little too loud when he spoke. "Especially if it gets you choice puss—"

"*Boys*," Dad said automatically, not looking up from his phone. "Your mother is here."

"Sorry, Mom," we said in unison.

She waved us off. Thirty-plus years of four boys had made her immune to pretty much everything.

Ryan sloped into the room, mumbling something to Dad about wanting the car keys, and Sean and Aiden leaned closer again.

"I'm going next week," Sean confided. "I'll tell you everything."

Aiden, younger than me by a couple years and still very much a junior in the business world, sighed. "I want to be you when I grow up."

"Better me than Mr. Celibacy over here. Tell me, Tyler, you got carpal tunnel in your right hand yet?"

I tossed a throw pillow at his head. "You volunteering to come help me out?"

Sean dodged the pillow easily. "Name the time, sugar. I bet I could put some of that anointing-of-the-sick oil to good use."

I groaned. "You're going to hell."

"Tyler!" Dad said. "No telling your brother he's going

to hell." He still didn't look up from his phone.

"What's the use of all those lonely nights if you can't condemn someone once in a while, eh?" Aiden asked, reaching for the remote.

"You know, Tinker Bell, maybe I *should* find a way to take you to the club. There's nothing wrong with looking at the menu, so long as you don't order anything, right?"

"Sean, I'm not going to a strip club with you. No matter how fancy it is."

"*Fine.* I guess you and your St. Augustine poster can spend next Friday night alone together. Again."

I threw another pillow at him.

The Business Brothers left around ten, driving back to their tie racks and home espresso machines, and Ryan was still out doing whatever thing he had needed the car so badly for. Dad was asleep in his recliner, and I was stretched out on the couch, watching Jimmy Fallon and thinking about what movie to pick for the middle school lock-in next month, when I heard the sink running in the kitchen.

I frowned. The Business Brothers and I (and a complaining Ryan) had done all the dishes after dinner expressly so that Mom wouldn't have to. But when I got up to see if I could help, I saw that she was scrubbing the stainless steel in savage circles, steam clouding around her.

"Mom?"

She turned and I could immediately see that she'd been crying. She gave me a quick smile and then shut the water off, swiping at her tears. "Sorry, hon. Just cleaning."

It was Lizzy. I knew it was. Whenever we were all together, the whole Bell brood, I could see that look in her eyes, the way she was picturing the table with one more setting, the sink with one more set of dirty dishes.

Lizzy's death had nearly killed me. But it *had* killed Mom. And every day after that, it was like we kept Mom artificially alive with hugs and jokes and visits now that we were older, but every now and again, you could see that a part of her had never fully healed, never really resurrected, and our church had been a huge part of that, first driving Lizzy to kill herself and then turning their backs on us when the story went public.

Sometimes I felt like I was fighting for the wrong side. But who would make it better if I didn't?

I pulled Mom into a hug, her face crumpling as I wrapped my arms around her. "She's with God now," I murmured, half priest, half son, some chimera of both. "God has her, I promise."

"I know," she sniffled. "I know. But sometimes I wonder…"

I knew what she wondered. I wondered it too, in my darkest hours, what signs I missed, what I should have noticed, all the times she seemed about to tell me something, but then sank into a fog of silence instead.

"I think there's no way we can't wonder," I said quietly. "But you don't have to feel this pain alone. I want to share it with you. I know Dad would too."

She nodded into my chest and we stayed like that a long time, swaying gently together, both of our thoughts twelve years away and in a cemetery down the road.

It wasn't until I was driving back home, listening to my usual cocktail of brooding hipster songs and Britney Spears, that I made the connection between Sean's club and Poppy's confession. She had mentioned a club, mentioned that most people would classify it as sinful. Could that be it?

Jealousy slithered inside of me, and I refused to acknowledge it, clenching my jaw as I maneuvered my truck onto the interstate. I didn't care that Sean would get to see this club, this place where Poppy had possibly exposed her body. No, I didn't.

And that jealousy had nothing to do with my sudden, out-of-the-blue decision to find her the next day and follow up on her request for a conversation during my office hours. It was because I was worried about her, I reassured myself. It was because I wanted to welcome her to our church and give her comfort and guidance, because I sensed that she was someone who was not easily lost, not easily broken, and for something to send her into a strange confession booth and bring her to tears...well, no one should have to bear those kinds of burdens alone.

Especially someone as sexy as Poppy.

Stop it.

It wasn't too hard to find Poppy again. In fact, I did literally nothing except jog past the open tobacco barn on my morning run and collide into her as she rounded the corner. She stumbled, and I managed to stop her fall by pinning her between my chest and my arm.

"Shit," I said, yanking the earbuds out of my ears. "I'm so sorry! Are you okay?"

She nodded, tilting her head up and giving me a small smile that gave me chills; it was so perfectly imperfect with her two front teeth peeking behind her lips and a sheen of sweat covering her face. At the same time, we both realized how we were standing, with my arms wrapped around her and her only in a sports bra and me without a shirt. I dropped my arms, immediately missing the way she felt there. Missed the way her tits pushed against my naked chest.

In the future: only sideways hugs, I told myself. I was already seeing another cold shower in my future.

She put her hand on my chest, casually, innocently, still giving me that small smile. "I would have fallen if it wasn't for you."

"If it wasn't for me, you wouldn't have been at risk of falling at all."

"And yet I still wouldn't change a thing." Her touch, her

words, that smile—was she *flirting*? But then her smile widened, and I saw that she was just teasing, in that safe, playful way that girls do with their gay friends. She saw me as safe, and why shouldn't she? I was a man of the cloth, after all, bound by God to be a caregiver of his flock. Of course, she would assume that she could tease me, touch me, without bothering my priestly composure. How could she know what her words and voice did to me? How could she know that her hand was currently searing its outline onto my chest?

Her hazel eyes flickered up to mine, green and brown pools of curiosity and intelligent energy, green and brown pools that reflected grief and confusion if you cared to look long enough. I recognized it because I had worn such a look for years after Lizzy's death, except in Poppy's case, I suspected that the person she was grieving—the person she'd lost—was herself.

Let me help this woman, I prayed silently. *Let me help her find her way.*

"I'm glad I saw you," I said, straightening up as her hand fell away from my skin. "You said earlier this week that you wanted to meet?"

She nodded enthusiastically. "I did. I mean, I do."

"How about my office in, say, half an hour?"

She gave me a mock salute. "See you there, Father."

I tried not to watch her run away, I really did, but I promise I only looked for a second, an infinitely long second, a second long enough to catalog the gleam of sweat and sunscreen on her toned shoulders, the taunting movements of her ass.

Definitely a cold shower then.

CHAPTER FOUR

Half an hour later, I was back in my uniform: black slacks, Armani belt (a hand-me-down from one of the Business Brothers), long-sleeved black shirt with the cuffs rolled up to the elbows. And my collar, of course. St. Augustine gazed austerely out over the office, reminding me that I was here to help Poppy, not to daydream about sports bras and running shorts. And I wanted to be here to help her. I remembered her soft crying in the confessional and my chest tightened.

I would help her if it killed me.

Poppy was one minute early, and the easy but precise way she walked through the door told me that she was accustomed to being prompt, took pleasure in it, was the kind of person who could never understand why other people weren't on time. Whereas three years of waking up at seven o'clock had still not transformed me into a morning person and more often than not, Mass started at 8:10 rather than 8:00.

"Hi," she said as I indicated a chair next to me. I'd chosen the two upholstered chairs in the corner of the office, hating to talk to people from behind my desk like I was a middle school principal. And with Poppy, I wanted to be able to soothe her, touch her if I needed, show her a more personal church experience than the Ancient Booth of Death.

She sank into the chair in this elegant, graceful way that was fucking mesmerizing…like watching a ballerina lace up her slippers or a geisha pour tea. She had on that igniting shade of lipstick again, bright red, and was in a pair of high-waisted shorts and a blouse that tied at the neck, looking more ready for a Saturday yachting trip than a meeting in my dingy office. But her hair was still wet and her cheeks still had that post-run flush, and I felt a small swell of possessive pride that I got to see this polished woman slightly unraveled, which was a bad impulse. I pushed it down.

"Thanks for meeting with me," she said, crossing her legs as she set down her purse. Which was not a purse but a sleek laptop bag, filled with strata of brightly colored folders. "I've been thinking a lot about seeking something like this out, but I've never been religious before, and part of me still kind of balks at the idea…"

"Don't think of it as being religious," I advised. "I'm not

here to convert you. Why don't we just talk? And maybe there will be some activities or groups here that match what you need."

"And if there's not? Will you refer me to the Methodists?"

"I would never," I said with mock gravity. "I always refer to the Lutherans first."

That earned me another smile.

"So how did you end up in Kansas City?"

She hesitated. "It's a long story."

I leaned back in the chair, making a show of settling in. "I've got the time."

"It's boring," she warned.

"My day is a praxis of liturgical laws that date from the Middle Ages. I can handle boring. Promise."

"Okay, well, I'm not sure where to start, so I guess I should start at the beginning?" Her gaze slid over to the wall of books as she worried her lower lip with her teeth, as if she were trying to decide what the beginning really was. "I'm not your typical runaway," she said after a minute. "I didn't sneak out of a window when I was sixteen or steal my father's car and drive to the nearest ocean. I was dutiful and obedient and my father's favorite child right up until I walked across the stage at Dartmouth and officially received my MBA. I looked at my parents, and I finally really realized what they saw when they looked at me—another asset, another folder in the portfolio.

"*There she is, our youngest,* I could picture them saying to the family next to them. *Graduated magna cum laude, you know, and only the best schools growing up. Spent the last three summers volunteering in Haiti. She was a shoo-in for dance at Juilliard, but of course she chose to pursue business instead, our level-headed girl.*"

"You volunteered in Haiti?" I interrupted.

She nodded. "At a charity called Maison de Naissance. It's a place for rural Haitian mothers to get free prenatal care, as well as a place for them to give birth. It's the only place besides the summer house in Marseille that my boarding school French has come in remotely useful."

Dartmouth. Marseille. Boarding school. I had sensed that Poppy was polished, had guessed from her mention of Newport that she had known privilege and wealth at some point in her life, but I could see now exactly how much privilege, how much wealth. I studied her face. There was a thriving confidence there, an old-fashioned bent toward etiquette and politeness, but there was also no pretentiousness, no elitism.

"Did you like working there?"

Her face lit up. "I did! It's a beautiful place, filled with beautiful people. I got to help deliver seven babies my last summer there. Two of them were twins...they were so tiny, and the midwife told me later that if the mom hadn't come to MN, she and the babies almost certainly would have died. The mother even let me help her pick out names for her sons." Her expression turned almost shy, and I realized that this was the first time she'd gotten to share this pure form of joy with anyone. "I miss it there."

I grinned at her. I couldn't help it, I just rarely saw anyone so excited by the experience of helping people in need.

"My family's idea of charity is hosting a political fundraiser," she said, matching my grin with a wry one of her own. "Or donating enough to a pet cause so that they can take a picture with a giant check. And then they'll step over homeless people in the city. It's embarrassing."

"It's common."

She shook her head vehemently. "It shouldn't be. I, at least, refuse to live like that."

Good for her. I refused as well, but I also had grown up in a household of religion, of volunteering. It had been easy for me; I didn't think this conviction had come easily to her. I wanted to stop her right then, hear more about her time in Haiti, introduce her to all the ways she could help people here at St. Margaret's. We *needed* people like her, people who cared, people who could volunteer and give their time and talents—not just their treasure. In fact, I almost blurted all this out. I almost fell to my knees and begged her to help us with the food pantry or the pancake breakfast that was so chronically short-staffed, because we needed her help, and (if I was being honest) I wanted her at everything, I wanted to see her everywhere.

But maybe that wasn't the best way to feel. I steered us back to her earlier and safer topic of conversation. "So you were at your graduation…"

"Graduation. Right. And I realized, looking at my parents, that I was everything they had wanted. That they had groomed me for. I was the whole package, the manicured, sleekly highlighted, expensively dressed package."

She was all those things. She was indeed the perfect package on the surface…but below it, I sensed she was so much more. Messy and passionate and raw and creative—a cyclone forced into an eggshell. Small wonder the shell had broken.

"I adorned the life that already had too many cars, too many rooms, too many luncheons and fundraiser galas. A life already filled with two other children who'd also graduated from Dartmouth and then proceeded to marry fellow rich people and have little rich babies. I was destined to work someplace with a glassed-in lobby and drive a Mercedes S-Class, at least until I got married, and then I would gradually scale back my work and scale up my involvement with charity, until, of course, I had the little rich babies to round out the family portraits." She looked down at her hands. "This probably sounds ridiculous. Like a modern Edith Wharton novel or something."

"It doesn't sound ridiculous at all," I assured her. "I know exactly the kind of people you're talking about." And

I really did—I wasn't just saying that. I'd grown up in a fairly nice neighborhood and—on a much smaller scale—the same attitudes had been at work. The families with their nice houses and their two point five children who were on the honor roll and also played varsity lacrosse, the families that made sure everyone else knew exactly how successful and delightfully American their healthy Midwestern offspring were.

"I rejected that entire reality," she confessed. "The Wharton life. I didn't want to do it. I *couldn't* do it."

Of course, she couldn't. She was so far above that life. Could she see that about herself? Could she sense it, even if she couldn't see it? Because I barely knew her, and even I knew that she was the kind of woman who couldn't live without meaning, powerful and real meaning, in her life. And she wouldn't have found it on the other side of that Dartmouth stage.

"I was heartbroken over Sterling, yes," she continued, still examining her hands, "but I was also heartbroken over my life...and it hadn't even happened yet. I took the fake diploma they give you before they send you the real one, walked off that stage and then right off campus, not staying for the requisite hat-throwing or the pictures or the too-expensive dinner that my parents would insist on. And then I went to my apartment, left a definitive voicemail on my father's phone, stuffed my things into my car and left. There would be no more internships for me. No more $10,000-a-plate fundraisers. No more dates with men who weren't Sterling. I left that life behind—along with all of Daddy's credit cards. I refused to touch my trust fund. I would stand on my own two feet or not at all."

"That was brave," I murmured. Who was this Sterling she kept mentioning? An ex-boyfriend? A former lover? He had to have been an idiot to let Poppy go, at any rate.

"Brave or foolish," she laughed. "I threw away a lifetime of education—expensive education. I assume my parents were devastated."

"You assume?"

She sighed. "I never spoke to them directly after I left. I still haven't. It's been three years, and I know they'd be furious..."

"You don't know that."

"You wouldn't understand," she said, her words chastising but her tone friendly. "You're a *priest*, for crying out loud. I bet your parents were ecstatic when you told them."

I looked down at my feet. "Actually, my mom cried when I told her, and my father didn't speak to me for six months. They didn't even come to my ordination." It was not a memory I liked reliving.

When I looked up at her, her red lips were pressed in a line. "That's awful. It sounds like something my parents would do."

"My sister..." I stopped and cleared my throat. I'd

talked about Lizzy countless times in homilies, in small groups, in counseling sessions. But somehow, explaining her death to Poppy was more intimate, more personal. "She was abused by our parish priest for years. We never knew, never suspected…"

Poppy put a hand over mine. The irony of *her* comforting *me* was keenly palpable, but at the same time, it felt nice. It felt good. There had been no one to comfort me when it had happened; we'd all been in our separate worlds of pain. There had been no one to just *listen*, like it mattered how I felt about it. Like it mattered that I *still* felt about it.

"She killed herself when she was nineteen," I went on, as if Poppy's touch had triggered a response to share that couldn't be stopped. "She left a note, with the names of other children he'd hurt. We were able to stop him, and he was put on trial and sentenced to ten years in prison."

I took a breath, pausing a moment, because it was impossible not to feel those twin dragons of rage and grief warring in my chest, heating my blood. I felt a fury so deep whenever I thought of that man that I honestly believed myself capable of murder, and no matter how many times I prayed for this hatred to be lifted from me, no matter how many times I forced myself to repeat *I forgive you I forgive you* as I pictured his face, it never truly went away, this anger. This pain.

Finally mastering myself again, I went on. "The other families in the parish—I don't know if they didn't want to believe it or were humiliated that they'd trusted him, but whatever it was, they were furious with us for calling for his arrest, furious with Lizzy for being the victim, for having the gall to leave a note outlining in sick detail what had happened and who else it was happening to. The deacons tried to block her having a Catholic funeral and burial, and even the new priest ignored us. The whole family stopped going to church then—my dad and brothers stopped believing in God altogether. Only my mom still believes, but she will never go back. Aside from visiting me up here, she hasn't been inside a church since Lizzy's funeral."

"But you have," Poppy pointed out. "You still believe."

Her hand remained on mine, warm in the drafty air-conditioning of the office. "I didn't for a long time," I admitted.

We sat in silence for a while, jostling shoulders with dead girls and disapproving parents and tragedies that lingered like the smell of old leaves in a forest. "So," she said after a while, "I suppose you do know what it's like to face your parents' disapproval."

I managed a smile, trying to keep it from faltering when she withdrew her hand. "What did you do after you left Dartmouth?" I asked, needing to talk about something else, anything other than Lizzy and those painful years after her death.

"Well," she said, shifting in her chair. "I did a lot. The

thing was that I was able to find tons of work on my own, work using my MBA, but how could I be sure that it wasn't my scores of fancy internships and my expensive degree they wanted and not to have a Danforth working in their office? After six months in a New York office, feeling like DANFORTH was tattooed across my forehead, I left, as abruptly as I'd left New Hampshire, and I drove until I didn't want to drive anymore. Which was how I ended up in Kansas City."

She took a breath. I waited.

"I never meant to end up at the club," she finally said, her voice going low. "I thought maybe I'd find a small nonprofit to work at or maybe I'd do something prosaic, like waiting tables. But I heard from a bartender that there was a club hidden somewhere in this city—private, exclusive, discreet. And they were looking for girls. Girls who looked expensive."

"Girls like you?"

Poppy wasn't offended. She laughed that throaty laugh again, the laugh that kindled a low heat in my belly every time I heard it. "Yes, girls like me. WASP-y girls. The kind that rich people like. And you know what? It was perfect. I got to dance—I hadn't danced anywhere other than a gala for so long. It was, all told, a fairly classy place. A mandatory $500 coat check. $750 for a table, $1000 for a private dance. No patron-initiated touching. A two-drink maximum. It catered to a very specific clientele, and so I found myself stripping for the same men who would have employed me, married me, donated to my pet charities, in another life. I loved it."

"You loved it?"

Filthy girl.

The thought came out of nowhere, unbidden but refusing to leave, whispering itself over and over again in my mind. *Dirty, filthy girl.*

She turned those hazel eyes back to me. "Is that wrong? Is that a sin? No, don't answer, I don't really want to know."

"Why did you like it?" I was asking merely out of a counselor's curiosity, of course. "If you don't mind me asking."

"Why would I mind? I offered to tell you, after all." She adjusted herself, the shorts exposing more of those firm legs. Dancer's legs, I now knew. "I liked how it felt. Having men watch me with hooded eyes, wanting me and only me—not my education or my pedigree or my family's connections. But even more than that, on this raw, primal level, I loved the way the men responded to my body. I loved that I made them hard."

I loved that I made them hard.

I nearly choked, my mind fracturing into twin minds—one determined to see this meeting through with grace and compassion and the other determined to let her know how hard she made *me*.

She was oblivious to my internal struggle. "I loved that

they would become almost wild with the need to touch me, so wild that they would offer me astounding sums of money to come home with them, to leave the club and become their mistress. But I never accepted. Even though many of them were handsome, even though I wasn't in a place where I could pretend money was no object. But something about it was antithetical to my very nature, and I couldn't imagine accepting any of those offers. Isn't that a ridiculous notion? A stripper insisting on preserving her virtue?"

She didn't seem to expect an answer and kept going. "The sad thing was that I was actually starved for sex while I was turning down all these offers. I'm sure you know the feeling, Father, like the slightest breeze is enough to send you over the edge, like your skin itself is combustible."

God, did I know that feeling. I was feeling it right now. I offered her a weak smile, which she returned.

"I was so combustible, Father Bell. I would get wet watching the men stroking themselves through their custom-tailored trousers. In the private rooms, I'd pull my thong to the side and let them watch as I brought myself off. They liked that, they liked it when I teased myself and rubbed myself and rode my hand until I shuddered and sighed."

I realized my hands were gripping the arms of the chair very hard now, and I tried to flush out all the images her words were conjuring, but I couldn't and she continued on, oblivious to my sudden discomfort, innocently secure in the mistaken notion that I was simply an input for information, an output for advice, and not a twenty-nine-year-old man.

"But it wasn't the same, getting myself off," she said. "I wanted to be *fucked*, fucked and used. I wanted to be filled with someone's dick, I wanted to have fingers in my mouth and in my cunt. In my ass." She took a breath.

I, on the other hand, couldn't breathe.

"What's that sin called? I know it has to be one. Is it just lust...or is it something worse? What kind of prayer should I pray for that one? And what if I don't feel bad about what I've done, the things I wanted to do? Even now, even after what happened last month, I still want it. I still feel lonely, I still want to be fucked. Which is confusing as hell because I have no idea about anything else I want out of my life."

Despite everything, I still wanted to respond to her last sentence, the ultimate motivation for her being here in this office. I wanted to take her hand and give her soft intimations of wisdom, but fuck, nothing about me was soft right now.

Her words.

Her fucking words.

It had been bad enough listening to her talk about working at that club, but then when she'd described touching herself, coaxing her pussy into orgasm, and I had imagined myself as one of those hungry businessmen watching it, offering everything in my wallet just to see that glistening cunt pulse with pleasure. I bet I could see it now if I wanted. I could stand her against the wall and yank down those shorts, kick her legs open so that she would be exposed to me…

There was no earthly way I could last another minute in this meeting.

God must have heard my unspoken prayer because her phone chimed then, a businesslike little tone, and she fished it out of her bag. "I'm so sorry," she mouthed as she answered the call.

I indicated that it was okay, trying to solve the bigger problem of how to stand up without revealing what her words had done to me.

She ended the call quickly. "I'm sorry," she apologized again. "Some work stuff has come up and—"

I held up a hand. "Don't worry about it. I have a parish meeting coming up soon anyway." That was a lie. The only meeting that was about to happen was between my hand and my dick. But probably not good form to tell a hopeful convert that. (I made a mental note to ask forgiveness for that lie as well as what I was about to do.)

"I, ah, I hope to see you soon though."

She gave me a gorgeous smile as she stood and grabbed her bag. "Me too. Bye, Father."

I couldn't even wait until I was sure she was out of the church. As soon as Poppy left, I got up and locked the door, taking the time only to move over to my desk so I could brace one hand on the surface as I fumbled with my belt.

There wasn't time to feel guilty or question my motives or for anything remotely resembling thought. I didn't even pull my slacks down any farther than it took to free my dick, and then I was jacking myself hard and fast, nothing in my mind but release.

I tried to think of someone else—anyone else—other than the woman who had come to me seeking God's forgiveness and reassurance. But my mind kept wandering back to her, imagining her at the club, but moving for me and only for me, pulling her thong aside to show me the thing I most wanted.

Christ help me.

I felt it building, taut electricity in my pelvis, and I was thrusting into my hand now, wishing I was fucking Poppy Danforth—her mouth or her cunt or her ass, I didn't care—and then I shot all over my desk, pulsing and spurting and imagining that each and every drop of myself was being spilled onto her white skin.

My hand stilled and my breathing slowed and reality came crashing back down. Here I was, dick in hand, cum all over my liturgical desk calendar, and a picture of St. Augustine looking at me reproachfully from the wall.

Shit.

Shit.

Numb, I zipped up my slacks and tore off the top sheet of the calendar and threw it away, the crinkling of the thick paper loud and almost accusatory, and fuck, what the hell had I done?

I sat in the chair and stared at St. Augustine.

"Don't pretend you don't know what it's like," I mumbled. I braced my elbows on the desk and ground the heels of my palms into my eyes.

Poppy Danforth was not going to go away. She lived here. She was going to come back, and I had no doubt that we'd only scratched the surface of her "carnal" confessions. And I would have to listen to it without getting aroused like a teenage boy. More than listen, I would have to respond with grace and empathy and compassion when all I would be able to think about was that mouth with those slightly imperfect teeth.

Stars were now dancing behind my eyelids, but I didn't move my hands. I didn't want to see this office right now or St. Augustine. I didn't want to see the newly ragged edges of my calendar or my newly filled wastebasket.

I wanted to pray in complete darkness. I wanted nothing in between my thoughts and God, in between this woman and my vocation. I wanted everything but my sin and these starbursts in my eyes stripped away.

I'm sorry, I prayed. *I'm so sorry.*

I was sorry that I'd betrayed the trust of one of God's flock. I was sorry that I'd betrayed the holiness of this place and this vocation by lusting after someone seeking solace and guidance. I was sorry that I hadn't even controlled my desire long enough to step into a cold shower or go for a run or any of the other tricks I'd learned over the past three years to stifle my urges.

Mostly…

Mostly, I'm sorry that I'm not sorry.

Dammit, I wasn't sorry at all.

CHAPTER FIVE

"And here I thought priests only drank communion wine."

My head snapped up to see Poppy standing in front of my table. I was at the little coffee shop across the street from the church, trying to make sense of the renovation budget and failing, basically accomplishing nothing except for checking *The Walking Dead* forums and putting a major dent in the shop's coffee supply.

I wanted to think of a witty reply to Poppy's greeting, but she was wearing another dress—a cream vintage affair with three-quarter sleeves and a skirt that brushed the middle of her thighs—and while it wasn't revealing or especially clingy, it did nothing to hide the perfect nip of her waist or the soft swells of her breasts. She was close enough that I could reach out and take her hips in my hands and pull her to me; close enough that I could grab her and ruck up her skirt and then bury my face in the heaven she kept under there.

(Plus there was the distracting fact that the last time I saw her, I'd ended up jizzing all over my desk.)

Luckily, she took the chair opposite me before I lost all control and broke my vows in front of everyone in the coffee shop.

"What are you working on?" she asked, nodding at the laptop.

I breathed a silent *thank you* to God that she hadn't noticed—or at least was willing to overlook—my lack of reply, and then another *thank you* for the very safe topic of budget spreadsheets.

"We are working to raise money to renovate the church," I told her. "And we've already had a few bids put in for the job, it's just a matter of allocating the funds in the right places, after we meet our initial goal."

"May I take a look?" she asked, canting her head toward the screen.

Before I'd even nodded, she'd already slid the laptop over to her side of the table and was scrolling through my sheets. A small smile creased the corners of her red mouth, making her look sexy and knowing and mischievous all at the same time.

"What did you go to school for, Father Bell?" she asked, still scrolling, pausing to click every few seconds.

"Before my mDiv? Classical languages. *Si vis amari, ama.*"

"I'm guessing they didn't teach you a lot about spreadsheet formulas in Latin class."

"I was usually busy in the other kind of sheets." I'd meant it as a lighthearted quip, but it came out lower than I'd intended, more intense. It came out like a warning.

No. It came out like a *promise.*

Her hazel eyes flashed up to mine, and she drew in a breath when she saw my face.

Fuck, what was wrong with me? Why couldn't I keep any interaction with her normal and well away from implications of sex? "You were saying about the formulas?"

"Um, right." Her eyes flicked back to the screen, and she swallowed. Her smooth throat moved with the motion, and I wanted that throat arched up in offering to me.

I wanted that whole body arched up in offering to me.

"Doesn't the church have real bookkeeping software?" she asked, stopping to fix a row of data that I'd accidentally cloned.

"Yes, our office manager does, but I don't know how to use it."

"So you can quote Seneca but you can't use Quicken."

"You knew that was Seneca?" I smiled despite myself. I didn't meet very many people who even knew who Seneca was, much less who were able to recognize a quote from one of his letters.

"My parents paid a lot of money when I was a girl to make sure I knew all sorts of useless things."

"You think it's useless? *Non scholae sed vitae.* 'We learn not for school, but for life.'"

"But *si vis amari, ama*? 'If you wish to be loved, love?' I tried that once. It didn't work out so well." Her voice was bitter.

I put my hand on her wrist. It was pure instinct, to comfort someone who was hurting, but I hadn't counted on the heat rippling up from her hand, on the way that my touch would send goose bumps crawling up her arm. I hadn't counted on how perfect her delicate wrist would feel with my fingers wrapped around it, as if God had made it for the sole purpose of me holding.

I should let go. I should apologize.

But I couldn't. And I couldn't stop myself from saying, "Maybe you loved the wrong person."

Because who wouldn't love this gorgeous creature? This over-educated, over-sexed woman who oozed intelligence and sensuality? This woman of white skin and red lips and a brain built for running financial empires?

She met my gaze again. "Maybe you're right," she whispered.

We stayed like that a moment, our eyes locked, my hand gripping her wrist, and then—*may I be forgiven*—I slowly ran a thumb along the underside of her wrist, a motion that nobody could see, but that she definitely felt because she took in a shuddering breath.

Fuck, she was so smooth, her skin so silky. I wanted to

kiss that part of her wrist, press my lips against her pulse point, right before I tied a rope around it. In fact, I got as far as lifting her wrist off the table before the hissing of the espresso machine brought me back to my senses.

What the fuck was I doing?

I let go of her hand and shut the laptop closed, standing abruptly. "Sorry. It's none of my business."

"You're a spiritual advisor," she said, peering up at me. "Isn't everything your business?"

I was too busy pushing my stuff into my laptop bag to answer, desperate to leave, trying to convince myself that it was okay, it was *fine*, I had just comforted her, I had basically done nothing more than hold her hand, which I wouldn't think twice about doing with any other parishioner.

It was *fine.*

But when I turned around, Poppy was standing next to me with her own bag all packed up. "Can I walk with you back to the church?" she asked. "My house is on the same block."

Of course it was.

"Sure," I said, hoping I sounded normal and not like a priest trying to fight an erection in public. "No problem."

We stepped out into the heavy summer heat, crossing the street. The silence between us felt odd, laden with whatever strange moment had just happened, and so I spoke, trying to stave off the fantasies that continued to crowd at the edge of my mind.

"How long have you lived here?"

"Not long," she said. "I just closed on the house two weeks ago, actually. Once the owner of the club I worked at found out I had an MBA and a lot of experience, he asked me to come on board as a marketing and financial consultant, which I could do remotely and which pays—well, it pays a lot. And then last month, when *he* found me…"

Her voice broke and she squinted at the sidewalk, as if examining something. I wasn't sure exactly what had upset her, but I gave her a moment to collect herself.

We walked several feet before she continued. "So now I make good money, working for a nice guy, and I have the freedom of starting over in a sweet little town. It's what I had wanted before Sterling came to the club."

Sterling. I recognized that name from our conversation about her past, and damn it all if it didn't trigger a ridiculous spike of jealousy, as if there were any universe in which I'd be allowed to feel possessive of Poppy Danforth.

We reached the church.

"It was nice to run into you, Father," she said with another one of those small smiles, making as if to keep walking.

"Which one is your house?" I was stalling. I knew I was, but I couldn't help it. I needed just one more glimpse of those red lips, one more word in that breathy voice.

"That one." She pointed to a house across the park, a

snug bungalow with a large tree in the front yard and an overgrown garden in back. I would be able to see it from the rectory. I would be able to see if her lights were on, if her car was in the driveway, if she was moving through her kitchen early in the morning making her coffee.

That didn't seem like it would be a very healthy opportunity for me to have.

"Well, if you need any help moving furniture around or anything…"

Shit. Why did I offer that? As if being alone with her, in her house, was a great thing for me to do.

But then her face lit up and my stomach constricted at the sight. Because she was beautiful all the time, but happy? Happy, she was fucking *radiant*.

"That would be amazing," she said. "I don't know anybody here and my friends in the city are all so far away… Yes, I will definitely let you know if I need help."

"Okay," I said, still captivated by her smile and her suddenly lively eyes. "Any time."

She leaned forward, pushing up on her toes, and I had no idea what she was doing until I felt her soft lips press against my cheek. I froze, every detail, every sensation etching itself into my soul, imprinting itself while she imprinted my skin with her crimson lipstick.

"Thank you," she murmured, her words and her breath near my ear, and then she bit her lip and turned away, walking towards her house.

And I went inside the rectory for another twenty-minute cold shower.

I would be lying if I said I wasn't both dreading and looking forward to Monday's confession hours with equal measure. I'd spent Mass on Sunday searching the pews for Poppy, and when I didn't see her, a brief balloon of hope and despair had risen in my mind. Maybe she was gone, maybe her brief flirtation with religion had flamed out, and maybe this unwinnable test of my self-control was over.

Maybe she was done with me, I would think, and the balloon would fill with relief.

Maybe she was done with me, I would think again, and this time the balloon held only pain.

And so when Rowan finally left the booth that Monday and someone else slipped inside, the balloon burst with a vengeance, and my pulse began to race (with trepidation or arousal, I didn't know).

"Father Bell?" a low voice asked.

"Hello, Poppy," I said, trying to pretend that her voice didn't go straight to my dick.

She let out a laugh, small and relieved, and the sound conjured up her smile from Friday, the way she'd beamed at me when I'd offered to help her settle into her house.

"I don't know what I expected. It's just—it feels too good to be true sometimes. I left Kansas City looking for a new start, some meaning in my pointless life, and then here's this unbelievably handsome priest, practically in my backyard, willing to listen to all of my problems."

"It's my job," I said gruffly, trying to ignore the boyish jolt of happiness that came when she called me handsome. "I'm here for everyone."

"Yes, I know. But right now, 'everyone' includes me and I can't tell you how grateful I am for that."

Tell her you can't do it, my conscience demanded, thinking of the other day in my office. *Help her find someone else—anyone else—to confess to.*

Yes. I should do that. Because she was making it clear that she trusted me, all while I was betraying that trust over and over again in my mind. (In lots of different positions. On every surface in my house.)

But just as I'd resolved to bite the proverbial bullet and tell her how it had to be, she said, "Are you ready?" and then no other words came to mind except:

"Yes."

POPPY

Things went on like that for about a year and half. Between helping Mark with the business end of things and the dancing, I was making almost as much money as I would have at one of those offices in New

York. I loved that I got to dance, loved it. Even if it wasn't ballet or jazz, it was still my body and rhythm and music. And I loved how much sex there was in the job–even if no one was having sex there, it still hung everywhere, this fog of desire, and I couldn't get enough of it.

But I was lonely. The men at the club kept begging to take me home, offering way more than one-night stands, offering penthouses and yachts and stipends, but I refused to be a mistress. I may love sex, but I also have a mind and a soul. I want to have a husband one day and kids and grandkids and the whole thing… I couldn't bear to have any substitute for it, no matter how good it might make me feel temporarily.

But the trade-off for my self-respect was a cold bed and an overused vibrator, and it was starting to wear thin. Not to mention all the things I just talked about–the husband and the kids and all that. I began to miss my old life. Not the monotony or the hypocrisy, but the guarantee at least. If I had stayed, I would've never been alone. I would have been married by now, possibly pregnant. And what if I'd made the wrong decision? What if I'd ruined my chances at a happy life, because let's face it, what man is going to marry a stripper–no matter where she came from or who she is?

And that was when Sterling came to the club.

Sterling Haverford III. Yes, I know it's a ridiculous name, but where we came from, it was par for the course (especially if your estate had its own golf course).

I was doodling Mrs. Sterling Haverford in my flimsily locked diaries ever since I could remember. He was my first kiss, my first cigarette, my first orgasm. Of course, I know now that I wasn't his first anything, and that even while he was dating me, he was fucking other girls. But at the time, I was convinced we were getting married. That he loved me.

I was convinced of it right up until my parents got the invitation to his wedding. To Penelope Fucking Middleton.

We'd been off and on, for sure, but I thought it was the distance and how dedicated I was to school and charity, and fuck, I'm crying now, I'm so sorry. I'm not even sad about it, I'm just pissed still, that I'd given so much time to this asshole, and then when I was feeling so low about everything, he had the nerve to show up at the club.

I assumed he was in town for a business meeting and that maybe a potential client had brought him to the club for a little extra wooing–not an uncommon scenario where I worked, especially when it came to the private rooms in the back. And of all the girls that could have been working that particular room that night, it was me.

It was fucking me.

I had on six-inch heels and a bright blue wig and he still knew me the moment I entered, just as I'd known from one glimpse of his profile that it was him.

"Jesus Christ," he said, his words carrying like a poisonous melody over the throbbing music. "Is it really you?"

I stood in the doorway, having no idea what the fuck to do. I knew I could go find Mark, explain to him that I knew the client and couldn't dance for him—Mark would understand. But even three years after he'd dumped me via wedding invitation to another girl, I still couldn't force myself to walk away. Or stop listening when he started talking.

He said he couldn't believe it—everyone had thought I'd absconded off to Europe or someplace exotic and all the while, I had been here. He gestured to me, to indicate the skimpy outfit I wore, to indicate all the things that came along with here, the dancing and the alleged disgrace, but I saw the moment he was done making his point, the moment his pupils dilated and he took in my nearly naked body.

He'd married fucking Penelope but he was here and he was here for me, and fuck it all, I wanted that. That moment where he chose me over her. No matter how wrong it was.

"Come inside," he said, and I did.

Will God forgive me for that? Because I could have left. Without any consequences. I could have found another girl and left the club without another moment spent with Sterling Haverford III. But deep down, I wanted to stay. Deep down, I wanted what I knew would happen if I stayed.

I closed the door behind me and crossed my arms, and then told him exactly how much of an asshole he was. To his credit, he didn't deny it.

He asked me to come closer. It was a command, and Lord help me, I've always responded to commands. I walked over to him, and he ran a hand up my flank to where my skirt hung just below my ass. His wedding ring glinted in the low neon light of the room. His fucking wedding ring from his fucking marriage to Penelope Fucking Middleton.

I tried to pull back, but he reached up and grabbed my arm.

And then he said, "You know why I didn't marry you, Poppy?" He was caressing the inside of my thigh now and I couldn't help it, I took a tiny step to the side, just to widen my legs the smallest bit.

He smiled and went on. "It's not because I didn't want to be married to a Danforth. God knows that with your family and your money and your brains, on paper you would have been the perfect wife. But we both know better, don't we, Poppy?"

His fingers finally found what they were looking for, my lace thong, and he curled his fingers around the fabric and ripped, the flimsy material tearing easily, granting him access to my cunt.

"Deep down," he said, continuing his earlier train of thought, touching me, touching me so much now, "deep down, we both know that you're a little slut. Yes, with a perfect background and a perfect education, but you were made for being a whore,

Poppy, not a wife."

I told him to fuck off, and then he said, "Do you think I just showed up here accidentally? I've been looking for you for three years. You're mine or have you forgotten?"

How could I be his when he had a fucking wife? I asked him that.

And he responded that he didn't give a shit about her–which is probably the truth. But he told me he married her because he needed someone proper, someone he wouldn't worry about his clients wanting to fuck.

And then he said that wasn't me. Said I screamed sex with my tits and my mouth, and not only did I always want it, but I always looked like I wanted it. And he couldn't have that in the precious Haverford family portrait.

The worst thing was, I knew he wasn't saying it like an insult. Those were just the facts. People like us weren't supposed to be this way. We were supposed to be reserved and cold. Thin and bloodless. Sex was either a necessity or a calculated affair. And now Sterling wanted me to be his calculated affair. I had loved him and he wanted to keep me as his pet mistress, in a box that had no place for real love or a real future.

But while I was thinking all of this, he was unzipping himself, and he was so hard, so mouthwateringly hard, and I couldn't help it–I knew he was married, I knew he was an asshole, but it had been so long, too long, and I had loved him once...

Are you judging me right now, Father Bell? Are you thinking about what a dumb bitch I am? I know you aren't, you aren't like Sterling and me. The words dumb and bitch have probably never even come out of your mouth in the same sentence. But I was thinking it then, just like I'm thinking it now. I was stupid. But I was also lonely and heartbroken and so fucking wet it was dripping down my thighs.

Then I let him fuck me. Because he was right, I do like it, I do always want it. And as he slammed into me over and over again, I told him to tell me the fantasy, this life he was offering me. And he did, goddamn him, and it all sounded so perfect coming from his lying businessman's mouth. He told me about the lazy afternoons we'd spend together, the expensive restaurants he'd take me to, the orgasms he'd give me on top of smooth Egyptian cotton sheets. He told me about the flowers and jewelry and vacations in Bora Bora and expensive cars and everything else that would fill up our illicit life together, all while I ground myself on his cock, ground myself towards the best orgasm I'd had since college.

He was cursing by this point, folding me over the bench and driving into me from behind while he pressed my face against the leather and I felt the cold metal of his wedding ring against my hip. It was degrading and terrible and I came almost immediately.

And then I came again.

CHAPTER SIX

"And that's my real sin," Poppy finished. "That's my real shame. I can't sleep at night knowing that I let him—let myself—" She broke off and there was a moment of silence which I didn't interrupt, both out of respect for her and also because I didn't trust my voice. Her confession had been so raw—so fucking detailed—and I was filled with rage at this Sterling asshole and sorrow for her and also a fierce, unshakable jealousy that just weeks ago, he got to be inside her and he didn't deserve it, not one bit.

But mostly I was so fucking hard I couldn't think straight.

"I let myself come," she said finally, in a quiet, sad voice. "He is a married man and he cheated on me for years and he wasn't even *sorry*, but I still not only fucked him, but I came. I came twice. What does it matter that I made him leave right after it happened? What kind of girl still does that?"

I needed to say something, needed to help her, but fuck, it was so difficult to focus on anything other than the image of her face pressed into the seat as she gasped her way through multiple orgasms. I was going to hell for even thinking this, especially since I wanted to punch Sterling in the windpipe for acting on it, but it was almost unbearably sexy that those rough kinds of things got her off. Because they got me off too, and it had been so long since I'd had a woman whimpering under my touch…

You're no better than him, I castigated myself. *Fucking get it together. Feelings, focus on her feelings.* "How did it feel?"

"How did it feel? It felt amazing. Like he was claiming me from the inside out, and when he came inside of me, it felt like he was marking me as his property, and it was his climax that made me orgasm again. I can't help it—a guy coming is the hottest fucking thing, especially when I can feel it inside of me…"

My head fell back against the wood of the booth with an audible *thud.* "I meant," I said in a strangled voice, "how did it feel *emotionally*?"

"Oh," and then the breathy little laugh, and then fuck it, I'd go to hell, because I couldn't not rub myself now. I was so hard that I could feel every ridge and slope of myself through my pants. My other hand toyed with my zipper as I stroked, trying to keep my breathing silent. Could I unzip myself quietly enough that she wouldn't hear? Could I jack myself right here in the booth without her knowing?

Because there was no way I could live without it at this point. Her words were carved into my mind, and they would be there forever.

"I guess it made me feel like Sterling was right. I am a whore, aren't I? I had a debutante ball and my family was listed in the Social Register and I have dressage trophies—but that doesn't change who I am on the inside. I think deep down, I always knew that Sterling didn't really love me, but I was willing to accept sex in lieu of love because I wanted that just as much as I wanted the romance, and what woman thinks like that, Father? That I'd rather have sex without love than have no sex at all? So what do I do now? How do I carry the shame of all this while at the same time knowing it's a fundamental part of who I am?"

Shame. Yes, I knew that feeling; I was feeling it right now, in fact. I forced my hands to my thighs, well away from my erection. *Concentrate*, I told myself. *And when you're alone, you can take care of your...problem.*

"God made us as sexual creatures, Poppy," I said, wishing my words sounded more soothing than they did. With my choked voice and barely controlled breathing, they came out sounding like a dark threat. A dark, imminent threat.

"Then He made me too sexual," she whispered. "Even now, I—"

But she stopped.

"Even now, what?" And I was using that voice again, and there was no mistaking the danger now.

I could hear her shifting in her seat. "I should go," she said. I heard her reaching for her purse and then the door handle clicking open, but I was out of the booth and over to her side in an instant, standing there as her door swung open. I braced my hands on either side of the door (what in the actual fuck was I *doing*?) blocking her escape because I had to know, I had to know what she was going to say, and if I didn't, I would go crazy.

She looked up at me looming over her, her hazel eyes growing wide. "Oh," she breathed. We stared at each other for a moment.

It could have ended right there. It would have, even with her red lipstick and her bright eyes and her nipples in tight little points under the thin silk blouse she wore. Even with my wide shoulders blocking the door to the booth, even with the surge of power and satisfaction and lust that came from positioning my body against a woman's in this primal, dominating way.

It would have, I swear.

But then she bit her lip, those slightly-too-big teeth digging into her full lower lip, all pure white digging into the sharpest, bloodiest red imaginable, and then she rubbed her thighs together, a tiny noise coming from somewhere in the back of her throat.

I stopped seeing a penitent.

I stopped seeing a child of God.

I stopped seeing a lost lamb in need of a shepherd.

I saw only a woman in need—ripe, delicious need.

I stepped back, drawing a deep breath, some valiant part of my conscience trying to flicker back online, and she took a tentative step out of the booth, her eyes still pinned to mine. I let her walk past me, but it wasn't because I wanted her to leave or because I wanted this temptation to end. No, it was more like I was giving her one last chance to escape, and if she didn't then Jesus help her, because I had to touch her, I had to taste her and it had to be right the fuck now.

She backed up a few paces until she bumped against the baby grand piano set below the choir platform. She still didn't speak, but she didn't have to, because I could read every tremble of hers, every breath, every goose bump. Her teeth still bit her bottom lip and *I* wanted to bite that lip, bite it so hard that she would squeal.

I advanced on her, and she watched every step of mine with a hunger that was beyond palpable, it was oppressive, it was ferocious.

"Turn around," I ordered her, and fuck if she didn't comply right away, turning and bracing her hands against the edge of the black wood. She was still rubbing her thighs together when I reached the piano and stood directly behind her. I ran my index finger from her hand to her shoulder, feeling every pebbled inch of skin on her arm. "Now what were you going to say in the booth?" I asked her in a low voice. "And remember that lying is a sin."

She shivered. "I can't say it. Not here. Not to you."

My hand reached her shoulder. She'd worn her hair up in a loose twist, exposing the ivory nape of her neck, and I caressed it now, wanting to devour every shudder, every hitched breath. And then I placed the flat of my palm in the space between her shoulder blades and pushed her down against the piano, so that she was bent over, the side of her face pressed against the glossy wood. She was so petite that she had to stand on tiptoe, her leather ballet flats tugging free of her heels, her calf muscles bunching into tight balls.

She'd worn a high-waisted pencil skirt, and once she was bent over, the slit rose high enough to expose a narrow glimpse of pink flesh.

"Poppy," I said dangerously, "did you come here without underwear?"

My hand was still on her back, my fingers resting against her neck, and she nodded.

"Was that on purpose?"

A pause. Then another nod.

The crack resounded through the sanctuary, and she jumped at the feeling of my hand smacking her ass. Then she moaned and pushed her ass up farther.

I didn't spank her again, although Lord knows I wanted to. Instead I ran my hand from her shoulder to her hip, feeling the curve of her breast where it was pressed against the piano, the dip of her waist, the firm swell of her ass. And then I repeated the action with both hands this time, letting my hands drift down to the hem of her skirt. She drew in a breath, and then I abruptly yanked it up to her waist.

I knelt down behind her and spread her legs, spread them so that her cunt was gloriously bared to me. "My little lamb," I whispered. "You are so very, very wet right now."

She was, wetness slicking almost every part of her. Her pussy wasn't just wet either—it was fucking *quivering*, pink and soft and quivering right in front of my face.

I grabbed her ass in my hands and dug my fingers in, leaning forward so that my breath tickled her sensitive flesh.

She whimpered.

"This is so wrong," I said, moving my mouth even closer. I could smell her, and she smelled like heaven, like soap and skin and the delicate female scent that every man hungered for. "But just one taste," I murmured, talking more to myself than to her now. "God wouldn't punish me for just one taste."

I traced my way from her clit to her cunt with my tongue and (forgive me, my God) but no communion wine, no salvation had ever tasted sweeter than this, and one taste would not be enough.

"Please," I whispered against her skin, "just one more." I flattened my tongue against her clit and sampled her again, my dick now so hard that it hurt.

She cried out against the wood of the piano, and I almost died, because those noises and *fuck me* that taste. I dove into her like a man possessed, my fingers burrowing into her ass cheeks to hold her open for my assault. I fucked her with my tongue and my lips and my teeth, *eating* her, eating her like a starving man. Her cunt was exactly as perfect as I'd imagined all those nights in my frozen showers, that time I'd shot off thinking about doing this very thing.

She *would* come, I decided right then. I would make her come on my face, and just the thought made my balls draw up and my dick jolt in my pants. It was a very real possibility that I myself might orgasm without even touching my cock.

I let one finger drift over to her pussy and then I slid it inside, crooking it down to find the soft, textured spot that would push her over the edge. She was shamelessly grinding back into my face now, her fingernails scratching against the piano wood, little sighs and moans issuing from her throat.

All I could breathe and taste was her, and then I looked up and saw the crucifix at the front of the church—a tragic, agonized god hanging in sacrifice—and my heart lurched. What the hell was I doing? Anybody could walk in right now, walk in the front door, and see their priest with a woman bent over the piano, kneeling as if he was praying to her cunt, kneeling with his face buried in her ass.

What would they think? After I had worked so hard to repair this town's hurt, after I'd finally helped this community trust the Church again?

And more than that—what about my vow? A vow I had

made before my family and God? What does an oath mean to me if only three years after swearing chastity, I'm shoving my tongue up a woman's wet cunt?

But then Poppy came, her cry the most beautiful hymn I've heard in my life, and everything else vanished except her and her smell and her taste and the feeling of her clenching around my finger.

Reluctantly, I pulled back, wanting one more orgasm from her, wanting to bury my face in her ass again, but knowing I couldn't, I shouldn't, and then I stood and saw her looking over her shoulder like I was the most wondrous thing she'd ever seen.

"No one's ever done that to me before," she whispered.

Tongue-fucked her in a church? Bent her over a piano and licked her until she couldn't stand anymore?

My eyebrows drew together, and she answered my unspoken question. "No one's ever made me come with their mouth before, I mean," she said. There was still a flush high on her cheeks, creeping down her neck.

I didn't understand. "No guy has ever gone down on you?"

She shook her head and then closed her eyes. "That felt so good."

I was shocked. How could she have never received oral?

"That's a shame, little lamb," I said, and I couldn't stop myself, I pressed my covered erection into her ass. "No one's taken care of you properly before." I dropped a hand down and around to find her clit again, groaning inwardly when I found that it was still a swollen, hot button of need. "But I won't lie. It makes me hard as fuck knowing that I was the first man to taste you."

I heard the words as I said them and suddenly reality slammed back into me.

What the fuck was I doing? What the fuck had I done?

And why had I done it here, of all places?

I stepped back, breathing hard, no thought in my mind other than to get away, somewhere else, before I was laid low by guilt and regret.

Poppy spun around, her skirt still bunched around her waist, her eyes flashing. "Don't you dare," she said. "Don't you dare check out on me now."

"I'm sorry," I said. "I…I can't."

"You can," she said, stepping forward. She pressed a palm to my erection, and I looked down to see her unbuckling my belt.

"I can't," I repeated, still watching as she drew out my cock. The moment her fingers brushed over my bare skin, I wanted to die, because I hadn't exaggerated how good that felt in my memories and my fantasies, no, I had not.

"You are a good priest, Father Bell," she said, her hand moving down to explore lower, cupping me. "But you're also a good man. And doesn't a good man deserve a little indulgence every now and then?"

She gripped me tighter, started to stroke in earnest now.

I watched her hand moving up and down my shaft like a man hypnotized. "We won't have sex," she promised. "No sex, and then it's not really breaking any rules, right?"

"You're equivocating now," I said raggedly, closing my eyes against the sight of her pumping my dick.

"Then how about another confession," she said, dragging her fingernails from my pelvis to my navel, making my abs tighten. "After the first day I talked to you, I looked you up online. I couldn't stop thinking about your voice, like I could still hear it in a way, echoing in my mind. And then I saw your picture on the website and you looked...well, you know how you look. That was the first time I got off thinking about you."

"You've touched yourself thinking about me?" The last remaining shred of my self-control frayed, threatening to snap.

"More than once," she admitted, still running her fingers over my abs underneath my shirt. "Because seeing your body that first time we met while running...and then your face the last time we talked. God, your face, it was so damn dark, like you wanted to gobble me up right there...I had to fuck myself three times before I could focus on anything else."

There it went, any self-discipline that remained, and all that was left was a male—not Tyler, not Father Bell—but something more primal and more demanding.

"Show me," I ordered.

"What?"

"Lie down on this floor, spread your legs, and show me what it looks like when you fuck yourself thinking of me."

Her mouth parted and her cheeks reddened and then she was laying on the carpet, her hand on her cunt. I stood over her, fisting my cock, giving in to it all, giving in to everything, as long as it ended in her covered in my climax.

"Why didn't you wear underwear today?" I asked, watching her trace circles around her clitoris.

"The last time, when we talked, I got so hot talking to you. I thought if it happened again today, it would be easier if I didn't wear panties. To…take care of it. And it was easier."

I knelt down between her legs and then took her slender wrists in my hand. I stretched out over her, pinning her wrists to the floor above her head, my dick brushing against her pussy and her bunched-up skirt. "Are you telling me," I asked, "that you were masturbating in the booth next to me?"

She nodded fearfully. "You make me so wet," she said. "I can't stand it."

It took everything I had not to shove into her right there and then. Every time I rocked my hips, my dick slid against her folds, and they were so *warm*. So *wet*.

I dropped my head, burying my face in her neck. She smelled like clean skin and the barest hint of a lavender perfume—something that probably cost more than what I made in a month. For some reason, this excess, this possible decadence, fueled my need to tear her apart. I bit her neck, her collarbone, scored her shoulders with my teeth, all while I ground my cock against her clit and palmed her breast, driving her to a second orgasm as if I were punishing her with pleasure. Punishing her for showing up here and knocking my carefully constructed life over as if it were a house of cards.

She squirmed underneath me, panting and gasping, her hands flexing uselessly against the floor as I kept them pinned there with only one hand. She was so wet, it would be so easy, just a slight change in angle, and then I could thrust in.

I wanted to. I wanted to, I wanted to, I wanted to. I wanted to fuck this woman more than I'd ever wanted anything in my life. And perversely, the fact that I couldn't, that it would be wrong on every single level—moral, professional, personal—made it even hotter. It made the image, the imagined feeling of it, a single bright point of obsession, until I was mindlessly rutting against her, sucking and nibbling at her as if I could burn out this need by devouring every inch of her skin.

"Oh God," she whispered. "I'm going to—*oh God*—"

I would have flogged myself every day for the rest of my life if I could have been inside of her right then, felt her tightening on my dick, felt her shuddering convulsions from the inside out. But being on top of her was almost as good, because I felt every seizing, jerking breath, every wild buck of her hips, and when I met her eyes, they were fierce and penetrating, but also surprised, as if she'd been given an unexpected gift and wasn't sure if she should be grateful or suspicious.

But before I could delve further into that look, she'd arched her back and unseated my balance, tipping me so that I rolled to my back and she was on top of me.

Without hesitation, she tugged my shirt up so she could see my stomach, and I didn't miss the way her jaw clenched and her eyes flared. She scratched my stomach—hard—as if furious that it was firm and muscled, as if angry that it turned her on. (And I'd be lying if I said that didn't turn *me* the fuck on.)

She sat on me, her slick cleft sliding against the underside of my dick, and then she started stroking me that way, as if she were jacking me off with her pussy. I raised up on my elbows so I could watch it, watch the way her flesh pressed against mine, the way her bare cunt allowed me to see her ripe clitoris peeking out. It was so goddamn wet, and with all the pressure, her full body weight pressing against my cock, it was such a close approximation to the real thing, maybe too close, but it still wasn't technically sex, I lied to myself, maybe it wouldn't count, maybe I wasn't sinning.

But even if I was, holy fuck, I was not stopping.

It was so *dirty*, the way her skirt was still hitched up to her hips, the way my pants were yanked down just far enough to free my balls, the way the old carpet abraded my ass and lower back. The way she shamelessly angled herself so that my shaft would press on her in all the right places, the way it was just our arousal lubricating us and nothing else, and God, I wanted to marry this woman or collar her or cage her; I wanted to own her, make her, *take* her; I wanted us on this old carpet forever, with her hair coming undone and her nipples hard and her naughty pussy milking my dick for everything it was worth.

"Come," she told me hoarsely. "I have to see you come. I *need* it."

My jaw was too tight to answer, because it was close, something more intense than I'd felt in years gnawing at the base of my spine and rending its way through my pelvis.

"Don't hold back," she begged now, pressing down even more, and *fuck*, there it was. "Give it to me. Give me every drop."

Shit, this woman was filthy. And perfect. And it was pure instinct that made me grab her hips and work her harder and faster over me, my mind filled with the sight of her straddling me and her pale pink clitoris, still plump and needy, and the memory of her taste and smell on my mouth and face, and then it flooded through me—no, it burned and chewed through me, and she let out a low moan at the sight of my cum spurting onto my stomach. There was so much, and it felt like hours instead of seconds that I was suspended in pulsing, total-body release.

And at that moment—at the peak of my high, at the peak of her greedy triumph—our eyes locked and we surged past every barrier—stranger and stranger, priest and penitent, Tyler and Poppy. We were simply male and female, as God had made us, Adam and Eve, in the most elemental and fundamental form. We were biology, we were creation incarnate, and I saw the moment she felt it too—that we were fused somehow. Irrevocably and undeniably fused together into something singular and whole.

My climax abated, but I could barely breathe, barely process what the fuck I had just felt, and then Poppy bit her lip and dragged one finger across my stomach, coating it in my orgasm, and then brought it to her mouth. My cock jumped as I watched her suck it off her finger.

I rested my head back against the floor, overcome with the sinking realization that I would probably not ever be able to dig this woman out of my system. She was the kind of woman that could make me hard over and over again, the kind of woman I could spend a week fucking nonstop and then still want more, and that was bad news for my self-control, which was slowly resurrecting back into life, along with my defeated, gnashing conscience.

"Will it drive you crazy," she asked after a moment, "knowing that I'll be touching myself, just inches from you, every time I come in to confess?"

I groaned. Fuck yes, it would.

"Poppy," I said, but then stopped. What could I possibly

say in this moment that would have any value? That would encompass the rushing torrents of shame and guilt, and also express how deeply this woman had gotten under my skin?

"I know," she whispered. "I'm sorry too."

She stood and rearranged her clothes as I wiped my stomach with my shirt and sat up. Had it been only a minute ago when the entire universe had shrunk to just me and her, to our noises and our sweat, our fucking without really fucking? And now the sanctuary seemed vast and hollow, a cave with only the overtaxed air conditioner to chase away the dull silence.

The church was empty. The townspeople weren't gathered in the narthex, ready to throw stones at me or exile me. I'd gotten away with it.

And somehow that made me feel worse.

Poppy and I didn't say goodbye. Instead, we looked at each other, rumpled and damp, reeking of sex, and then she left without another word.

I slowly made my way back to the rectory, sticky and hard again and hating myself relentlessly.

CHAPTER SEVEN

My screen door slammed shut, and I jumped out of my kitchen chair, expecting Poppy or an angry horde of parishioners or the bishop here to excommunicate me, but it was just Millie, her arms laden with frozen casseroles.

She bustled past me into the kitchen, the late afternoon light shining through her stiff, brick-red wig as she started unloading her cargo.

"You are too clean," she said by way of greeting, scowling at the fastidiously neat countertops. "Boys your age should be messy."

"I'm hardly a boy, Millie," I said, walking over to help her move the food into the freezer.

"At my age, anyone under sixty is a boy," she said dismissively, shooing me out of the way so she could put one of the dishes in the oven.

Millie was approximately one hundred and thirty years

old, but she was not only one of my most active parishioners, but the sharp-as-a-tack bookkeeper for the church. She'd been the one to insist that we upgrade to iPads and Squares for our bake sales and Fish Fry Fridays, and the one who spearheaded the installation of fiber optic internet when nowhere else in town had it yet.

She'd also adopted me as a sort of project when I moved up here, new to town and new to living any place other than a trendy Midtown apartment in walking distance to a Chipotle. She'd clucked her tongue at my age and my appearance (her nickname for me was "Father What-a-Waste") and showing up once a week with food (even though I'd protested a thousand times that I could cook for myself [mostly ramen noodles, but still]). And after she'd met my mother and they'd spent an hour talking about the best temperature of water to use in pie crust dough, it was all over. Millie adopted my mother as well, along with my brothers, who got packages of cookies sent to their sleek offices in downtown Kansas City every week.

Except today I felt unworthy of her bustling, fussing attentions. I felt unworthy of everything—this house, this job, this town—and I just wanted to sit here at my kitchen table until I died.

No, that was a lie. I wanted to *do* something—run or lift weights or scrub the tile until my hands bled—I wanted penance. Funny how many times I had counseled my flock about the real nature of penance, the real weight of God's unconditional love and forgiveness, and my first reaction to sinning with Poppy was to punish myself.

Or at the very least, exhaust myself so that I couldn't think actual thoughts anymore.

"Something's bothering you," Millie decided, sitting at the table and folding her hands together into a bundle of papery skin and old rings. Someone once told me that she'd been one of the first female engineers in Missouri, doing surveying for the government when they built the interstate system through the Midwest. And it was easy to believe now, with the no-nonsense look she was leveling at me, with those sharp eyes searching my face for every detail.

I did my best attempt at an easy smile. I have a nice smile, I admit. It's one of my most effective weapons, although I lobby it more against congregants than co-eds these days. "It's just the heat, Millie," I said, making to stand.

"Uh-uh. Try again," she said and nodded back to the chair. I sat again, fidgeting like a kid. (Millie has that effect on me. Our bishop once joked after meeting her that she should have been the Mother Superior at an abbey a hundred years ago, and all I have to say about that is that I would feel sorry for any nun working under her.)

"Nothing's wrong," I said, keeping my voice light. "I promise."

She reached across the table, covering my large hand with her thin, wrinkled one. "The thing about being old is that I know when people are lying. Now, last time I checked, you were in charge of an entire parish. You wouldn't lie to one of your parishioners, would you?"

If it was about having almost-sex on the sanctuary floor? A fresh wave of guilt flooded through me as I realized that I was compounding my sins now. I was lying (and lying to a good person who'd done nothing but take care of me). Suddenly, I wanted to tell Millie about this afternoon, about the past couple of weeks, about this new temptation that was the oldest temptation on earth.

Instead, I stared down at our hands and didn't answer. Because I was prideful and defensive and furious with myself. And that wasn't all.

I wanted to do it again. I wanted Poppy again. And if I told someone my sin, I'd be accountable. I'd be bound to obey my vows, I'd be bound to behave.

Nothing about Poppy Danforth made me want to behave.

But I'd be risking everything by not behaving, my job and my community and my duty and my sister's memory and maybe even my eternal soul.

I lowered my head onto Millie's hand, careful not to rest the full weight against her fragile bones, but desperately needing comfort. "I can't talk about it," I said into the table. I wasn't going to lie. (Except how often did I tell my youth group about lies of omission? When exactly had I started making the sharp left turn into being a hypocrite?)

Millie patted the back of my head. "This wouldn't have

anything to do with the pretty young woman who bought the old Anderson house?"

My head snapped up. I don't know what my face looked like, but she laughed. "I saw you two at the coffee shop last week. Even through the window, I could see you guys made quite a couple."

Fuck. Did she suspect? And if she did, did she judge me for it?

"She was looking at the renovation spreadsheets. She's got a background in finance and an MBA from Dartmouth." I didn't mention that she also had a background in seducing wealthy men by dancing on a platform. Or that her cunt tasted sweeter than heaven.

"Maybe she and I will have to get together for coffee sometime," Millie said. "Since you can barely add two communion wafers together. Unless, of course," she said, watching my face, "you'd rather keep the meetings just between the two of you."

"*Rem acu tetigisti,*" I said, sliding my eyes away from hers. *You've hit the nail on the head.*

"I'm going to assume that means, 'You're right, Millie, I am deplorable at math.'"

It didn't.

"I've always said that you were too young and too handsome to lock your life away. 'Trouble will come of it,' I said. 'Mark my words.' And nobody marked my words."

I didn't answer. I was staring at our interlocked hands

again, thinking of the silence in the sanctuary after I'd come all over my stomach, the feeling of Poppy's wet heat pressing down on me. I'd taken two showers, scrubbing myself to the point of pain, but nothing could erase the feeling of her skin on mine. The feeling of warmth splattering on my stomach as she watched with hungry, feral eyes.

"My dear boy, you do realize this is perfectly natural. What was the homily you preached your first month here? That part of healing would be celebrating normal, consensual, Godly sex?"

I *had* preached that. Setting aside the fact that I had enjoyed my share of consensual sex in college (consensual, but not always normal, mind you), I had a firm theological belief in the importance of human sexuality. Almost every variation of Christianity had been in the business of suppressing sex and its enjoyment, but suppressed desires didn't just disappear. They festered. They created guilt and shame and, in the worst cases, deviancy. We weren't ashamed to enjoy food and alcohol in moderation—why were we so afraid of sex?

But obviously, I had meant this message for my congregation, not for me.

"What was it you quoted?" Millie asked. "*Mere Christianity*? 'The sins of the flesh are bad, but they are the least bad of all sins…that is why a cold, self-righteous prig, who goes regularly to church, may be far nearer to hell than a prostitute.'"

"Yes, but Lewis ends that paragraph with: 'Of course, it's better to be neither.'"

"You *are* neither. Did you really think that by wearing a collar every day you would stop being a man?"

"No," I said, agitated. "But I thought I would be able to control my desires with prayer and self-discipline. It's my vocation. I *chose* this life, Millie. And am I going to abandon it at the first temptation?"

"Nobody said anything about abandoning. I'm simply saying, my dear boy, that you could choose not to flagellate yourself over this. I've lived a long time, and a man and a woman wanting each other is by far one of the least sinful things I've seen."

I'd set out the Bible study curriculum for the men's group at the beginning of the year, so it was nothing more than awful coincidence that tonight was the beginning of our discussion on male sexuality. Despite Millie's practical advice, I spent the rest of the afternoon and early evening cultivating a very robust form of self-loathing, doing push-ups in my basement gym until I couldn't breathe or move or think, until it was time to come to the little faux-wood-paneled classroom on the far side of the church.

I knew Millie had been trying to make me feel better, but I didn't deserve to feel better. She didn't know how far I'd already gone, how much of my vow I'd already broken.

Probably because she would never assume her priest would be so weak as to actually act on his desires.

I rubbed my face vigorously. *Wake the fuck up, Tyler, and figure this out.* It had only been a couple weeks, and I'd completely failed at keeping my shit together. What would I do for the next two months? The next two years? She was here to stay and so was I, and there was no way I could let what happened this afternoon happen again. I mean, if Millie seeing us together once (innocently and in public) had given her ideas, then what would happen if we started actually sneaking around?

I lifted my head and greeted the men as they drifted in. Of all the groups and activities, I was the most proud of this group. Typically, women were the driving force behind church attendance; most men only came to Mass because their wives wanted them to. And especially after my predecessor's crimes, I knew that the men in particular—many of whom had sons who were the same age as the victim—would harbor a deep anger and a mistrust that would not be overcome by typical methods.

So I hung out at the local bars and watched Royals games. I enjoyed the occasional cigar at the town tobacco shop. I bought a truck. I organized a hunting club at the church. And all the while, I continued to be open about my own family's past and all the ways that the church needed to—and would—change.

And gradually this group coalesced, growing from two

old men who'd been going to church so long that they'd forgotten how to stop, to a group of forty, ranging from recent graduates to the recently retired. In fact, we'd grown so big that next month we were starting a new group.

But what if I had just undone three years of hard work? Three years of toil thrown away for half an hour with Poppy?

If I seemed distracted, nobody noticed or commented on it, and I managed to not choke on my own words as we read through passages in 2 Timothy and Song of Songs. At least, I managed not to choke until we reached one verse in Romans, and then I felt my throat close and my fingers shake as I read.

"I do not understand what I do. For what I want to do, I do not do, but what I hate I do...for I have the desire to do what is right, but I cannot carry it out. What a wretched man I am."

What a wretched man I am.

What a wretched man I am.

I had come to a town cracked wide open by the vile actions of a predator and I had vowed to fix it. Why? Because when I looked up at the stars at night, I could feel God looking back down. Because I felt the wind as His breath on my neck. Because I had bought my faith with a great deal of struggle and pain, but I knew that my faith was also what gave my life shape and purpose, and I didn't want the Church's failures to deprive an entire town of that gift.

And then what had I done today? I had betrayed all of that. Betrayed all of them.

But that's not what made my hands shake and my throat tighten. No, it was the realization that I had betrayed God, perhaps more than I'd betrayed the people in this room.

My God, my savior. The recipient of my vehement hatred after Lizzy's death and also the presence that had patiently awaited my return a few years later. The voice in my dreams that had comforted me, enlightened me, guided me. The voice that had told me what I needed to do with my life, where I needed to go to find peace.

And the worst thing was that I knew He wasn't angry with me. He'd forgiven me before it had even happened, and I didn't deserve it. I deserved to be punished, a hail of fire from above, bitter waters, an IRS audit, something, anything dammit, because I was a miserable, loathsome, lustful man who'd taken advantage of an emotionally vulnerable woman.

What a wretched man I am.

We wrapped up Bible study, and I cleaned up the coffee and chips robotically, my mind still dazed by this newest wave of shame. This feeling of being too small, too awful, for anything less than hell.

I could hardly bear walking past the crucifix on my way back to the rectory.

CHAPTER EIGHT

I slept perhaps three hours total that night. I stayed up late reading the Bible, perusing every passage about sin that I knew of until my tired eyes refused to focus on the words any longer, sliding over them like two magnets with the same charge. Finally, I crawled into my bed with my rosary, mumbling prayers until I drifted off into a restless sleep.

A strange kind of numbness settled over me as I said Mass that morning, as I laced up my running shoes afterwards. Maybe it was the lack of sleep, maybe it was emotional exhaustion, maybe it was simply the shock of yesterday carrying over into today. But I didn't want numb—I wanted peace. I wanted strength.

Taking the country road out of town to avoid Poppy, I ran farther than I normally did, pushing myself harder and faster, moving until my legs cramped and my breath screamed in and out of my chest. And instead of going straight to my shower, I staggered inside of the church, my hands laced above my head, my ribs slicing themselves apart with pain. It was dark and empty inside the church, and I didn't know what I was doing there instead of my rectory, didn't know until I stumbled into the sanctuary and collapsed onto my knees in front of the tabernacle.

My head was hanging, my chin touching my chest, sweat everywhere, but I didn't care, couldn't care, and I couldn't pinpoint the moment my ragged breathing turned into crying, but it was not long after I went to my knees, and the tears mingled with the sweat until I wasn't sure which was which.

The sunlight poured through the thick stained glass, jewel bright patterns spilling and tumbling over the pews and my body and the tabernacle, and the gold doors glinted in darker shades, somber and sacred, forbidding and holy.

I leaned forward until my head pressed against the floor, until I could feel my eyelashes blinking against the worn, industrial carpet. Saint Paul says we don't have to put words to our prayers, that the Holy Spirit will interpret for us, but interpreting wasn't needed this time, not when I was whispering *sorry sorry sorry* like a chant, like a mantra, like a hymn without music.

I knew the moment I was no longer alone. My naked back prickled with awareness and I sat up, flushed with embarrassment that a parishioner or a staff member had seen me crying like this, but there was no one there. The sanctuary was empty.

But still I felt the presence of someone else like a weight, like static along my skin, and I peered into every dim corner, certain I'd see someone standing there.

The air-conditioning powered on with a thump and a whoosh, the change in air pressure slamming the doors to the sanctuary closed. I jumped.

It's just the air-conditioning, I told myself.

But when I looked back up at the tabernacle, golden and stained with color, I suddenly wasn't so sure. There was something anticipatory and sentient about the silence and emptiness. It suddenly felt as if God were listening very intently to what I was saying, listening and waiting, and I lowered my eyes back to the floor.

"I'm sorry," I whispered one last time, the word hanging in the air like a star hangs in the sky—glimmering, precious, illuminating. And then it winked out of existence, at the same moment I felt my burden of sorrow and shame wink out of existence.

There was a beat of perfect completeness, a moment where I felt as if I could pluck each and every atom out of the air, where magic and God and something sweetly beyond complete understanding was real, completely real.

And then it was all gone, all of it, replaced by a deep feeling of peace.

I exhaled at the same time the building seemed to exhale, the prickling on my skin disappearing, the air vacant once again. I knew a thousand explanations for what I had just felt, but I also knew that I really believed only one.

Moses got a burning bush, and I get the air-conditioning, I thought ruefully as I got to my feet, rising as slowly and unsteadily as a small child. But I wasn't complaining. I had been forgiven, renewed, released from guilt. Like Saint Peter, I'd been tested and found wanting and forgiven anyway.

I could do this. There was life after fucking up, after all, even for those who lived without fucking.

The next two days passed without event. I spent Thursday lounging on my couch while watching *The Walking Dead* episodes on Netflix and eating Cup of Noodles that I'd made by using hot water from my Keurig.

Sophisticated, I know.

And then Friday. I got up and prepared myself for the morning Mass as I always did, a few minutes late, reminding myself for the thousandth time to rearrange the sacristy, and then readied myself to walk into the sanctuary. Weekday Masses are short—no music, no second reading, no homily—sort of like drive-thru Eucharist for the extremely faithful. Like Rowan and the two grandmothers and—

Jesus help me.

Poppy Danforth.

She was sitting in the second row, in a demure dress of ice blue silk with a Peter Pan collar and flats, her hair in a loose bun. She looked prim, composed, modest…except for that fucking lipstick, fire engine red and begging to be smeared. I looked away as soon as I saw her, trying to recapture that holy sense of peace I'd been given on Tuesday, that sense that I could master any temptation as long as I had God on my side.

She needed something from this place, from me, something way more important than what we had done on Monday. I needed to honor my office and give it to her. I focused on the Mass, on the words and on the prayers, pleased to see Poppy doing her best to follow along, praying especially for her as I performed the ancient rites.

Please help her find guidance and peace.

Please help her heal from her past.

And please please please help us behave.

When it was time for Eucharist, she lined up behind the grandmas and Rowan, looking a little uncertain.

"What do I do?" she whispered when she got to the front of the line.

"Cross your hands over your chest," I whispered back.

She did, her eyes still on mine, her long fingers resting on her shoulders. She cast her eyes back down, looking so lovely and yet so frail, and I wanted to hug her. Not even sexually, just a regular *hug*. I wanted to wrap my arms around her and feel her breathe into my chest, and I wanted to tuck her face into my neck as I kept her safe and protected from her past, from her ambiguous future. I wanted to tell her and have her know—really know—that it would be all right, because there was love and because someone like her was meant to be out in the world sharing that love, like she had done in Haiti. All that joy she had felt there—she could feel it anywhere, if only she'd open herself to it.

I placed my hand on her head, about to murmur a standard blessing, and then her eyes lifted to mine and everything shifted. The floor and the ceiling and the cincture tight around my waist to encourage pure thoughts and her hair feather-soft under my fingertips and my skin on her skin. Electricity skimmed down my spine, and every sense memory of her—her taste and her feel and her sounds—shocked through me.

Her mouth parted. She felt it too.

I could barely get the blessing out, my throat was so dry. And when she turned to walk back to her pew, she also looked stunned, as if she'd been blinded.

After Mass, I practically bolted back to the sacristy, not looking at anyone or anything as I did. I took my time removing my vestments, hanging the way-too-expensive embroidered chasuble on its hanger and folding my alb into a precise, neat square. My hands were shaking. My thoughts were incomplete fragments. Things had been so good this week. And things were going so well during the Mass, even with her all adorable and devout and so fucking close, and then I touched her…

I stood for a minute in my slacks and shirt and stared at

the processional cross (feeling a bit betrayed, if I was being honest). If I was forgiven, why hadn't God also removed this temptation from me? Or given me more strength to bear it? To resist it? I knew it wasn't fair to hope that Poppy would move away or become a Baptist or something, but why couldn't God eliminate my attraction to her? Deaden my senses to the way she'd felt under my blessing...deaden my eyes to those red lips and bright hazel eyes?

Father, if you are willing, take this cup from me. Even Jesus had said those words. Not that they had worked out so well for him... Why was God so willing to leave bad cups all over the place?

I left the sacristy in a strange mood, trying to summon that ethereal, distinctly nonphysical tranquility I'd felt earlier, and then I turned the corner and saw Poppy standing in the center aisle, the sole parishioner remaining.

I honestly didn't know what to do. We were urged to flee temptation, but what if my job was helping the temptress? Was it more wrong to sneak away, to leave her without help, and avoid the lust and desire? Because of course, the lust was my own problem, not hers, and no excuse to be cold to her.

But if I did go to her, what else was I risking?

More importantly, was I risking it because I *wanted* to risk it? Was I only telling myself I cared about her spiritual development, so that I could be near her?

No, I decided. That for sure wasn't true. It was just that

the actual truth was so much worse. I cared about her as a person, as a soul, *and* I wanted to fuck her, and that was the recipe for something much worse than carnal sin.

It was a recipe for falling in love.

I would go to her. But I would put her in contact with the leader of the women's group, direct Poppy to seek guidance from her instead of me, and hopefully the occasional Mass would be the extent of our interactions.

Poppy stared at the altar as I approached.

"Aren't there bones inside there?"

"We prefer the term *relic.*" My voice had that unintentionally deep timbre again. I cleared my throat.

"Seems a little macabre."

I gestured towards the crucifix, which depicted Jesus at his most bloody, broken, and tortured. "Catholicism is a macabre religion."

Poppy turned toward me, face thoughtful. "I think that's what I like about it. It's gritty. It's real. It doesn't gloss over pain or sorrow or guilt—it highlights them. Where I grew up, you never dealt with anything. You took pills, drank, repressed it all until you were an expensive shell. I like this way better. I like confronting things."

"It's an active religion," I agreed. "It's a religion of *doing*—rituals, prayers, motions."

"And that's what you like about it."

"That it's active? Yes. But I like the rituals themselves too." I looked around the sanctuary. "I like the incense and the wine and the chants. It feels ancient and holy. And there's something about the rituals that brings me back to God every time, no matter how foul my mood is, no matter how badly I've sinned. Once I start, it all sort of fades away, like it's not important. Which it isn't. Because while Catholicism can be macabre, it's also a religion of joy and connection, of remembering that sorrow and sin can't hold on to us any longer."

She shifted, her flat bumping against my shoe. "Connection," she said. "Right."

In fact, I was feeling connection right now. I liked talking religion with her; I liked that she got it, got it in a way that a lot of lifetime churchgoers didn't. I wanted to talk to her all day, listen to her all day, have her breathy words whisper me to sleep at night…

Noooooo, Tyler. Bad.

I cleared my throat. "What can I help you with, Poppy?"

She held up the church newsletter. "I saw that there was a pancake breakfast tomorrow and I wanted to help."

"Of course." The breakfast was one of the first things I'd started doing after coming to St. Margaret's, and the response had been overwhelming. There was enough rural poverty and poverty in nearby Platte City and Leavenworth to guarantee a steady need for the service, but there were never enough volunteers and we were slammed the two times a month we hosted it. "That would be so much appreciated."

"Good." She smiled, the hint of a dimple appearing in her cheek. "I'll see you tomorrow then."

I prayed extra last night. I woke up at dawn and went on an even longer run than the ones I'd been taking, crashing into my kitchen sweaty and exhausted, causing a casserole-unloading Millie to *tsk* at me.

"Are you training for a marathon?" she asked. "If so, it doesn't look like you're doing a very good job."

I was too out of breath to even sputter a protest at that. I grabbed a bottle of water and drank the entire thing in several long gulps. Then I stretched out facedown on the cold tile floor in an attempt to lower my core temperature.

"You do realize it's dangerous to run in the heat, even in the morning. You should get a treadmill."

"Mmphm," I said into the floor.

"Well, regardless, you need to shower before the breakfast. I ran into that delightful new girl last night in town, and she said she was going to help us today. And surely you want to look nice for the new girl, right?"

I lifted my head and looked up at her incredulously.

She dug the toe of her purple pump into my ribs before stepping easily over me. "I'm going to the church now to help them mix the batter. I'll be sure to help Miss Danforth get settled if I see her before you get there."

She left and I peeled myself off the floor, taking a minute

to clean the sweaty torso-print with paper towels and a cleaning spray. And then I went back and showered.

It ended up being surprisingly easy to stay focused at the breakfast itself. It was so busy, and I tried to make a point to sit down at every table over the course of the morning and get to know the people who visited. Some had children who I could send home with backpacks stuffed with school supplies and peanut butter, some had elderly parents I could refer to local eldercare services and charities. Some just were lonely and wanted someone to talk to—and I could do that too.

But every so often, I'd see Poppy out of the corner of my eye, smiling at a guest or bringing a fresh stack of trays out, and it was hard not to notice how at home she looked in this environment. She was genuinely kind to the visitors, but she was also efficient, focused, and able to ladle scrambled eggs at a rate that made Millie declare her an honorary granddaughter. She seemed so at peace, so unlike the troubled woman who had confessed her sins to me.

I ended the morning batter-splashed (it was my job to carry the giant bowls of batter over to the stove) and finger-burned (ditto with cooking the bacon) and happy. While I probably wouldn't see any of these people at Mass anytime soon, I would see them again two weeks from now, and that was the important thing—it was about filling bellies, not winning souls.

I told Millie and the other two grandmothers to go

home and rest while I cleaned up, not seeing Poppy and assuming she'd already left. I hummed as I folded up the tables and stacked the chairs, and as I wheeled the mop bucket out onto the floor.

"How can I help?"

Poppy was at the foot of the stairs, tucking a piece of paper back into her purse. Even in the dim basement light, she looked unreal, too rare and too lovely to gaze at for longer than a few seconds without pain.

"I thought you'd left?" I said, moving my gaze back to the very safe mop and bucket in front of me.

"I went up with a family earlier—I heard the mother mention some issues with late taxes and since I'm a CPA, I offered to help."

"That was really generous of you," I said, again feeling that frantic, squeezing feeling that I'd felt yesterday, that feeling like I was losing my footing with her and starting to flirt with something much worse than pure lust.

"Why are you surprised that I did something nice?" she asked, stepping toward me. The words teased and joked, but the subtext was clear. *Don't you think I'm a good person?*

I immediately felt defensive. I always assumed the best of people, always. But I guess I was a little surprised at the depth of her earnestness to help—I had been when she'd told me about Haiti too.

"Is it because you think I'm some sort of fallen woman?"

I dropped the mop in the bucket and looked up. She was

closer now, close enough that I could see where a small cloud of flour had settled on her shoulder.

"I don't think you're a fallen woman," I said.

"But now you are going to say that we are all fallen sinners in a fallen world."

"*No*," I pronounced carefully. "I was going to say that people who are as smart and attractive as you don't typically have to cultivate skills like kindness unless they want to. Yes, it surprises me a little."

"You're smart and attractive," she pointed out.

I flashed her a grin.

"Stop it, Father, I'm being serious. Are you sure that it isn't because I'm a smart, attractive, advantaged *woman* that you don't feel that way?"

What? No! I had been one class short of a Women's Studies minor in college! "I—"

She took another step forward. Only the mop bucket was in between us now, but the bucket couldn't stop me from noticing the elegant curve of her collarbone under her sundress, the faintest suggestion of cleavage before the bodice began.

"I want to be a good person, but more than that, I want to be a good woman. Is there no way to be both completely *woman* and completely good?"

Shit. This conversation had gone from taxes to the darkest corners of Catholic theology. "Of course, there is, Poppy, to the extent that anyone can be completely good," I said. "Forget the Eve and the apple stuff right now. See yourself as I see you—an openly loved daughter of God."

"I guess I don't feel so loved."

"Look at me."

She did.

"You are loved," I said firmly. "Smart, attractive woman that you are—every part of you, good and bad, is loved. And please ignore me if I fuck up and make you feel any differently, okay?"

She snorted at my swearing and then gave me a rueful grin. "I'm sorry," she said softly. "I didn't mean to corner you like that."

"You didn't corner me. Really, I'm the one who's sorry."

She took a step back, like she was physically hesitating about telling me what she was about to say. Finally she said, "Sterling called me last night. I think…I guess I maybe let it fuck with my head."

"Sterling called you?" I asked, feeling an irritation that was way beyond the scope of professional concern.

"I didn't answer, but he left a voicemail. I should have deleted it, but I didn't…" She trailed off. "He repeated all those things he'd said before—about the kind of woman I am, where I was meant to be. He said he's coming for me again."

"He's coming for you? He said that?"

She nodded and red rage danced at the edge of my vision.

Poppy evidently saw this, because she laughed and put her fingers over mine, where they'd been gripping the mop handle so tightly that my knuckles had turned white. "Relax, Father. He'll come here, try to woo me with more stories about vacations and vintage wine, and I'll reject him. Again."

Again…so like last time? Where you let him make you come before you made him leave?

"I don't like this," I said, and I said it not as a priest or a friend but as the man who had tasted her just one flight of stairs away from here. "I don't want you to meet with him."

Her smile stayed but her eyes changed into cold shards of green and brown. I suddenly appreciated what a weapon she would have made in a boardroom or on the arm of a senator. "Honestly? I don't think it's any of your business if I do meet with him or not."

"He's dangerous, Poppy."

"You don't even know him," she said, removing her hand from mine.

"But I know how dangerous a man can be when he wants a woman he can't have."

"Like you?" she said, and the mark was so ruthlessly and perfectly aimed that I nearly staggered back.

The weight of the overtones collapsed onto us like a rotten ceiling—Poppy and Sterling, yes, but Poppy and me, my childhood priest and Lizzy.

Men wanting what they shouldn't: the story of my life.

Without another word, Poppy turned and left, her strappy sandals clacking on the stairs. I forced myself to take several deep breaths and try to figure out what the fuck had just happened.

CHAPTER NINE

Knock.

Knock.

Pause.

Knock knock knock.

"Stop," I muttered, rolling out of bed, sleep making me slow and fumbling. "I'm coming, I'm coming."

Knock knock BOOM.

The deafening thunder and preceding flash of light did nothing to alleviate my disorientation, and I stumbled into the table, the sharp corner burrowing into my hip. I swore, blindly reaching for a T-shirt (I was only in a loose pair of sweatpants) and groped my way down the hall to the living room where the front door was. I was just awake enough that I was beginning to register that someone really was at my door at three in the morning, and it was either a police officer coming to tell me that Ryan had finally rammed his car into a tree while texting or one of the parishioners needing last rites. Whatever reason they had for coming to the rectory, it probably wasn't good, and I steeled myself for tragedy as I opened the door, awkwardly also trying to tug my T-shirt over my head.

It was Poppy, rain-soaked with a bottle of scotch in her hand.

I blinked like an idiot. For one thing, after our fight this morning, the literal last thing I expected was Poppy at my door in the middle of the night bearing gifts. For another, she was wearing what I assumed were her pajamas—a pair of dancing shorts and a thin *Walking Dead* T-shirt—and the rain had thoroughly wetted both. She wasn't wearing a bra and the rain had made her thin shirt almost transparent, her nipples dark and hard under the fabric, and once I noticed that, it was hard to think about anything else than those wet breasts, probably pebbled with goose bumps, and how that cool flesh would feel against my hot tongue.

And then I came back to myself and for a terrible moment, I warred between two impulses: shutting her out into the rain or shoving her to her knees and making her swallow my cock.

Flee the temptations of youth, we'd read at the Bible study earlier tonight. *Pursue righteousness.* I should shut the door and go back to bed. But then Poppy shivered, and a lifetime of respect and politeness intervened. I found myself stepping back and gesturing for her to come inside.

Pursue righteousness, the author of Timothy said. But did righteousness carry a bottle of Macallan 12 in her hand? Because Poppy did.

"I couldn't sleep," she said, stepping into the living room and then turning around to face me.

I shut the door. "I gathered." My voice was gravelly from sleep and something less innocent. Predictably, my dick started to swell; despite everything that had happened, I hadn't seen her breasts yet, and they were more tempting than ever under that wet shirt.

Fuck. I didn't mean *yet.* I meant never. I was never going to see her breasts. *Accept it,* I mentally chastised my groin, which refused to heel, and instead kept sending these painfully vivid sense memories back to my brain, like how it had felt to grope Poppy's tits when she was bent over the church piano.

Her eyes dropped to my hips, and I knew my sweatpants were not doing a very good job hiding my thoughts. Clearing my throat, I turned away from her to walk over to the kitchen. "I didn't know you liked *The Walking Dead,*" I mentioned lightly, sliding my hand over the switch. A pale yellow glow wafted from the postwar-era light fixture, casting angled shadows into the living room.

"It's my favorite show," Poppy said. "But I don't know why you act surprised that you didn't know. We haven't known each other that long, and most of our conversations have involved me telling you my darkest secrets—not what's on my Netflix queue."

She had come up to me and extended the bottle of scotch, which I took, moving into the kitchen to search for glasses, trying to piece together a response—any response—but I literally couldn't think of a single thing to say.

"It's a peace offering," she said, nodding towards the Macallan. "I couldn't sleep and I wanted to say I'm sorry for our fight today and I thought maybe scotch..." She took a deep breath and for the first time, my still sleep-fogged brain realized that she was nervous. "I'm so sorry for waking you up," she said quietly. "I should go."

"Don't," I said automatically, my mouth operating on instinct before my mind could catch up. A gratifying flush spread up her cheeks, and something clicked in my mind, and now I was fully and completely awake. "Go to the living room," I said—not asked. "Turn on the gas fireplace and sit on the hearth. Wait for me."

She obeyed without question and that simple act of obedience stirred up the old me, the me that was known on campus for a certain type of experience in the bedroom. I couldn't help it, it felt so damn good to have a woman pliant to my demands, to see a woman as smart and independent as Poppy let me take care of her, trust me to direct her in exactly the right way. And then I felt like an idiot. I gripped the countertop, remembering my women's studies classes in college, the feminist nun at the seminary who outlined every painful instance of misogyny in the Church's history. I was being a pig, for more reasons than one. I needed to regain my control, go out there and tell her that after her drink, she needed to go. I would be honest about my struggle and hope that she would understand.

Even if she hated me for it.

Because I deserved her hatred.

But first, the drinks. While I enjoyed scotch, I usually drank it alone or with my brothers, so I didn't have the right glasses for it. In fact, I didn't have any drinking glasses at all. So I brought the scotch out in two chipped coffee mugs.

Be good be good be good, I told myself as I approached her. *Don't jump her bones. Don't fantasize about fucking her tits. Be a good priest.*

I offered her the scotch. "Sorry about the mugs."

She grinned. "But they're so classy."

I rolled my eyes and sat in the chair next to the fire, which was a bad idea because it meant that she was basically sitting at my feet and that was just reinforcing all the bad thoughts.

Now or never, Tyler, I told myself. *You have to do this.*

"Poppy—" I started but she interrupted.

"No, I'm the one who needs to apologize," she said. "That's what I came here to do, after all." She tilted her head up to meet my eyes and the fire glowed through her hair, showing where it was drying into messy waves. "I feel terrible about this afternoon. I'm fucked up from what happened with Sterling, and for some reason, when you got all protective of me this afternoon, I panicked."

You and me both.

"And I'll be honest—since I am talking to a priest after all. It's complicated by the fact that I can't stop thinking about you all the goddamned time, and it's killing me."

Everything in me lit on fire, because these were both the first and last words I wanted to hear, and I flinched.

She cast her eyes down in a wounded way that knifed through my ribs. She thought I was rejecting her attraction, rejecting *her*. Shit, nothing was further from the truth, but there was no way to explain that without making things more tangled than they already were.

"Anyway," she continued in a small voice, "I'm sorry for lashing out at you this afternoon. And I'm also sorry for what happened last Monday. I took advantage of you. I have all this shit in my life and I inflicted it upon you because you were here and you were kind."

I leaned forward, trying to summon the strength to say what needed to be said. "I'm glad that you came here and that you're sorry—not that you should be sorry, because the blame of what happened after your last confession rests squarely on my shoulders. But I'm glad because it means that you understand why it can't happen again. I have a vow to uphold, to honor God by honoring his children, his lambs. You came to me for help and instead I—" I stopped, unable to utter the words. But the heat rushed to my groin anyway, as words from that one afternoon shot through my mind like bullets through ballistic gel. *Cunt. Clit. Cock.*

Come. I didn't need to look to know that my sweatpants were dangerously close to revealing these thoughts.

"—I took advantage of you," I finished instead.

She pressed her lips together. "You did *not* take advantage of me. Yes, I've got some shit going on in my life right now, but I am my own person, capable of making my own choices. I'm not damaged, I didn't grow up unloved. I'm not a blank slate for males to exert their agency on. I *chose* to sleep with Sterling. I *chose* to let you go down on me. I wanted those things, and you don't get to tell me that I didn't. You don't get to tell me that I was nothing more than an unwilling bystander."

She stood, the red in her cheeks not just from the fire. "Don't worry. I won't bother you with my body again. I'll respect your vow and your outdated chivalry along with it."

That stung. That stung like hell, actually, because I had just been trying to summon up all of my postmodern, feminist ally thoughts, trying to squash down the part of my brain that fantasized about making her crawl naked across my floor with a glass of single-malt balanced on her back.

And that's why—I think—I grabbed her arm and tugged her between my legs. She gasped, but she didn't pull away. I was at the perfect height to sit up and suck on her nipple through her shirt, which I did. Her hands laced through my hair as she moaned.

"I thought—you just said—" She writhed as I bit gently down and then resumed my sucking.

"You're right," I said, pulling back. "I shouldn't do this."

Her face fell ever so slightly, but she nodded, pulling away, and then I grabbed her hips and tugged her down so that she straddled my thigh, her pussy immediately starting to grind against me in an adorably needy way.

"I shouldn't put you over my lap and spank your ass for being a brazen little slut and coming here without a bra," I growled in her ear. "I shouldn't twist ropes around your wrists and ankles until your cunt is exposed and then screw you until you can't walk anymore. I shouldn't flip you over and fuck your ass until your eyes water. I shouldn't drive you down to the strip club and fuck you in the back room, so that you'll forget all about Sterling and the only name you'll remember to say is mine." I lightly bit her nipple again. "Or God's."

I tucked two fingers into the waistband of her shorts and pulled down, the elastic stretching and giving me a peek at what I had already suspected. There was the smooth rise of her pubic bone, her clit visible as a tiny, soft bud of flesh, a bud just begging to be touched.

"Why did you come here tonight, Poppy?" I asked as I palmed her breast, quietly groaning at the feeling of its unsupported weight in my hand. I kept my other hand where it was, still staring at her bare cunt. "Did you really come to say sorry? Or did you come here, in the middle of the night, without a bra or panties, to tempt me? That's a sin, you know. Willfully leading another person into wrongful action or thought. No, don't pull away now."

She had started to twist away, and I knew I was sending signals so mixed that they were beyond confusing, they were blended, incomprehensible, but then I murmured, "One more. Give me one more."

One more what? I wondered even as I spoke. One more orgasm? For her? For me? One more chance? One more glimpse, one more taste, one more minute to pretend that there was nothing in the way of us being together?

And then I blanched. That was a stupid way to phrase it—being together—as if my attraction to Poppy Danforth was more than three years of celibacy encountering the sexiest woman I'd ever met. As if there was some secret part of me that wanted to do more than fuck her, it wanted to take her to dinner and make her breakfast and fall asleep with her in my arms.

She was staring at me the whole time I thought this, staring with hungry hazel eyes and a hungry mouth and those tits so perky and soft under her shirt.

"Tonight," I told her. "We have this. Then no more."

She nodded, then swallowed, as if her mouth were dry. I watched her throat move.

"Get on your knees," I said hoarsely.

She scrambled to obey, kneeling in between my legs and peering up at me through the long, dark lashes that haunted my waking thoughts.

"Take your shirt off."

She pulled the cotton shirt over her head and dropped it on the floor, and I had to fist my hands in my sweatpants to keep from tackling her and screwing her brains out, because holy *fuck*, were those breasts perfect. Cream-pale with dark pink nipples, small enough to cover with a fingertip, but large enough that I'd be able to draw them easily into my mouth. I wanted to see my cock slide between those tits, I wanted to jet my climax all over them, I wanted to feel them pressed against my chest while I stretched my body on top of hers.

But there would be no end to the things I wanted to do to this little lamb, no matter how many times or how many ways I had her. She was creating this insatiable pit in me, a yawning chasm of need, and even in my haze, I could see how destructive that would be if I didn't stop it.

And the stopping would happen soon…just not right *now*.

I lowered the waistband of my own pants just enough to free my dick, leaving my shirt on as well. I liked being dressed when I fucked, I always had; there was no bigger turn-on than having a naked woman climbing all over you, purring at your feet and squealing in your lap, all while you were fully dressed. (And yes, I recognize that's also fucked up in terms of feminism and all that. I'm sorry.)

Poppy squirmed now, her hand drifting to the thin fabric between her legs, caressing herself.

"You left a wet spot on my leg, lamb," I said, glancing

down to my thigh, where her arousal had soaked through the fabric of her shorts and my pants. "Do you want something?"

"I want to come," she whispered.

"But you can make yourself come any time you want. You came here tonight because you want something else. What is it?"

She hesitated then answered. "I want you to make me come."

"But you know it's wrong to ask."

"But I knew it was wrong to ask…or to want."

I let out a breath. It was wrong. All of it, so very wrong.

And Jesus help me, for some reason that made it all the sweeter.

"Lick," I said, indicating my cock. My hands were still by my thighs; I didn't bother holding myself for her. Instead, I sat back and watched as she ran her tongue from my base to my tip in one long motion. My fingers dug into the chair, hissing as she did it again. I'd forgotten how good this was too, how smooth and slick and soft a woman's tongue could be, how perfect it felt tracing lines along the sensitive underside of my dick, tracing delicate circles around the crown.

Obedient lamb, she didn't do any more than lick, her hand still between her legs, her eyes pinned to mine in the dim light.

"Suck now," I told her. A quick flash of a smile—a smile

that screamed Ivy League and financial analysis and a taste for good champagne—and then her head was nothing but a bobbing mass of dark waves between my legs.

I really did groan now. Was there any sight I'd missed more than this? A head moving eagerly between my thighs? But then I thought of that Monday in the church, her bent over the piano and her cunt the only thing in my vision. Her sitting on me, grinding her clit against my shaft.

There were a lot of sights I'd missed.

My hips and legs were practically vibrating with the suppressed need to thrust into her mouth, and I indulged myself just a little, threading my hands through her hair and holding her down over my cock, pushing up with my hips until I hit the back of her throat, shuddering as I slid back out, lips and teeth and tongue and palate, all of it stroking me, stoking me to further flame. I'd never been harder than this before, I was sure of it, and when I pulled her lips off my cock, I could see every vein, could feel the painfully swollen crest as it flared out then back in to my tip.

That's when I knew I had to feel her cunt. If it was going to be the last time, if this was it, then I had to. I mean, I was already committing a mortal sin by letting her suck me off. Would it be so much worse if I had her rub her pussy against me again?

Or if I slid just partway inside? That still wasn't really sex, not really *really*, and I would pull it right back out. I just wanted to feel it once. Only once.

Shit, I sounded like a teenager. I also didn't care at that moment, with the hardest dick in the world and with the most beautiful woman I'd ever seen still kneeling in front of me, mouth parted, cunt wriggling in undisguised want.

"Take your bottoms off and get on the counter," I ordered. She stood, took off her shorts, and walked to the kitchen (where thankfully all the blinds were drawn) and hopped onto the counter.

I approached her slowly, my blood at a low, dangerous boil, because I knew that I was walking oh so close to the edge, to the point of no return, but I wanted to, I wanted to fling myself into the unknown if the unknown was Poppy. It was hard to give a shit about anything else.

I smelled her as I stepped up to the counter, a mix of her arousal and clean soap and just a hint of lavender. I spread her legs as far apart as the counter would allow, reaching behind her and scooching her right up to the edge, so that when I pressed myself against her, my cock nestled against her folds.

She licked her red lips as she met my eyes. Licked her lips, as if she were a predator about to devour me, but that was not how this worked, not at all, and suddenly I was obsessed with smearing that red lipstick, still perfect at three in the morning, as if she'd reapplied it before she'd come over. Yes, when I was done with her, that carefully applied color would be everywhere, and she would feel marked, taken.

I leaned forward and kissed her for the first time.

Her lips were as soft as I expected—softer even—but they were firm in a way that I had not expected, not immediately yielding to me. Had I not lived the life I'd lived before the robe, I wouldn't have understood her reluctance. But I had, and I did.

"You want me to fight for it, lamb?" I murmured against her lips.

She nodded breathlessly.

"You want me to steal it from you?"

Another nod.

"Force it from you?"

A shuddering exhale. And then finally another nod. My little lamb wanted it rough, and what do you know, I wanted to give it to her that way.

My lips became an inexorable force, an act of nature—an act of God—and I gripped the back of her head as hard as I dared, pressing her face to mine. I ground my hips into her, rubbing myself against her, and used my free hand to claim her breast—pressing it into her chest, grabbing it so fiercely that I knew she could feel every fingertip as a bright point of discomfort. Slowly, oh so slowly, her mouth opened up to me, and the first time our tongues slid together in a tangle of silk and promise, I nearly lost it right then and there.

Her mouth was greedy, but mine was greedier, and we fought each other, who would devour whom the fastest, who could take what they wanted first, who could take the most, and before long, she was a writhing form of smooth muscle and soft curves, her hips jerking against mine and her hands fisting my hair and scratching my back.

When I finally, finally broke our kiss, I was satisfied to see that the lipstick was indeed smeared. It matched her smudged eyeliner and her wild hair, it matched her hands gripping my ass like two hot brands.

"I want to be inside you," I said. "Just a little. Just to feel it."

"Oh God," she breathed. "Please. It's all I've thought about since we've met."

"You have to hold really, really still," I warned her. "Will you behave?"

She bit her lip and nodded, and then I took myself in my hand. I couldn't believe I was doing this, and in the kitchen of my own fucking rectory—not that it was any worse than the sanctuary floor. But with her legs spread, with her practically whimpering from that kiss, I couldn't have stopped myself if I tried. And I definitely didn't want to try.

Holding myself, I pressed the head of my cock against her clit, brushing down past her entrance to her ass. She shivered in a way that told me she had no objection to that either, and I'd have to add that to the things I'd bitterly regret never having. I moved up, again grazing past her opening and up to her clit. She gave me an agonized expression and I wanted to kiss it right off her face—or come all over it, either one. After a few more passes, I couldn't wait any longer, I had to do it or I might actually die on the spot.

I leaned my forehead against hers, both of us looking down to watch as my tip pressed against her and slowly slipped inside. I stopped when the crest of my cock was in her, and then froze, muscles quivering.

Both of us just stared down at it, this impossible sight: me inside of her, a priest tasting the forbidden fruit and barely able to keep himself from eating it all.

"How does it feel?" she whispered.

"It feels…" my voice was barely more than a gasp at this point. "It feels like heaven."

She was so tight, her cunt squeezing my tip, and there were no words to describe what that wet, slippery skin was doing to me, because it was rewriting my mind and my soul, my future and my life. It was a sensation so base and primal, so delicious, that I would have killed to feel it, I would kill somebody right now if it meant I could have my dick inside this woman again.

One and a half inches of damnation, and all I could think about was sinking deeper into hell.

She rocked forward the tiniest bit, unable to help herself, greedy lamb, and I grabbed her neck, my legs shaking with the effort not to come from that single little movement alone. "Stay the fuck still, or I'm going to come before I want to, and if that happens, then I will take you over my knee and spank your ass until you learn how to listen," I said sternly.

My command had the predictable effect of sending goose bumps rippling up her arms. Her breathing was loud and harsh sounding in the small kitchen. "Fuck," she whispered. "*Fuck*. I—this—this is the hottest thing I've ever done."

It was possibly the hottest thing I'd ever done too, and I'd done a lifetime's worth of hot things to many hot women—but none of them had been like Poppy.

Red-lipped and blue-blooded. And fuck, the horniest woman I'd ever met.

"I want to feel you come around me," I said, my forehead still against hers, our eyes going back to the place where we were joined. I would never forget this as long as I lived, I knew, and I didn't want her to forget either.

"That won't take long," she said and then gave a little husky laugh that made her clench around me. I hissed, grabbing the countertop to keep myself from losing it.

"Sorry," she whispered, and in answer, I slid a hand over her leg to her clit and began rubbing.

"Stay still," I reminded her as we watched my large hand, tan and calloused from all the odd jobs I did around the church, pressing into her soft pink flesh, as we watched her quiver around the tip of my dick.

"I'm trying to stay still," she murmured, and I could tell she was, I could tell she wanted to see herself come around me as much as I did. I increased the strength and tempo of my fingers.

"Filthy girl," I whispered. "So dirty to let me stick it inside of you. Do you like this, being spread open and used this way? I bet you like being called dirty names too."

"P-please," she moaned.

"Please what, lamb?"

She could barely talk now, her head lolling back against the cabinets, her arched back shoving her breasts closer to me. "Names," she got out. "I like…the names…"

Fuck. She was really going to kill me. Death by turn-on. Death by perpetual erection.

"Are you a slut, Poppy?" I bent my head down and sucked on a nipple, loving the feel of it furling on my tongue, stiffening as I sucked. "You're sure acting like a slut, making me act this way. You're making me break all sorts of rules, and I hate breaking rules." I moved to her neck, kissing and biting. "You'll take it anywhere you can get it, won't you?"

"I'm—" She inhaled, unable to finish, but she didn't need to because she was coming now, her body undulating as if to chase the waves of pleasure that rolled through it. Again and again, her pussy clamped down on the head of my cock, squeezing and pulsing, and just knowing that I could make her come with only the shallowest of penetrations made me nearly wild.

She slumped in my arms as she came down, resting her

head on my shoulder. "Your turn," she said against my skin.

I started to pull out but she grabbed my hips and stopped me. "No," she said. "In me."

"Poppy," I started.

"I'm on the pill." Her jaw set as she looked up at me. "I want to see it spilling out around you. I want it where it belongs—in me. Please, Tyler. If this is the last time, give me this one thing."

Tyler. She'd never called me that before. And it was there at the base of my spine now, fueled by her dirty words—what woman begged for this? What woman was turned on by it?

But frankly, I would have agreed to anything, no matter how dangerous, so I nodded, my jaw clenching.

She leaned back against the cabinets, bringing her heels up to the counter. The change in her position didn't move me any deeper inside, but it made her flex and tighten around me, and my climax clawed closer. She slid her hands to the undersides of her breasts, running her thumbs along her still-stiff nipples, pressing her breasts together and moving them apart, highlighting how fucking luscious they were and nearly blinding me with lust at the same time.

God, I needed to pump.

Needed to thrust.

Needed to fuck.

Then her fingers went to her clit and she started getting herself off again, her other fingers going up to slide in and out of her mouth and I was fucking transfixed, those lips, that wicked mouth, the mouth that had gotten my cock from *hard as fuck* to *harder than fuck* by the fireplace earlier. And then—naughty girl—she moved her hips ever so slightly, bucking them just enough to push me in and out of her the smallest bit, so wet, so tight, and there it was, stabbing through my balls and up my cock, and we both watched as it happened, as my hips jerked and my stomach muscles jumped and then I ejaculated. My legs could barely support my weight and I could barely breathe as it ripped through me, my first climax in a woman in years, but I forced myself to stand stock-still because I wanted to memorize this moment forever, the semen dripping and her pussy so wet and her legs spread in hallowed welcome. The pulsing finally, finally slowed, and she laid her head against my chest, making this happy, contented little sigh, and my heart twisted inside my chest, demanding everything that it wanted now that it could be heard over my rampant lust.

"Shit," I mumbled, leaning forward and pressing my face into her sweet-smelling hair. "What are you doing to me?"

We stayed that way a long moment, neither of us wanting it to be over, but then the air-conditioning kicked on, blowing cold air over us, and Poppy shivered, still naked. I had her stay on the counter while I got a washcloth and cleaned her with warm water, and then I helped her find her clothes and walk to the door.

"So I'll see you at Mass tomorrow?" she said.

"Poppy—"

"I know, I know," she said with a sad smile. "Tomorrow, we'll start fresh. Chaste. Clean."

"Good, but that's not what I was going to say."

Her brows furrowed. "What were you going to say?"

I leaned in and brushed my lips against hers. *Last time. Last kiss.* "I wanted to say thank you. For the scotch and for…what just happened."

She blinked up at me and then her eyes fluttered closed as I deepened our kiss, tasting every inch of her mouth, licking into her as gently and lovingly as I had done ferociously earlier. I never wanted to move from this spot, I only wanted to taste her and breathe the air that we were sharing and feel her body warm against mine—and also pretend that I wasn't waiting for a tsunami of guilt and a lifetime of penance.

"Good night," she said against my mouth.

"Good night, little lamb," I said.

Stepping away felt like stepping onto shards of glass, and I couldn't help myself, she was so wide-eyed and so open to my love, and it was instinct more than anything else that led to trace a small cross on her forehead.

A blessing.

And hopefully a promise to do better.

CHAPTER TEN

My phone buzzed violently on my counter.

It was Monday, two days post-not-really-sex, and I was thinking about how I was meeting Poppy in just a few minutes for lunch. I was cleaning the counter and remembering what the view had been from this exact location two nights ago.

I didn't even try to puzzle out what the text said. It was from Bishop Bove, and my boss was not only terrible at texting but also really insecure about his terrible texting, so I knew he would call right after he sent the text to make sure I got it (and then translate it for me).

Sure enough, my phone rang a moment later, *The Walking Dead* theme song echoing in my kitchen. Normally I would hum a couple of bars, normally I would be more than happy to talk to the gruff, principled man who was reforming our diocese and fighting for reform alongside me, but today, I only felt a prickling trepidation, as if he knew somehow what I had done two nights ago. As if he would guess it the minute he heard my voice. "Hello?"

"Are you going to the Mid-America Clergy Convention next year?" Bishop Bove asked, skipping straight to business. "I want to put a panel together. And I want you on it."

"I haven't decided yet," I said, and I realized my palms were actually getting sweaty, like I'd been called to the principal's office or pulled over or something. Shit. If I felt this nervous on the phone with him, what would I do when I saw him in person?

"I think this is finally the year we'll get the panel we want in there," the bishop said. "You know how long I've pushed for it."

The panel we want…the panel on abuse. Bishop Bove had submitted proposals to the continuing clergy education organization for the last four years and had been shot down every time. But the leadership within the organization had shifted, younger organizers were in charge, and I knew that Bove had been told privately that he would finally get his controversial panel.

But how was I going to sit in a hotel ballroom staring at a sea of priests and presume to lecture them on the perils of errant priest sexuality? I glanced down at my countertop, where I'd slipped inside Poppy. Not all the way. Not all the way, but enough to come. Enough to make her come. I rubbed my eyes, trying to block out the sight.

Could a vow be not all the way broken? Could a sin be not all the way committed?

Of course not. And even if no one ever knew about it, I realized that I'd destroyed my legitimacy with myself, and maybe that was worse than my public legitimacy being destroyed. What had I gotten myself into? Was I ever going to be able to let myself speak about—preach about—the things I cared the most for again?

"Tyler?"

"If you get the panel, I'll be there," I mumbled, still rubbing my eyes. I was seeing sparks.

Better than seeing my sins.

"I knew you would. How's St. Margaret's? How's Millie? She gave the diocesan bookkeeper hell last week for misplacing your quarterly tithe reports. I heard she reduced the poor man to tears."

"Everything's good here, everything is going really well," I lied. "Just gearing up for all the fall youth stuff."

And you know, halfway fucking hopeful converts.

"Good. I'm proud of you, Tyler. I don't say that often enough, but the work you've done in that town has been nothing short of a miracle."

Stop, I begged him silently. *Please stop.*

"You are doing Christ's work, Tyler. You are such an example."

Please, please stop.

"Well, I'll let you go. And the panel—I'll text you the moment I hear."

"Are you sure about that?"

"Fine, I'll *call*. Goodbye, Tyler."

I hung up and stared at my phone a minute. I had woken up telling myself that yesterday was my starting-over day. My being-chaste day. And that today would be even easier. So why did I feel like my sins were still haunting me? Still dogging my steps?

Because you haven't confessed them, Tyler.

I was an idiot. I should have done this at the very beginning. I sat on one side of the booth every week—why hadn't it occurred to me to seek out the other side? To seek out the absolution and accountability that every person needed?

Next week. I would go down to Kansas City next Thursday to visit my confessor—a man I went to seminary with—and then I would have dinner with Mom and Dad and everything would be so much better.

I felt a little swell of relief at this plan. It was all going to be okay.

Poppy had come to Mass yesterday morning and sought me out afterwards to arrange our lunch plans for today. I'd wanted to have lunch with her right then—or have her for lunch, I hadn't been sure—but she'd ducked away the moment our plans were figured out, and then I'd been swarmed by the usual crowd of after-service lingerers. Was she trying to keep her distance? And if so, was it because she wanted to? Or as a perceived favor to me?

The thought that this would be how we would behave around each other from now on—businesslike and abrupt—made me acutely miserable.

Which was stupid, because it was what I had wanted—no, what I should want—but I didn't. I wanted both lives—the life where we were believer and priest and the life where we were man and woman—and every moment that passed without my mouth on Poppy's skin, more and more of my willpower bled away, until I was left with the uncomfortable knowledge that I would endure whatever guilt or punishment I had to in order to touch her again.

Today these thoughts still clouded my head when I gathered my things and walked the two blocks to the nearest winery. I had expected to see Poppy by herself but was pleasantly surprised to see her chatting animatedly with Millie in the wine garden, an open bottle of something white and chilled on the table.

Poppy waved me over. "I invited Millie—I hope that's okay?"

"Of course, it's okay," Millie interrupted before I could answer. "This boy can barely tell time, let alone budget for a major project."

I mock-frowned at her. "I'll have you know that I've got

a very organized pile of Post-it Notes and bar napkins in this bag."

Millie huffed, as if I'd confirmed every one of her darkest fears. I glanced over to Poppy, some immature part of me wanting to make sure that she had laughed and then wishing I hadn't once I took in how marvelous she looked. She wore turquoise skinny jeans and a nowhere-near-loose enough T-shirt, a soft thin cotton that reminded me of the shirt she wore Saturday night...the shirt I'd sucked her nipples through. Her hair was in a messy braid thrown over one shoulder, and her eyes were more green than brown in the sunlight filtering in through the vines covering the pergola, and her lips were back in their trademark red, and why did she have to be so fucking sexy all the damn time?

"Sit, my boy, before the Riesling gets warm," Millie told me. "Now, Poppy, tell Father Bell what you just told me."

I pulled out a wrought iron chair and settled in, already sweating in the early September heat. Millie poured a third glass of cool wine and I accepted it, grateful to have something I could stare at other than Poppy.

"Well," Poppy started, "to start off, I'm not familiar with what you guys are doing for fundraising or what you have done in the past, so I don't want to step on any toes or anything."

"You won't," I promised.

"But tell me if I do. This is your project after all."

"It's the church's project," I said. "And since you've

been coming to St. Margaret's, I'd say that makes it your project too."

She flushed a happy little flush, as if this pleased her, tracing circles around the edge of her iPad as she talked. I remembered my thoughts about her during our meeting, that she was a born volunteer, someone who loved to help. I saw it in her eyes as she talked, the excitement and the purpose. "I've noticed that Weston has a huge number of seasonal festivals, which isn't unusual for a bed-and-breakfast town," she was saying. "And I noticed on the church website that you advertise that you keep your doors open for visitors during these festivals—have you ever done more?"

"Not really," Millie said.

"And how many visitors do you usually get?"

I tried to remember. "Three? Four?"

Poppy nodded, as if I'd proved her point. "I think a festival is a perfect opportunity to bring in more donors, if we take advantage of it the right way. This building is over one hundred years old—and that kind of old charm is exactly what people are coming for. That and booze. So you set up on the sidewalk, you give away local wine and whiskey from the distillery, but you stay away from the usual church sale fare. They're not coming in to buy recipe books or rosaries—they are coming in to *see*. And you give them the booze for free, so they feel unconsciously obligated to you."

I could see the Business Poppy right now as she layered through her points efficiently and easily, rolling her stylus through her fingers as she talked. I saw the wealthy boarding-school girl, the Dartmouth grad, the woman engineered for large boardrooms and corporate victories.

"So anyway, you make the church a destination for the people wandering around. That's step one. But more importantly, you reach out to the local newspapers and the Kansas City television stations. You turn St. Margaret's into a local interest news story, the kind that goes viral on Twitter and Facebook. The church is about preserving Midwestern tradition—you emphasize the things Millie says you are planning to do—keeping the original windows, restoring the original hardwood floors and repairing the old stonework. People love that stuff. And then, step three, which is really step zero because you do this part before you do anything else, you make a Kickstarter for the renovation, so that when the stories air and the posts get reposted, there's an easy link for people to follow. You'll increase your fundraising footprint from the Weston area to the entire Kansas City Metro—and possibly even farther out than that."

This woman was so damn smart. "So why not just do the Kickstarter and the news thing?"

"Because," Poppy said, leaning forward, "you need to bring a crowd of people into the church, to see it with their own eyes, to learn about its history and potential restoration. You need them to go back to wherever they came from and seed the push. They're the ones who will be the most likely to start sharing and tweeting, they're the ones who will help you overcome that first clutch of inertia, because they are invested now, they've spent time and energy in St. Margaret's. They are your disciples. You teach them, and then you say, 'Go thou and do likewise.'"

"You've been reading up on your Bible," I said approvingly.

She smiled. "Just a little. Millie invited me to the Come and See meeting next week. That verse was on the back of the brochure."

The Come and See meetings were for people interested in joining the Church, and now it was my turn to hide my happy reaction. Despite everything that had gone wrong between us, she was still sincerely interested in exploring the faith.

"I think your idea sounds fantastic," I said. "We've pretty much exhausted all of the usual means, and I think our own parish is tapped dry of funds. You make it sound so easy though—how expensive will it be to offer free wine? How do I even get in touch with the news people?"

Poppy tugged the cap off her stylus with her teeth and starting jotting notes onto her iPad. "I'll take care of it. The wineries here will donate the wine—that's easy. And the news stations are always looking for stuff like this, it'll be little more than sending an email, which I'll do this week.

And I'll set up the Kickstarter too. You will see—it's not that much work."

"It feels like a lot of work," I admitted. "I mean, I think you're right and I want to do this, but it does feel like a lot."

"Okay, it does look like a lot, but really, I promise it won't be. Especially with me doing the setup—all you'll have to do is be charming and square-jawed for the cameras."

Millie patted my arm appreciatively. "He's good at that. He's our secret weapon."

Poppy's eyes flicked to mine. "Yes, he is."

We spent the rest of the hour planning, deciding on what festival made the most sense for our fundraiser (Irish Fest) and who would do what (Poppy would do mostly everything, but Millie and I agreed to be conscripted wherever we were needed, giving Poppy our personal email addresses and phone numbers). And then Millie climbed in her gold Buick sedan and drove the two streets over to her house while Poppy and I walked back in the direction of the church.

"I won't be able to come to confession today," she said out of nowhere. "I have a conference call. I hope that's okay."

"Most Catholics only go to confession once a year. You're fine." But I was a little disappointed. (And of course for all the wrong reasons.)

"I was wondering…"

"Yes?" I asked hopefully.

"This is going to sound stupid. Never mind."

We were crossing the main street now, from shady sidewalk to even shadier sidewalk, and all around us was the noise of the breeze in the leaves and the birds and the faint roll of cars far away. I wanted to tell her that right now I'd give her anything, I'd give her everything, so long as we could stay in this peaceful bubble of early autumn forever, just the two of us and the leaves and the green warmth that made it so easy to feel loved by God.

But I couldn't tell her that. So instead, I said, "I don't think you're capable of asking a stupid question, Ms. Danforth."

"You should reserve judgment until I ask, Father," she said in a voice that was half laugh, half sigh.

"I'm Catholic. Judging is my thing."

This earned me a real laugh. She squinted up at the brick edifice of the church as we approached and then squared her shoulders, as if deciding to go for it. "Here's the thing. I want to do this…this God stuff. I think maybe it's the first choice that's felt right since I walked off that stage at Dartmouth. But I have no framework for even thinking about living a religious life. I know I'm supposed to show up at Mass and I'm supposed to read the Bible and that all seems straightforward enough. But praying…I feel foolish. I feel clumsy. I've never really done it before and I'm not sure I'm doing it right." She turned to me. "So I guess I wanted to know if you can help me with that. With the praying."

I meant to tell her that prayer wasn't a test, that God wasn't grading her on how well or how eloquently she prayed, that even sitting in silence counted. That we Catholics had prescribed prayers to circumvent exactly this kind of crisis. But then the breeze blew a strand of hair across her face, and I without thinking reached up and brushed it back behind her ear, and her eyes drifted closed at my touch, and fuck fuck fuck, what had I been about to say?

"Tonight," I said. "After the men's group. Come find me and we'll work on it."

CHAPTER ELEVEN

After men's group, I stopped by my office to grab a rosary and a small pamphlet containing some basic prayers and walked into the sanctuary, knowing that Poppy would probably be there early.

What I didn't know was that she'd be standing directly in front of the altar, staring at the cross, the late-dusk light pouring through the windows and staining her in dark jewel tones, sapphire and crimson and emerald. I didn't know that her shoulders would be shaking ever so slightly, as if she were crying, and I didn't know that all the doors and windows would be closed, trapping the lush, incense-scented air inside.

I stopped, the greeting on my lips stalled by the stillness, by the heavy weight of the quiet.

God was here.

God was here, and He was talking to Poppy.

I felt every kiss of air across my skin as I walked closer to her, heard her every exhale, and when I reached her, I saw how goose bumps peppered her arms, how tears ran silently down her cheeks.

There were a thousand things I should say, but I couldn't bring myself to interrupt whatever moment this was. Except that it wasn't truly interrupting, because I felt invited into it, like I was supposed to be part of it, and I did what felt right: I wrapped my arms around her.

She leaned back into me, her eyes still pinned to the cross, and I just held her as we both let the moment wash over us, bathe us in the dying light and the silence. Shadows crept along the floor and pooled around our feet, and the seconds ticked into minutes, and slowly, slowly, we drew incrementally closer, until every inch of her back was pressed against me, until my nose was in her hair and her hands were twined through mine.

The closeness of her and the closeness of the divine all at the same time was euphoria, bliss, and I was almost dizzy with it, feeling both at once, intoxicated by her and intoxicated by my God. And in the face of this numinous encounter, there was no room for guilt, no room for critical self-analysis and recrimination. There was only room to be present, be there, and then she turned in my arms, tilting her face up to mine.

"You feel it too?" she asked.

"Yes."

"Is it always like this for you?"

I shook my head. "Once a week, maybe. Sometimes twice. I know people like my confessor who feel it every moment and people like my bishop who feel it never."

"It's beautiful."

It was full dark now, and there was nothing but different shadows, but even in the shadows, the tear tracks on her face glistened. "*You're* beautiful," I whispered.

We were talking in hushed voices; the air was still heavy with holiness and presence. And I should have felt wicked for holding Poppy like this in the face of God, but our burning bush of a silent room somehow made everything seem more right, like it was the most perfect thing to do, holding her in my arms and staring down at her face.

I slid my fingers under her chin, keeping her face angled to mine, and leaned down just enough so that our noses brushed together. I could kiss her right now. Maybe I should kiss her right now. Maybe it was God's plan all along for us to end up here, alone in this sanctuary, and forced to face the truth, that this was more than friendship, this was more than lust. This was something raw and real and undeniable and it was not going to go away.

She was trembling against me now, her lips parted and waiting, and I allowed myself a narrower margin now, lowering my mouth to a mere fraction of an inch above hers, tightening my arm around her lower back. We were so close that we were sharing breath, literally, our hearts beating in the same dizzy rhythm.

In spite of everything that had happened between us, this moment somehow felt more intimate, more vulnerable, than anything we'd yet shared. Everything else had happened while I pretended God wasn't watching, but this—there was no pretending now. Sacred and profane were blending and blurring together, fusing and welding themselves into something new and whole and singular, and if this was what love was, then I didn't know how anyone could bear the weight of it.

"I can't stop myself, I'm sorry," I said at the same time she said, "I tried to stay away from you."

And then I kissed her.

I brushed my lips against hers once, just to feel the softness of her skin glancing past mine, and then pressed my mouth to hers in earnest, tasting her in the slowest, deepest way possible, until I felt her knees weaken and she made little noises in the back of her throat.

I kissed her until I saw static at the edges of my vision, until I couldn't remember a time when we hadn't been kissing, until I couldn't feel where my mouth ended and hers began. I kissed her until it felt like we'd exchanged something—a promise maybe or a covenant or a piece of our souls. And when I finally pulled away, it was as if I pulled away reborn, a new man. A baptism by kiss rather than a baptism by water.

"More," she begged. "More."

I kissed her again, this time with hunger, with need, and

I could tell by the way she made little sighs into my mouth, the way her fingers twisted in the fabric of my shirt, that she was as far gone for me as I was for her, and I never wanted to stop, never wanted this to end.

But it had to.

When we broke apart, she stepped back and wrapped her arms around herself, shivering a little in the blast of the air-conditioning. The clouds outside had parted, sending a shaft of silver through the windows, and we were in a fairy pool of glowing moonlight. The God feeling was still there, but rather than a weight from the outside, it felt like sparks on the inside, as if the divine had seeped into my blood. I felt light-headed and drunk with it.

"I'm tired," Poppy said, though she didn't sound tired so much as dazed. "I think that I should go home."

"I'll walk you," I offered. She nodded, and together we left the mystery behind, as if by walking to the sanctuary doors, we were walking away from what had just happened.

"That was incredible," she murmured.

"I've been told I'm a good kisser."

She bumped my shoulder. "You know what I mean."

We were in the narthex now, but I couldn't shake the image of her standing in front of the cross, so open and receptive to an experience that most people would dismiss outright. "Poppy, I have to ask. Did something happen to draw you to the church? Did you go as a child and now you're circling back?"

"Why?"

"It seems like…" I searched for the right phrasing, wanting to express how much a good thing I thought her interest was. "I think it's marvelous that you're jumping in feet first. It's just not the way a lot of people do it."

"It feels a lot more gradual on my end," she said as we walked outside. I kept a careful space between us as we took the stone stairs down the hill the church was perched on. "My family isn't religious—in fact, no one we knew was religious. I think they were always suspicious of it, like anything that could inspire such fervor in people was gauche, at best. Dangerous, at worst. I guess I was always a bit more open to it. In college, I went with a friend to her Buddhist temple almost every week and in Haiti, I was working side by side with missionaries. But it wasn't until the day I came in for confession that I'd ever sought it out on my own."

"What made you come back after that?"

She paused. "You."

I processed this as we hit the bottom of the stairs and walked into the wooded park between the church and her house. It was bright with closely spaced lamps and moonlight. I cleared my throat, wondering if my question ultimately made a difference, but deciding to ask anyway. "Was it me as a priest? Or me as a man?"

"Both. I think that's what is so confusing."

We walked in silence now, together but not together,

our minds on the beauty of that moment in the sanctuary, on the way it felt to kiss when our souls were on fire.

Fuck. It was all so confusing to me too, except that parts of the confusion were starting to fall away, which should have been clarifying, but I worried that it was actually the opposite, that I was forgetting things I was supposed to remember.

Like my promise to be better.

"I want to hold your hand right now," I said abruptly. "I want to wrap my arm around your waist and pull you close."

"But you can't," she replied softly. "Someone could be watching."

We were at the garden behind her house now.

"I don't know what to do next," I said honestly. "I just…"

I had literally nothing else to say. I didn't know what I could do to explain how I felt about her, and also how I felt about my vocation and my responsibilities, and about how I was so ready to abandon them all because I wanted to kiss her again. I wanted to hold her fucking hand in the park at night.

She peered up at the stars. "I wish you could hold my hand too." She shivered again and I could see that her nipples had pebbled in the slight evening chill, hard little furls just begging to be sucked.

The sweet feelings of a few minutes ago were starting to fuse with other, baser feelings that crowded up from my pelvis. It took every ounce of my self-control not to pin her up against the fence and kiss her again, not to yank down her pants and fuck her right here, outside, where anyone could see.

"I want to see you again," I said in a low voice. There was no mistaking my meaning and she shifted, rubbing her thighs together.

"Is that…I mean, should we…"

"I don't think I care anymore," I said.

"Neither do I," she whispered.

"Tomorrow."

She shook her head. "I have to go to Kansas City for some club stuff—we're switching over to new accounting software. But I'll be back Thursday night."

I wanted to groan out loud, but I managed to stop myself. "That's three days from now," I said.

She put her fingers on the latch to her back gate. "Come inside," she said. "Let's hang out tonight."

"It's late," I said. "And I want plenty of time for what I have in mind."

She exhaled slowly and her red lips parted, showing me those two front teeth, the tiniest glimpse of tongue.

I looked around to make sure we were truly alone, and then I grabbed her hand, opened the latch and tugged her inside the garden. I pulled her under the overgrown trellis, and then I spun her around so that her ass was pressed against me—pressed against my erection. I put one hand over her mouth and then unfastened her jeans with the other.

"Three days is a long time from now," I said in her ear. "I just want to make sure that you're taken care of until then."

And then I slid my fingers down her stomach, slipping under her silk panties. She moaned against my hand.

"Shhh," I said. "Be a good girl and I'll give you what you want."

She whimpered in response.

God, I loved her pussy. I'd never felt anything softer than the skin between her legs—and *fuck* she was wet. So wet that I really could pull these jeans down and take what I wanted, right here, right now. But no. She deserved better than that.

Not that I wouldn't fantasize about it as I got her off.

I started in on her clit in earnest now, circling it hard and fast, loving the way she bucked against my hand. I knew it was more pressure and speed than was comfortable, but I also knew that she would like it that way, savor that tiny, tiny bite of pain with her pleasure.

"I could do this all day, little lamb," I told her. "I love reaching down the front of your jeans, playing with your cunt, making you come. Do you like it?"

She nodded, her breathing jagged against my hand. She was getting close.

"Thursday night," I said, and I almost felt like I was having an out-of-body experience, listening to myself say these words. But I was beyond caring, or more accurately, beyond the place where the rules I cared about mattered. "I want to be with you. I want to fuck you. But only if it's what you want."

She nodded again, eagerly, desperately.

"I can't wait," and my voice was hoarse now. "I can't wait to be inside you. Feel me. Feel how hard I am just thinking about it." I ground my cock into her ass, and she shuddered against me, my words and my hard dick pushing her over the edge. She made a tiny cry that was muffled by my hand, quaked under my touch for a long minute, and finally came down, sagging against me.

I kept my hand in her panties for a minute or two longer, loving the way it looked, loving the way it felt, and then I reluctantly withdrew, zipping and buttoning her back up. I sucked on my fingers as she turned to face me, eyes bright and cheeks clearly flushed even in the dark.

"Go to bed, Poppy," I said when I could see that she would protest me leaving. "I'll see you Thursday night."

It hit me like a ton of obvious, kiss-sized bricks as I recited Mass the next morning: I was falling in love with Poppy Danforth.

I wasn't just desperate to fuck her. I wasn't just happy to help her find faith. I was well and truly on my way to being in love with her.

After a month.

Stupid, stupid, stupid.

And now that she wasn't here, not anywhere near here, I found my obsession spiraling out of control, like a drug addiction that demanded to be fed.

I imagined her voice filling the sanctuary after Rowan and the grandmothers left morning Mass. I pictured her face and her messy braid as I ran off copies of the Bible study worksheet for the next men's group. I found myself googling pictures of Dartmouth and Newport instead of trawling through *The Walking Dead* forums. I even (creepily, I know) googled her family, scrolling through pictures of polished people at polished charity events, finally finding an old picture of her at what looked to be some sort of fundraiser for a politician. Her and a cluster of attractive people who were obviously her parents and siblings—her father, silver-haired and broad-shouldered, and her mother, svelte and elegant. A brother and a sister with the same expensive clothes and expensive, high-cheekboned faces.

I clicked the picture to see the image on its own, see a larger version of Poppy's face. She was clearly younger, though not too young—in her early twenties maybe, and she was clearly unhappy. While everyone else flashed their wealthy, happy smiles at the camera, Poppy had only managed a firm press of her lips, her eyes directed somewhere behind the cameraman, as if absorbed with something only she could see.

A wave of unwanted jealousy and suspicion surged in my chest. Was she looking at Sterling? This seemed like the kind of event he would be at, from the little I knew. Or maybe she was merely gazing at the specter of her own unhappiness, her own dull future, spelled out in seating arrangements and menu cards?

I thought of the picture the rest of the evening, as I set up for the youth group. I also thought of *her*, of getting to see her on Thursday, and every few minutes I would catch myself smiling, smiling for no reason at all except that I would get to see Poppy again.

Tonight in youth group, we talked about Jesus being tempted in the desert, and in a dramatic turnaround from last week, I felt completely removed from the verses. I wasn't in a desert…I was in a place with rustling green leaves and clear, rushing water.

What had changed? I wondered. Between last week and this week, between yesterday and today?

It was last night. It was the praying, the magic, the smell of her hair. The kiss that had sealed something, something that transcended the physical and the spiritual. They were no longer separate and divided, but one…and with that, the experience of her had crossed over from being confusing as hell to wonderful. Awesome. Not awesome in the *cool* sense, but awesome in the sense that it filled me with awe.

She filled me with awe. She made me see the world with a new sense of wonder, every tree greener, every angle sharper, every face more pleasant and delightful to help.

It wasn't that the guilt had disappeared, however. I zigzagged from fantasy to recrimination, punishing myself with more runs, more push-ups, more chores around the church, spending hours in prayer searching for an answer.

Why would God bring Poppy here if I wasn't supposed to fall in love with her?

Was it truly so terrible for a man of God to have sex? The Protestants had been doing it for half a millennium and they seemed no more hell-bound than the Catholics for it.

And was it so wrong to want both? I wanted to lead this church, I wanted to help people find God. But dammit, I wanted Poppy too, and I didn't think it was fair that I had to choose.

God didn't answer. Whatever magic had been lingering in the sanctuary these past couple weeks hid itself from me, and in a way, that was its own answer.

I was meant to figure this out on my own.

CHAPTER TWELVE

I was as restless as a caged animal on Thursday.

I tried watching Netflix, I tried reading. My house was already perfectly clean, my lawn mowed. The only thing I could focus on was Poppy. On seeing her tonight.

And finally, I gave up and went to my room. I sat in the chair by my bed and unzipped my jeans. I had been in a state of semi-hardness all day, and just the thought of jacking off—something I'd mostly denied myself for the past three years—was enough to get me all the way there. I gave myself a couple of pulls until my cock was pointing straight up, remembering how it felt to have Poppy's wet cunt pressing against me. I leaned back, my jaw tight, finally giving up and reaching for my phone.

She picked up on the second ring. "Hello?" That voice. It was even huskier on the phone. I wrapped my hand around my dick and slowly stroked myself.

"Where are you?"

"I'm at the club." I could hear her moving around, as if she were walking into a more private place to talk. "But I'm almost done. What's going on?"

I hesitated. God, this was so fucking crass, but I wanted her voice in my ear as I did this. "I'm hard, Poppy. I'm so fucking hard that I can't think straight."

"Oh," she said. And then, her voice filled with understanding, "Oh, Tyler, are you—"

"Yes."

"How?" she said, and I could hear her moving again and then I heard a door close shut. "Where?"

"I'm in my room. My jeans are pulled down."

"Are your legs splayed? Are you leaning back or sitting up?" Her questions were laced with want, with hunger. It made me grip myself harder.

"I'm leaning back. Yes, my legs are wide. It makes me think of when you knelt between them and sucked me off."

"I want to do it again," she purred, and somehow I knew that she was touching herself too. "I want to lick you from base to tip. I want to suck you in deep."

"I want that too."

"Are you using your whole hand or just your fingers?"

"My whole hand," I said, and I was jerking myself in earnest now, wanting her to be here so badly.

"Hold on," she said, and there were a few seconds of

silence. Then my phone buzzed. "You have a text," she said silkily.

I held my phone away from my face and nearly passed out. She'd sent me a picture of her fingers buried in her cunt. "You're so fucking dirty," I said. And then another one came through, this one angled so that I could see her black high heel braced against the edge of a desk.

Holy shit.

"I can hear you now," she said. "I can hear your hand moving over your cock. God, I wish I could see it."

"I wish you could too," I said, and I managed to pull up the camera on my phone and turn on the video, all with one hand because no way was I slowing down now.

"I'm so wet," she confided. "I'm making a mess. I'm in my boss's office right now—*mmm*—it's all so slippery and I wish it was your cock instead of my fingers, I wish it so much. I wore these heels today knowing I'd be digging them into your back later."

I kept the image of her heels and that perfect cunt in my mind as I let her words work their magic. My climax jolted through me and I thrust up into my hand, groaning loudly as cum jetted out of my dick, exhaling a muttered *fuck* as the orgasm slowly backed down.

"I love hearing you," came her voice from the earpiece. "Your noises. I thought about them last night in my hotel room while I played with myself."

"Naughty girl." I sent her the video. "Now it's your turn

to check your messages."

There was a pause and then I could hear the unmistakable sound of myself jacking off as she played the video, hear my groan echoing in her boss's office. "Oh God," she whispered, and it was clear I was on speaker now. "Fuck, Tyler. That's so—if I were there, I would lick every last drop off you."

"If you were here, it all would have gone in your tight little cunt," I growled.

"*Jesus*," she moaned. And then, "Yes," which was followed by breathy little gasps that made my cock stir back to life. And finally silence, punctuated with a loud sigh and the chair squeaking as she sat up.

I heard the click as I came off speaker. "Tyler?"

"Yes?"

The smile was apparent in her voice. "Feel free to call me any time."

Somehow, I managed to make it through the rest of the day, running until I couldn't think, half-heartedly piecing together stuff for Bishop Bove's panel proposal while I impatiently watched the clock (and tamped down guilt as I gathered notes about sexual sin).

Around seven in the evening, my phone buzzed.

I'm home. Do you want me to come to the rectory?

I responded right away. **I'll meet you at the church.**

Thursday night was the one night a week without any activities, groups, or Bible studies going on, so the church was empty. It was still early enough in the evening to be light out, and I wanted the plausible excuse of counseling or budget stuff in case someone saw her walking into the church. Her coming to the rectory alone at night would be a little harder to defend.

I slipped in the back door and practically jogged down the hallway to the narthex, where the front doors were locked. I turned the bolt and opened the door, and there was Poppy in a short red dress and black high heels, lips red and ready for me.

I had wanted to be gentle at first, to share more of those deep sweet kisses that left us dizzy and stunned, but that dress and those heels…

Screw gentle.

I grabbed her wrist and pulled her inside, barely taking the time to lock the door before I pushed her against it and slanted my mouth over hers. I slid my hands under her ass and lifted her so that she was truly pinned between the wood and my pelvis, which I rocked against her as we kissed.

And that was when I discovered she wasn't wearing underwear.

"Poppy," I said, breaking our kiss to move a hand down between us. "What's this?"

"I told you," she said, trying to catch her breath. "You made me messy today. I had to take them off."

"So you spent the rest of the afternoon bare?"

She nodded, biting her lip.

I pulled away from the wall, still holding her, and carried her into the sanctuary, using my back to push open the door. She wrapped her legs around my waist, and it was so natural, so right, to have her in my arms that I never wanted to put her down.

"Am I in trouble?" she asked, a bit coyly.

"Yes," I growled, nipping at her neck. "Lots of trouble. But first, I'm going to bend you over and see exactly how bad you've been."

My plan had been to take her into my office, but I couldn't wait the five minutes it would take to walk back there; I was barely able to keep myself from unzipping my jeans and thrusting up into her right there and then. I could bend her over a pew, but I wanted her to be able to brace and balance herself. The piano was across the sanctuary, but the altar...the church's sacred stone table was only a couple of steps away.

Forgive me, I thought and then carried Poppy up the shallow stairs. I set her down and turned her to face the altar, happy to see that it would be the perfect height with her in those heels.

"The altar," she murmured. "Am I your sacrifice tonight?"

"Are you offering?"

In response, she put her hands flat on the altar cloth, a

move that curved her back and highlighted the round contour of her ass.

"Oh, very good, lamb, but not good enough." I pressed a hand against her back and pushed her down, watching the skirt ride slowly up the back of her thighs as she bent over. I pushed until her turned cheek was sideways against the altar, and then I found her wrists and stretched them above her head.

"Don't move an inch," I whispered low in her ear, then walked to the sacristy, where I found a cincture. When I came back out into the apse, she was still as I left her, which deeply pleased me. I would reward her for that later.

I made quick work of knotting the white rope around her wrists and hands, thinking of the prayer priests were supposed to say as they tied their cinctures. *Gird me, O Lord, with the cincture of purity, and quench in my heart the fire of lust...*

Wrapped around her wrists, binding this woman to my desires, the cincture was doing the exact opposite of its purpose, quenching nothing. My entire body was on fire for hers, flames already licking every inch of my skin, and the only way to douse them was to sink balls deep into her sweet cunt. I should feel bad about that.

I should.

I stepped back to admire my work: the way her arms looked stretched forward and bound together, like a captive in supplication; the way her black heels dug into the carpet; the way her ass was displayed and at my disposal.

I came back to her, lifting the hem of her skirt with one finger. "This shows an awful lot, little lamb. Do you know how much?"

She was staring at me over the curve of her shoulder. "Yes," she said. "I can feel the air on me…"

I knelt behind her as I had that time after her confession, but this time only to examine. The skirt indeed only just covered what it needed, and the slightest lift would have revealed the shell-pink seam of her cunt.

"Why did you wear this dress today, Poppy?"

"I wanted…I wanted you to fuck me in it."

"That's naughty. But not quite as naughty as being in public, at work, with your bare cunt so exposed." I stood up and then ran my hands up her thighs, catching the soft fabric in my fingers and moving it above her hips.

"What if the wind had blown your skirt up?" I caressed her ass as I spoke. "What if you'd happened to uncross your legs and someone was looking from just the right angle?"

Her voice was muffled by her arm. "I used to get naked for money. I'm not worried about it."

Crack.

She sucked in a deep breath, and I watched as a red handprint bloomed on her ass, clear even in the dim late-evening light.

"*I'm* worried about it," I said. "You know how fucking jealous I am of the men who got to see you like that? How jealous I am of Sterling?"

"You shouldn't be—"

Crack.

She shuddered and then widened her stance to push her ass closer to my hand.

"I know I shouldn't be," I said, "that's not the point. I don't hold your past life against you. But this"—I let my hand slide down to cup her pussy, which was hot and swollen and wet—"I'm taking this tonight. I'm making it mine. Which makes you a bad girl to be so reckless with it today."

I spanked her again, and she moaned against her arm. "I don't know what it is about you," I told her, leaning close to her ear. "But you bring out the fucking caveman in me. Look at me, Poppy."

She did, one beautiful hazel eye peeping up over her tied arm. I squeezed her pussy, and she was so slippery against my palm, it took everything I had not to show how wild that made me, that she could get this turned on by the spanking and the submission. But I had to check this one box, settle this final question, because I didn't want to go to feminist ally hell on top of the other hells I was destined for.

I squeezed her again and she struggled to keep her gaze on me. "Poppy, I…I want to be like this with you. Rough. Possessive. But you have to tell me it's okay." I rested my head on her back, rolling my face into her neck. "Tell me it's okay, Poppy. Say those words."

God, that lavender smell and the silky brush of her hair

against my cheek and the feeling of her wet cunt pulsing in my hand. "Just…fuck."

"Yes," she said, and her voice was urgent, clear, loud. "Yes, please."

"Please what?" I had to be sure. Because the things I wanted to do to this woman—Leviticus had not even come close to covering all the ways I wanted to defile her.

I could hear the smile in her voice along with the neediness. "Tyler, you are exactly what I want. Use me. Be rough. Leave marks." She paused. "Please."

That was all I needed. I kissed the back of her neck and then straightened so I could smack her ass again, rubbing the spot right afterwards to soothe away the burn. "Stand up and turn around," I ordered, and she complied right away. The look on her face as she turned around was enough to make me come on its own—she looked like she would do anything, *anything*, to be fucked just then, and I had a lot of things in mind for her to do.

But first.

I untied her wrists, kissing the faint indentations left behind by the rope, and then I reached behind her and unzipped her dress. It fell to her feet, leaving her completely naked with the exception of her heels. I took a minute to stare at her, at the ripe teardrops of her breasts, big enough to squeeze, small enough to support themselves. Her supple stomach, slender and soft and slightly rounded, with the kind of hips you could dig your fingers into. The naked V of her pussy, smoothly delicate, and the irresistible curve of her ass.

"I just realized you aren't wearing your…" she gestured at her throat.

"Day off," I said, my voice hoarser than I expected. I reached behind my neck and grabbed the fabric of my T-shirt, pulling it over my head and off my body, relishing the way her lips parted and her hand drifted to her mouth as she stared at me. I unbuckled my belt, sliding the leather through the loops of my jeans and dropping it on the floor. I kicked off my shoes and took off my jeans.

I normally liked to stay at least partly clothed during sex, but I wanted to give her this, my nakedness, as a gift. And selfishly, I wanted to feel every inch of her skin against mine. This was my first fuck in three years and I refused to miss a single thing.

"Come here," I said. "And kneel."

She did, her breath audible now, kneeling in front of me and crossing her ankles behind her, taunting me with those heels.

"Take them off," I said, jerking my chin down to indicate my black boxer briefs. She did, impatiently tugging them off my hips, and I groaned as my erection was finally, finally let free.

She pressed soft, red lips to the silky skin of my cock. "Let me suck you," she breathed up at me. "Let me make you feel good."

I found her lips with my thumb, running it along her lower one and pulling it down to open her up more. "Hold still," I told her, and then I guided my cock into her waiting mouth.

Holy shit.

Holy shit, that felt good.

It had only been since Saturday, and yet I'd forgotten that this woman's mouth was like a slice of heaven, warm and wet and with that flicking, fluttering tongue that danced along the underside of my dick.

I laced my hands through her hair—fucking up whatever adorable hairstyle she'd had it in—and then slowly withdrew, savoring every single second as her lips and tongue kissed against my skin. And then I slid in again, less gently this time, my eyes darting from her lips to her heels to the way her hand circled her clit as I slowly fucked her mouth.

She kept her eyes pinned to mine, peering up at me through those long dark eyelashes, and I thought about all the times they'd distracted the hell out of me and all the times that I'd wanted to fuck her brains out (and then paddle her sweet ass for making me so goddamned crazy about her).

I tightened my grip in her hair. I wanted to go hard, I wanted to make her eyes water, I wanted to thrust until I reached the point where I could barely hold back from shooting down her throat. "Ready?" I whispered to her, still wanting to tread on the side of consent and caution.

And then she groaned a frustrated groan, as if annoyed that I was asking again.

"Bad lamb," I said and thrust hard into her mouth. I heard her choke as I hit the back of her throat, but I only gave her a minute before I pushed in again, and again. I knew I was longer and wider than most men, I knew I was harder to take, but I wasn't going to cut her any slack unless she asked for it, not after that stunt.

"You like being bad? You like making me punish you?"

She managed to nod, her watery eyes blinking up at me in this honest, impeaching way, and I knew it was true.

I swore. "You're going to make me crazy."

She smiled around my cock, and *fuck*, I had to be absolved of all these sins because Saint Peter himself wouldn't have been able to deny himself this woman. I drove into her mouth several more times, right up until I could feel that familiar clench in my belly and then I pulled out, my breathing ragged from the effort it took not to come all over that gorgeous face.

Instead, I used my thumb to wipe at Poppy's eyes, which were now smudged with makeup and tears. The ever-so-slightly smeared lipstick I left the way it was.

In fact, it was too tempting not to kiss and lick and nibble at, and I picked her up so I could do just that while I walked her over to the altar. Her lips were swollen from my assault and yet so yielding to my kiss, so deliciously soft. I groaned into her mouth as she licked past my teeth and tasted my tongue, and I moved my mouth harder against hers. Harder and more and I could barely breathe for kissing this woman.

I set her down on the altar but didn't end the kiss, stroking around her breasts and hips. It was damn near impossible to stop, but I was getting to the point where little else mattered apart from getting inside her, and so I did stop.

"Lie back," I said as I broke our kiss, holding my hand behind her head so that she wouldn't hurt it accidentally.

It was a long altar, and she wasn't a tall woman, and so she was able to arrange herself comfortably with room to spare. I trailed one hand along her stomach as I walked around the back, facing the sanctuary as if I were beginning the communion rite. Except instead of the body and blood of Christ spread before me, I had Poppy Danforth.

I ran the tip of my nose along her jaw, oh so slowly down and across her body, loving the way she arched and tilted to my touch, so greedy. She was a feast to me—creases and hollows and supple curves—and having her like this was like the first gasp of oxygen after surfacing from the water, powerful and instinctual, and I didn't give a fuck about all the sins I was currently committing, I was going to revel in every minute of it.

I bit at the inside of her thighs. I circled every inch of her pussy with my tongue. I kneaded her breasts with rough hands until she squeaked, and I nibbled at the dip of her navel and sucked on each nipple until she was writhing on the altar. I took kisses *from* her rather than sharing them *with* her. I slid my fingers in her cunt not to make her feel good, but so that I could relish the sensation of the slickness against my fingertips.

I knew she was getting pleasure from all this, and I did want her to come, often and hard, when she was with me. But this moment? Where I was groping and squeezing and inhaling her scent and feeding on her sighs? This was for me.

And after I was done taking what I wanted, when I was so hard that I couldn't think straight, I climbed up on the altar with her, kneeling between her parted legs.

I waited, a hairbreadth of a second, waited for God's voice to come thundering down, waited for a heavenly intervention like when Abraham had his only child bound and ready for sacrifice. But it never came. There was only Poppy and her heaving chest as she murmured, "Please please please…"

I didn't know how anyone could so callously dismiss Poppy as simply a woman who always wanted it, as nothing more than a whore born into a debutante's body. Because right now, with her eyes so dark and her skin so flushed, she was the holiest thing I'd ever seen. A miracle made flesh, waiting for my flesh to join with it.

"You are truly beautiful," I said, running a finger down

her jaw. And then I reached for her hand, lacing my fingers through hers. "Whatever happens after this, I just want you to know that this was worth it. *You* were worth it. You were worth everything."

She opened her mouth and then shut it again, as if she couldn't find the right words to say. A single tear spilled out of the corner of her eye and I leaned over her to kiss it away.

"Tyler…" she started but I silenced her with a kiss.

"Just listen," I said, lowering myself between her legs. She shivered as the head of my cock pressed against her entrance.

"This," I said, and I pushed partly into her, barely able to breathe for how tight she was around me. "This is your body."

I leaned my head down and caught the delicate skin of her neck in my teeth. "This is your blood," I whispered in her ear.

I shoved all the way in, and she cried out as her back arched off the altar.

"This is you," I told her and the empty sanctuary, "this is you, given up for me."

We stayed still after that, absorbing the new feeling of each other, the feeling of my hips pressed to her softness, the feeling of her tight, tight channel around me. I was worried I was going to come just being like this, just being inside.

But then I noticed that she was biting her lip and

breathing shakily, and I realized that she was adjusting to my size. I could hardly fit, and what's worse, that was what made it feel so fucking good.

God, I was such an asshole. I hadn't made her ready enough and part of me found that hot, so hot that I was barely able to attend to her the way a good man should. I had to lean down and bite her neck and shoulders repeatedly to force myself to stay still—all I wanted to do was pound into her like she was a little fuckdoll, pump into her like nothing existed except for her pussy.

But no, this was not how our first time should be. I told her I wanted to be rough, but the rough fucking I was dying to give her would be too much, and I couldn't bear to abuse my lamb like that.

Finally mastering myself a little, I pulled out halfway, reaching down to rub her clit, thinking I would get her off and then finish another way that wouldn't hurt her. She caught my hand. "Don't," she said. "Don't be the good guy. I told you what I wanted. Now give it to me."

"But I want you to enjoy it too."

"I will," she said, her eyes wide and open and fervent. "Give me what I want, Tyler. I want this. Please."

I groaned at her words, my dick surging, and I sank back into her slowly. My thighs and arms were trembling with the suppressed need, but I couldn't be *that* guy, I didn't want to be that guy, the guy who used a woman for himself and didn't make it good for her. She said she wanted it, and

I know I'd asked for and gotten permission, but still, she didn't know how rough I could be, how hard I could go.

She slid her arms around my neck and pulled herself up to speak in my ear. "How can I push you over the edge? Hmm?" She wriggled underneath me, and I sucked in a breath, the sudden motion after the stillness almost too much.

"How can I convince you to tear me apart?"

Well, shit.

"I can tell that's what you want," she continued, purring in my ear. "I can feel you shaking. Do it. Just pull out and then push back in. Doesn't that feel good?"

Fuck yes, it did. It felt so good that I did it again, and again, closing my eyes and exhaling slow ragged breaths. Each time I pushed in, I ground myself against her clit, pulling out slowly to drag against her G-spot, some gallant voice telling me to make sure that she would come, the rest of me fighting that voice and pleading with me to screw her mindlessly.

"Where's the man who spanked me?" she asked. "Where's the man who fucked my throat until my eyes watered?"

My eyes were still closed, but I opened them now, meeting her gaze. "Don't want to hurt you," I said, my voice rough with the effort of my restraint. "I care about you too much."

"Tyler," she begged. "You've done it before with me."

"Not like this."

"Look," she demanded. "Look down at us."

I did, withdrawing out to the tip, and it was a mistake because seeing where we were joined was so hot, so primal, and it clawed its way up my spine, and I didn't even know what *it* was—lust or love or biology or fate—but my attempt at nobility fractured and the beast within broke through.

"Forgive me," I muttered and then rammed myself home. She moaned in surprise and then I laid my body on top of hers, supporting myself with only my forearms now, our chests and stomachs pressed together, my hips digging into her inner thighs. Pinning her down like this, I stabbed into her over and over and over again, burying myself repeatedly in that velvet pussy.

"More," she moaned, and I gave it to her.

I heard her heels tumble off and fall to the floor, and the altar cloth was sliding I was driving into her so hard, but I didn't care, I was lost to myself, lost to her, and lost to the world and everything except her grunts and squeals in my ear and the wet cunt underneath me.

It was perfect, and I was fucking that perfection, and I didn't give a fuck about anything else but it and my dick and filling this woman with my cum, and why the hell did damnation feel so fucking good?

I don't even know what I was saying as I rutted into her, *Jesus, please* and *I'm sorry* and *you're so tight* and *I have to I have to I have to.*

And she was saying words back, words that spilled out in gasps and grunts and pants, *right there* and *harder* and *close, I'm so close.*

Deeper, I had to get deeper even though I knew there was no actual, physical way I could be deeper, and then I took her mouth, kissing her with something violent and furious and worshipful. We could both hardly breathe but we refused to stop and I fucked her all the while, feeling her tighten and writhe and finally break underneath me. She bucked, crying out against my mouth, her fingernails gouging red lines of pain down my back, and we rode out her orgasm together because she was a wild thing, a woman possessed, and it was like having a tigress underneath me, but I kept riding her and then it was there, it was there, it was there and I still had her mouth as I jabbed in a final time and came.

Excruciatingly, I came.

Every pulse of my dick was like a pulse of my soul, and every muscle tightening and contracting was like a punch to the gut, and I was so *bare* with this woman in every way, my nerves flayed raw and my heart wide open and my eternal soul right alongside my bruising hips and thrusting dick and the cum that was now spilling everywhere, leaking onto the white altar cloth, and yes, this is why the Church wanted marriage and sex to go hand in hand because I felt as married to her right now as a man could be married to a woman.

I gave a few last thrusts, milking every last throb out of my climax, every last drop out of myself, and then I raised myself up on my hands to look down at her.

She was smiling a lazy, sated smile, and then she said, "Amen."

CHAPTER THIRTEEN

I went into the sacristy and came out with a small rectangle of white cloth, a purificator. It was normally used to wipe the communion chalice after every sip of wine.

Tonight, I used it to clean Poppy.

You might think that having sex on my altar, using sacred things normally meant for rituals of the highest order, meant that I wasn't taking my faith seriously, that I had slid straight past sin and into sacrilege, but that wasn't the truth. Or it wasn't the whole truth, at least. I couldn't explain it, but it was like somehow it was *all* holy, the altar and the relic within and us on top of it. I knew that outside of this moment there would be guilt. There would be consequences. There would be the memory of Lizzy and all the things I had wanted to fight for.

But right now, with Poppy's scent on my skin, with her taste on my lips, I only felt connection and love and the promise of something vivid and colorful.

After I finished cleaning her, I wrapped her in the altar cloth and carried her to the edge of the stairs, where I sat. I cradled her in my arms, brushing my lips against her hair and eyelids, murmuring the words I thought she should hear: how beautiful she was, how stunning, and how perfect.

I wanted to say *I'm sorry*, although my mind and soul still spun in dazzled wonder with it all, so I wasn't sure if I was sorry I'd lost control and gotten so rough with her, or if I was sorry that we'd had sex at all.

Except I wasn't. Because more than the transformative sex that we'd just had, *this* moment was worth sinning for. This moment where she was curled in my arms, her head on my chest, breathing contentedly against me. Where the altar cloth covered her in long, draping folds, but slips of pale skin still showed through.

She slid her fingers up my chest, resting them on my collarbone, and I held her close, as if I could press her straight through my skin and into my soul.

"You broke your vow," she said finally.

I glanced down at her; she was both sleepy and sad. I pressed my lips against her forehead.

"I know," I finally replied. "I know."

"What happens now?"

"What do you want to happen?"

She blinked up at me. "I want to fuck you again."

I laughed. "Like now?"

"Yes, like now."

She twisted in my arms until she was straddling my legs, and it only took one of her deep kisses to make me hard again. I lifted her up and guided myself inside, groaning quietly into her neck as she sat back down.

Slivers of sensation became known to me. Warmth and wetness. Her ass against my thighs. Her tits so close to my mouth.

"What do you want to happen next, Tyler?" she asked me, and I couldn't believe she was asking me this *now*, while she was riding me, but then as I tried to answer, I realized why. She didn't want me to be guarded, she wanted me to be honest and raw and like this, I couldn't possibly be anything else.

"I don't want us to stop," I admitted. She rolled her hips back and forth over me, and I did press my face in her chest then, feeling my climax building too fast, much too fast. "I feel like I…"

But I couldn't say it. Not even now, when she had me completely at her mercy. It was simply too soon—and not to mention ridiculous.

Priests weren't allowed to fall in love.

I wasn't allowed to fall in love.

Her fingers twined through my hair and she pulled my head back so she could look at me. "I'll say it if you won't," she said.

"Poppy…"

"I want to know everything about you. I want you to tell me what you think about politics, and I want you to read Scriptures to me, and I want to have conversations in Latin. I want to fuck you every day. I fantasize constantly about us moving in together, living every moment together. What is that, Tyler, if it's not—"

I clapped my hand over her mouth, and in an instant, had her on her back with me pushing into her.

"Don't say it," I told her. "Not yet."

"Why?" she whispered, her eyes wide and a little hurt. "Why not?"

"Because once you say it, once *I* say it, then everything has to change."

"Hasn't it already?"

She was right. It had changed the moment I kissed her in the presence of God. It had changed the moment I bent her over that piano. Maybe it had even changed the moment she stepped into my confessional booth.

But if I loved her…if she loved me…what did that mean for all of my work here? I couldn't carry on a secret affair and still crusade against sexual immorality in the clergy—but if I walked away from my vocation, then I would lose the ability to crusade at all. I would lose the man I was.

The only other choice was losing Poppy, and I wasn't ready to think about that yet. So instead of answering her question, I pulled out and flipped her over, driving into her from behind while I slid a hand around her hip and found her clit. Only three or four strokes like this and she was there, like I knew she would be; the more aggressive I was, the faster she came.

I followed her over the edge, chanting her name like a prayer and pumping the whole time, as if I could fuck the future and its horrible choices away.

Oh, God, what I would give for that to be true.

"I still can't believe how clean your house is," Poppy said.

We were in my bed after cleaning up the sanctuary and sneaking over to the rectory. I was fingering her hair with a fascination that bordered on reverence, worshiping those long, dark tresses with curls of my finger and brushes of my lips. We'd been talking lazy pillow talk, drifting from *The Walking Dead* speculations and favorite Latin texts to hushed recountings of all the ways we'd suffered in wanting each other this last month.

I had been about to kiss her again when she'd said that, so I settled for sliding a hand under the sheets and finding her breasts instead.

"I like things to be clean."

"I think that's admirable. You just don't see it very often in men like you."

"Men like me? Priests?"

"No," she shifted toward me, smiling. "Young.

Charming. Good-looking. You would have been a fantastic businessman, you know."

"My brothers are businessmen," I said. "But I was never interested in that stuff; I never wanted money or success or power. I loved old things—old languages and old rituals. Old gods."

"I think I can picture you as a teenager," she mused. "I bet you drove the girls crazy—hot, athletic, *and* bookish. And also really clean."

"No, I wasn't always clean." I debated for a moment about explaining, but we had just shared something so intimate, why would I hold this back from her? Just because it was depressing? Suddenly, I wanted to share. I wanted her to know every dark thing that I'd dragged around by myself, I wanted to show her all of my burdens and have her lift them from me with her clever mind and her elegant compassion.

I moved my hand from her breast and glided my fingers under her ribs, tucking her close against me.

"The day I found my sister," I said, "was a Saturday in May. There was a strong thunderstorm going on, and even though it was daylight, it was dim all around, like nighttime. Lizzy had taken Sean's car home from college—they were both at KU then—and so she was home for the weekend.

"My parents had taken Aiden and Ryan out for lunch, and I thought they'd taken Lizzy too. I'd slept in late, and I woke up to an empty house."

Poppy didn't say anything, but she nestled in closer, giving me courage.

"There was a bright flash of light and a huge noise, like a transformer had blown, and the power cut out. I went for the flashlight, but the stupid batteries were dead, so I had to go out into the garage to get more. We lived in Brookside, in an older house, so the garage was detached. I had to walk through the rain, and then when I got in there, it was so dark at first, I didn't see her..."

She found my hand and squeezed.

"I got the batteries, and it was only luck that the lightning flashed right as I was turning away, or I wouldn't have seen her. She was suspended there, like she was frozen in time. In the movies, they're always swaying, and there's a creaking noise, but it was so still. Just. Still.

"I remember running to her and tripping over a milk crate stuffed with cords, and then a tower of paint cans went rolling everywhere, and I picked myself up off the ground. There was a stepladder that she'd used—" I couldn't say the words, couldn't say *the stepladder that she'd used to hang herself.*

I swallowed and went on.

"I set it back upright and climbed it. It wasn't until I'd gotten her down and had her in my arms that I realized my hands were dirty from when I'd tripped. Wet from the rain, and then they'd rubbed against the dirt and oil and grime, and I'd left smudges all over her face—"

I took a deep breath, reliving the panic, the rushed 911 call, the choked conversation with my parents. They'd rushed home, and my parents and Aiden had run into the garage only steps ahead of the police, and no one had thought to keep Ryan out. He'd only been eight or nine when he saw his sister dead on the garage floor. And then the red and blue lights, and the paramedics, and the confirmation of what the cold skin and vacant eyes had already told us.

Lizzy Bell—animal shelter volunteer, lover of Britney Spears, and all of the other thousands of things that made up a nineteen-year-old girl—was dead.

For several moments, it was just the sound of us breathing, the slight rustle of the sheets as Poppy rubbed her foot against mine, and then the memories slowly bled back into the ground of my mind.

"My mom kept trying to wipe the smudges away," I said finally. "While we waited for the coroner's men to come get the body. The whole time. But you can't wipe off oil that easily, and so Lizzy had that smudge right up until we had to say goodbye. I hated that. I hated that so much. I made it my mission to scrub that fucking garage from top to bottom, and I did. And ever since then, I've kept everything in my life clean."

"Why?" Poppy asked, moving so she could prop herself on one elbow. "Does it make you feel better? Are you worried about something like that happening again?"

"No, it's not that. I don't know why I still do it. It's a compulsion, I guess."

"It sounds like penance."

I didn't respond to this, turning it over in my head. When she phrased it like that, it made it seem like I hadn't really let Lizzy go, that I was still grappling with her death, grappling with the guilt of sleeping in that day and not being awake to stop her. But it had been ten years and I wasn't holding on to it that much, was I?

"What was she like?" Poppy asked. "When she was alive?"

I thought for a minute. "She was my older sister. So, sometimes she was mothering, sometimes she was mean. But when I was scared of the dark as a kid, she always let me sleep in her room, and she always covered for me when I broke curfew when I was older."

I traced the backlit lines of the blinds on the comforter with my gaze. "She really, really loved terrible pop music. She used to leave her music in Sean's CD player when she borrowed his car, and he'd get so irritated when his friends would hop in the car and then some boy band or Britney Spears would start playing when he turned it on."

Poppy cocked her head. "Lizzy is the reason you listen to Britney Spears," she guessed.

"Yes," I admitted. "It reminds me of her. She used to sing so loudly in her room that you could hear it anywhere in the house."

"I think I would have liked her."

I smiled. "I think you would have." But then my smile slipped away. "The weekend of the funeral, Sean and I decided we were going to escape the relatives at the house for a few minutes and go out for Taco Bell. I'd wanted to drive, but we didn't think—we didn't remember that she'd been the last person to drive the car. Her music came on and Sean was…he was upset."

Upset wasn't the right word for what my older brother had been. He'd just turned twenty-one and so he was mourning Lizzy's death the Irish way, with too much whiskey and too little sleep. I'd turned the key in the ignition and the opening bars of "Oops, I Did It Again" came on, obnoxiously loud because Lizzy'd had the volume cranked all the way up, and we'd both frozen, staring at the radio as if a demon had just crawled out of the CD slot, and then he'd started yelling and swearing, kicking the dash so hard that the old plastic cracked, the whole car shaking with his fury and raw grief. They'd been the closest in age, Lizzy and Sean, and accordingly, they'd been best friends and bitter enemies. They'd shared cars and friends and teachers and finally a college, being only a year apart, and of all of us Bell siblings, her death ripped the biggest hole in his daily life.

So he ripped a hole in his car that day, and then we went and got Taco Bell and we never spoke of it. We still haven't.

"I've never told anyone this story before," I said. "It's easier to talk about Lizzy like this."

"Like what?"

"Like naked and snuggling. Just...with you. It's all easier with you."

She rested her head on my shoulder. We laid there for a while, and just when I thought she'd fallen asleep, she said in the darkness, "Is Lizzy why you are afraid to let go with me?"

"No," I said, baffled. "Why would she be?"

"It just seems like she's the motivation behind a lot of what you do. And she was hurt, sexually. I wonder if that makes you afraid of doing that—of making what happened to her happen to someone else."

"I...I guess I never thought of it that way." I found her hair again and played with it. "That might be why, I don't know. It was in college that I discovered how I liked it, but it was difficult. If I found a girl who was confident and smart and full of self-respect, then she didn't want the sex to be rough. If I found a girl who liked it rough, then the reason she liked it rough was because of some emotional issue, and yes, whenever I saw a girl like that, I thought of Lizzy. How many signs we'd missed. And if I ever found out that a guy had taken advantage of her when she'd felt like that..."

"It sounds like you had a lot of bad luck with women."

"Not necessarily. I had a few really great girlfriends in college. But it was easier to lock that part of me away, to have the healthy, confident girlfriends and the vanilla sex. It was safer."

"Then you became a priest."

"And that was *much* safer."

She sat up and looked at me, lines of shadow and streetlight across her face. "Well, you aren't hurting me. I mean it. Look at me, Tyler."

I did.

"I don't like it rough because I'm emotionally damaged. I've been treated like a princess my entire life, coddled and praised and protected from every single thing that could ever harm me. Sterling was the first person who didn't treat me like that."

Sterling.

My jaw flexed. I didn't like that he was so many of her firsts (which, I know, was totally unreasonable, but still. Maybe what I didn't like was that she remembered so many of her firsts with him so intently).

"Part of it is probably that it's taboo and therefore dirty, so it turns me on. But part of it is that it makes me feel unbreakable. Strong. Like the man I'm with respects me enough to see that. And I'm strong enough to have that experience in the bedroom and also have a perfectly healthy life outside of it."

"It's too bad it didn't work out with Sterling then."

Whoa, Tyler. Low blow. But I was agitated and jealous and feeling like I was being told off for something that wasn't my fault.

She stiffened. "It didn't work out with Sterling because

he can't differentiate between the two, the bedroom and real life. He thinks because I liked the way he treated me during sex that was how I wanted to be treated all the time. That I only wanted to be a whore, when really, I wanted to be a whore for him only when we were alone. Which is why I walked away from him at the club."

Not before you let him fuck you.

As if she could read my thoughts, she narrowed her eyes. "Are you jealous of him?"

"No," I lied.

"You aren't even supposed to be laying here with me," she said. "We can't hold hands in public, we can't do *anything* together without it being a sin. You could lose your job and essentially be exiled from the one thing that gives your life meaning, and you're worried about my ex-boyfriend?"

"Okay, fine. Yes. Yes, I'm jealous of him. I'm jealous that he gets to come back here for you, and I'm jealous that he *can* do that. He can pursue you. And I can't."

My words hung in the air for a long moment.

She dropped her head down. "Tyler…what have we done? What are we doing?"

She was there again. At that thing I didn't want to think about.

I reached for her and pulled her over me, laying down so that she knelt over my face.

"We should talk about this," she said, but then I flicked

my tongue up and over her clit and she moaned, and I knew that I'd managed to freeze this moment again, push the conversation and all its decisions forward to another time.

CHAPTER FOURTEEN

Jesus said that what is done in the darkness will be brought into the light. And when I woke up alone in my bed that morning, I knew exactly what He meant. Because everything that I had managed to push away last night crowded back, front and center, and not only did I have to face it, but I had to face it alone.

Where was she? There was no note, no text, no coffee mug in the sink. She'd left without saying goodbye, and that twisted sharp and splintery in my chest.

She's a layperson, I reminded myself. That was what laypeople did—they met, they fucked, and they moved on. They didn't fall in love at the drop of a fucking hat.

Last night, she had been about to say it, though. She'd been ready to profess it to me…or had I imagined that? Maybe I had imagined that this spark between us was something mutual, something shared. Maybe I'd been a curiosity to her—the handsome priest—and now that she'd satisfied her curiosity, she was ready to move on.

I had broken my vow for a woman who didn't even care enough to stick around for breakfast.

I shuffled into the bathroom, and when I looked up in the mirror, I saw two days' worth of stubble and hair that had been tugged on and the unmistakable stain of a hickey on my collarbone.

I hated the man in that reflection, and I almost punched the glass, wanting to hear it shatter, wanting to feel the bright pain of a thousand deep cuts. And then I sat down on the edge of the tub and gave in to the urge to cry.

I was a good man. I had worked very hard to be a good man, devoted myself to living my life the way God wanted. I counseled, I comforted, I spent hours upon hours in contemplative prayer and meditation.

I was a good man.

So why had I done this?

Poppy wasn't at morning Mass and I didn't hear from her all day, even though I walked by the window more often than necessary to double-check that her light blue Fiat was still in her driveway.

It was.

I checked my phone for a text about once every three minutes, typed several aborted messages, and then berated myself for doing so. I had just cried—like a baby—in my bathroom this morning. Stupid, echoing-off-the-tile, hiccuping cries. It was for the better if we had space from one another. I couldn't keep my focus when I was around her. I couldn't keep control. She made me feel like every sin and punishment was worth it just to hear one of her husky little laughs, and what I needed to do right now was triage this mess that I called my life and figure things out. Embracing this distance was prudence and sexual continence and the first scrap of wisdom I'd exhibited since I met her.

My hurt pride over her leaving without saying goodbye had nothing to do with it.

That night was the back-to-school party for the youth group, so I spent it eating pizza and playing video games and trying to keep the boys from making total asses of themselves as they tried to impress the girls. After the last teen left the church, I cleaned the basement and went home, undressing and pulling on a pair of sweats. I stared out my bedroom window at Poppy's driveway, lost in thought.

The Church said everything about her and me was wrong. It was lust and fornication. It was lying. It was betrayal.

But the Church also talked about the kind of love that transcended any and all boundaries, and the Bible was filled with stories of people who carried out God's will *and* had very human desires. I mean, what even was sin? Who was being hurt by Poppy and me loving each other?

It's a matter of trust, I reminded myself. Because while I wrestled with the epistemological nature of sin like the trained theologian I was, I was also a shepherd and shepherds had to be practical. The issue was that I had come here to build up trust in the church, to undo another man's wrongs. And no matter how consensual and otherwise unremarkable my relationship was with Poppy, it would still ruin that. My work, my goals, my memorial to Lizzy's death.

Lizzy.

It had felt so good to talk about her. We didn't talk about her much in my family. In fact, not at all, unless I was alone with my mother. And talking about it hadn't taken the pain away, necessarily, but it had made it different. Easier. I moved from the window and went to the bedside table to get the rosary I liked to use, an array of silver and jade beads.

It had been Lizzy's.

I didn't pray, but I ran the beads through my fingers as I sat, thinking and fretting and eventually letting my mind collapse into the worn runnels of worry and guilt.

Into the new thorny pain of her absence and all the fears that inspired. All of this to wrestle with, and the thing that haunted me most as I fell asleep was the possibility that Poppy was done with me.

The next day was the pancake breakfast, and Poppy did show up for that, although she avoided me, talking only to Millie and leaving as soon as the last guest walked up the stairs.

"She came to the Come and See meeting yesterday afternoon," Millie said. "She seems quite interested in joining. I explained to her how the catechism would work, and I think she's amenable, although she did ask if she could do it at another church." Millie looked hard at me. "You two didn't have a falling out, did you?"

"No," I mumbled. "Everything is fine."

"So that's why the both of you looked like you were in physical pain this morning?"

I winced. Millie was sharper than most people, but I didn't want *anyone* to notice the dynamic between Poppy and me, whether it be strained or friendly. We'd only had sex once, and already it was seeping through every possible crack in the dam.

"St. Margaret's needs her, Father Bell. I certainly hope you don't plan on fucking that up."

"Millie."

"What?" she asked, picking up her quilted handbag. "An old lady can't swear? Catch up with the times, Father."

And she left.

She was right. St. Margaret's needed Poppy. And I needed Poppy. And St. Margaret's needed me, and Poppy needed me. Too many people needed too many other people, and there was no way I could keep all the balls in the air; I would drop one and there would be catastrophic consequences.

It wasn't until Sunday evening that my angst got the better of me and I sent her a text.

Thinking of you.

My chest and throat felt like they'd been stitched together, and I nearly jumped to my feet when I saw the three rotating dots on the screen, meaning that she was typing a response. And then they went away.

I let out a long breath. She'd stopped typing. She wasn't going to answer.

I didn't even want to think about what that meant. So instead I treated myself to a warmed-up Millie casserole, three episodes of *House of Cards*, and a healthy slug of scotch.

I fell asleep with Lizzy's rosary woven between my fingers, somehow feeling further away from my own life than ever.

I hadn't seen Poppy at Mass that morning, so the last thing I expected after Rowan's confession was for her to slide in the other side of the booth.

It could have been the hesitant creak of the door or the unmistakable rustle of a dress against soft thighs or the electricity that immediately crackled across my skin, but I knew it was her without her even saying a word.

Her door closed and we sat in silence for a while, her breathing quietly and me anxiously tapping my thumb against my palm, hating that I was already half hard just being next to her.

Finally, I asked, "Where have you been?"

She exhaled. "Here. I've been right here."

"It didn't feel that way." I was embarrassed at how bitter and wounded I sounded, but I also didn't care. Tyler Bell at twenty-one would have never let a girl get under his armor of pride, never shown a girl that she'd hurt him. But I was almost thirty now, and well past college, and what would have meant next to nothing to me then meant a lot more to me now.

Or maybe it wasn't me who had changed. Maybe this was the effect that Poppy would have on me at any age, in any place. She did something to me, and I thought (a little petulantly) that it wasn't fair. Wasn't fair that she could just sit there and not be as torn up as I was about us, whatever us meant in our case.

"Are you angry with me?" she asked.

I leaned against the wall. "No." I reconsidered. "A little. I don't know."

"You are, then."

The words forced their way past my lips. "It just feels like I am risking everything, and you are risking nothing, and you are the one who's walking away and it doesn't feel fair."

"Walking away from what, Tyler? From a relationship we can't have? From sex that will destroy your career or worse? I've spent the last three days beating my head against the wall because I want you—I want you so badly—but if I have you, I'll ruin your life. How do you think that makes *me* feel? Do you think I want to shred apart your livelihood, your community, all for my sake?"

Her outburst lingered in my mind long after she'd stopped talking. This hadn't occurred to me—that she would feel guilty, that she would feel culpable. That she would want to avoid me because she couldn't bear the guilt of taking part in this thing that would ruin me.

I didn't know what to say to that. I was grateful and confused and still hurt all at the same time.

So I said the only thing that came to mind. "How long has it been since your last confession?"

An exhale. "So this is how this conversation will go?"

I didn't care how this conversation happened as long as it happened, as long as I got to keep talking to her. "If you want it to."

"You know what? I do."

POPPY

Premarital sex is a sin, right? And I'm sure having sex with a priest is a sin. And probably altar-fucking isn't anywhere in the Papal Encyclicals, but I'm guessing it's a sin too. So I'll confess those. I'll confess about how delirious I felt on that altar, having you between my legs. Finally coaxing you into letting go. We were more human than ever–more *animal* than ever—but somehow I still felt so close to God, like my entire soul was awake and alert and dancing. I looked up at the crucifix, at Christ hanging from the cross, and I thought, this is what it's like to be torn apart for love. This is what it means to be reborn. I stared at it over your shoulder, and you were piercing me, and Christ had been pierced too, and it all seemed like one secret and shimmering mystery—profound and acroamatic. I feel like we did something unfathomably ancient, stumbled onto some secret ceremony that fused us together—but how can I relish that feeling, how can I celebrate it, when it comes with such a high cost?

I told you I feel guilty, and that's true, but it's wrapped up in so much else that I can't tease apart the guilt from the joy and the want. Every moment I think I've come to a decision—that I am going to tell you that we must abide by your vows and choices, or that I'm going to tell you that we must figure out a way, *any* way, that we can still see each other—I change my mind.

Worry is a sin, even I know that, yet I am more than just a lily of the field. I'm a lily that's been plucked from the ground and laid at your feet. When it comes to you, I'm rootless and helpless and at your mercy for sunshine and water. And I'm not even supposed to be yours. How can I not worry?

Last night, I wanted to respond to your message so badly, but I didn't know what I could say, how to distill my thoughts into two or three cohesive sentences. I wanted to come over to your house and talk, but I knew if I did, then I wouldn't be able to keep myself from touching you and fucking you, and I didn't want to make things any more complicated than they already were.

But then I kept looking at your text, wondering exactly how you were thinking about me, and I wondered if you were thinking about the way I felt when you were inside. About the way I moved underneath you. I wondered if you were remembering your kitchen and both of us looking down as you pushed into me.

So here's my final confession. I knelt on my bedroom floor like I was going to pray, but instead of praying, I spread my legs and fucked myself with my fingers, pretending it was you.

And when I climaxed, I hoped to God that you would be able to hear me calling your name.

CHAPTER FIFTEEN

People might judge me for the way my breathing sped up. For the way I palmed myself through my slacks. But the image of Poppy on her knees, eyes closed and mind filled with me, all while her fingers played with that beautiful cunt, was too much to resist.

"Poppy," I said, unbuckling my belt. "Tell me more."

I knew she could hear the belt. I knew she could hear the zipper. Her breath shuddered in and then shuddered out.

"I used one hand to touch my breasts," she whispered. "And the other to work my clit. I wanted your dick so much, Tyler, it was all I could think about. How it stretches me. How you make it hit that perfect spot every time."

Still leaning back, I freed my cock from my boxer briefs and gripped it, moving my hand slowly up and down.

"What were you thinking about when you came?" I

asked. God, I wanted it to be dirty. I wanted it to be so fucking dirty.

Poppy didn't disappoint. "I thought about you taking my ass while you fingered me. About you pulling out to come on my back."

Shit. I was hard before, but now—now I was practically concrete. Who was I kidding with this? I needed to fuck her again and I was going to do it right here in the church in the middle of the day.

"My office," I said through gritted teeth. "Now."

She scooted out of the booth and I followed, tucking myself back in but not bothering to zip up. As soon as we were in the office, I shut and locked the door and rounded on her at the same time she rounded on me.

We came together like two storm clouds—a crash of separate beings that immediately become one entity. We were hands and lips and teeth, we were nips and kisses and moans, and I guided her backwards, meaning to put her over my desk, but our legs tangled and we fell to the floor, my arms a cage around her.

"Are you okay?" I asked, worried.

"Yes," she said impatiently, grabbing my collar to yank me back down to her lips. Her kisses drove me into a frenzy, the softness of her mouth echoing the silken heat below her skirt.

"I have to fuck you," I managed between kisses. It was a statement of fact. A warning. I slipped a hand down and found that once again, she was without underwear.

"Filthy," I said. "Fucking filthy."

She twisted under my touch, tilting her hips up to grant my fingers better access, and I kissed her neck as I jabbed two fingers inside her cunt. She was so wet already, and my rough treatment of her only seemed to arouse her more, because her hands fisted in my shirt and she panted as I continued my assault, awful words coming out of my mouth, *cocktease* and *slut* and *you want it, you know you want it.*

She moaned, my words teasing her more than my fingers ever could, and part of me was ashamed at how much it aroused me to say these degrading things to her and another part of me was telling that part to shut the fuck up and just do it already.

I sealed my mouth over hers as I yanked my boxers down far enough to free my dick, and then I blindly shoved my hips forward, burying myself in one rough stroke.

She wrapped her legs around my waist and her arms around my neck, her scorching mouth everywhere, and it was like holding a live wire, the way she moved and squirmed under me as I rammed into her, letting every doubt and jealousy and fear possess me. I would fuck her until she felt like she was mine. I would fuck her until she couldn't walk away.

I would fuck her until *I* couldn't walk away.

Every thrust brought me closer and closer, but one

thought wouldn't let go of me and I pressed my body into her and ground down against her clit, feeling her writhe and coil around me. She was close.

"Let me put it in your ass, Poppy," I said. I ran the tip of my nose along her jawline, making her shiver. "I want to fuck you there."

"Oh God," she whispered. "Yes. Please."

There was no time to think the logistics through, no time to even consider relocating to a more prepared place. I had something only a few steps away that would work, and I wasn't going to waste any time looking for something else.

I pulled out, my cock so hard it hurt, and stood. "Stay," I ordered, and I tucked myself back inside my boxers to make the short walk to the ambry in the back of the sanctuary, the small cabinet where we kept our sacred oils.

My hands shook as I opened the door. These were oils that had been blessed during Holy Week by my bishop, oils used only for sacraments like baptism and confirmation and the anointing of the sick. I selected a glass vial of oil—the Oil of Chrism—and went back to Poppy, studiously avoiding the crucifix and the tabernacle with my eyes as I did.

She'd stayed on the floor, her skirt still bunched up around her waist, her cheeks flushed. After I'd locked the door again, I stood over her and pulled at my collar, trying to take it off.

"No," she said, her pupils large and dark. "Leave it on."

My dick surged. *Dirty girl.*

"You're going to kill me," I told her as I knelt down. I flipped her over on her stomach, so that her delicious ass faced me and also so that she could rest her head on her arms if she needed.

I unstoppered the vial and drizzled some of the oil on my fingertip, which I then used to paint a slick circle around the tight rosebud of her ass. She quivered under my caress, involuntarily tensing every time my touch grazed her there. But her pussy clenched too, and I could see how she was starting to press her hips into the floor, trying to alleviate some of the ache building in her clit.

I added more oil to my fingers and started teasing and testing at her rim, massaging her, loosening her. The smell of balsam—an ancient, churchy smell—filled the room.

"Do you know what this is, Poppy?" I asked.

She shook her head against her arms.

"It's a sacramental oil. It's used for baptisms and ordinations. It's even used to anoint the walls of a church when it's built." I ran a hand down the smooth, firm slope of her back, feeling her sigh against my touch, and at that moment, sliding a finger inside.

She gasped.

"I'm anointing you now," I informed her. "I'm sanctifying you from the inside out. You feel that? That's my finger fucking your ass. And in just a minute, it will be my cock. It will be my cock consecrating you. No, don't touch yourself, sweetheart. We're going to get there together."

I took her hand, which had been sliding underneath her stomach, and put it up by her head, all while I kept working her ass with the oil and my finger. Her channel was so damn snug, and just knowing my dick would take its place in a matter of minutes was enough to make me into a wild man.

I couldn't wait any longer. I poured a healthy amount of oil on my palm and then fisted my cock, the view in front of me and my own slick, strong hand pushing me close to the edge.

"Tyler," Poppy said, looking back at me. "I've done this before. But never with someone your size." She looked a little worried, but she was also still grinding herself against the floor, desperate to be fucked.

I wanted to tell her I'd be gentle with her ass, but I also didn't want to make a promise I didn't know I could keep (because *fuck*, I could barely hold it together just looking at it). Instead, I told her, "You tell me when to stop and I'll stop that very instant, okay?"

She nodded and laid her head down, canting her hips up to meet me. I leaned down, one hand guiding my cock to her entrance and the other reaching for the oil, pouring more over her ass and over my dick until we were both slippery as fuck.

I set down the vial and then started caressing her back as I pushed against her tightness, feeling her open gradually to me, slowly welcoming me in.

The head of my dick pushed and pushed and finally

eased past the initial resistance, and all of a sudden, I was inside and her ass was gripping me in a tight heat unlike anything I'd ever felt before, even with the other girlfriends I'd done this with. I had to hang my head and take several deep breaths, counting to ten, before I could be sure that I wasn't going to lose it too early to savor her properly.

I pushed in a little more. "Oh lamb, this is going to be a tight fit," I warned.

And it was.

The moment I sank all the way home, I paused, giving her a moment to adjust to my size. She breathed in and out, and then sucked in a sharp, needy inhale as I found her clit and began working it. I didn't move for several long moments, simply let her feel the fullness of me while I exploited all that tension I'd built up in her, leading her to the precipice so we could jump off together.

I wanted to ask her if she was ready for more, but I knew how frustrated she got with Good Guy Tyler always asking for permission, so instead I moved slowly, waiting at every movement for her to signal that she needed time or that she needed to stop.

I lifted her hips, guiding her to rest up on all fours. *Pause.*

I straightened my own body as I kept rubbing her clit. *Pause.*

I withdrew just an inch and then pushed in just an inch. *Pause.*

And bit by bit, she went from adjusting to wanting, pushing back into me like the greedy kitten she was, whimpering in protest whenever my hand left her clit. And I gave her slightly more and more, until I was pulling out to the tip and gliding back in, still unhurriedly—calmly even—but building steam now.

The whole time, I stroked her legs and back and rubbed her clit, I told her what a good girl she was, such a good little slut for letting me fuck her sweet ass, my own obedient little slut, and she belonged to me, wasn't that right? She only wanted me inside her, she only wanted my dick and my fingers and my mouth.

She nodded at my words, all of them, and she was trembling as I fucked her, covered in sweat and shivering like she had a fever. I had meant to hold her back until the very end, but seeing her like this drove me crazy, obsessed me with the thought of her coming while I was in her ass, and so I finally settled in on her clit in earnest, pressing the pad of my middle finger against it and circling her in the hard, fast way that she liked.

Within seconds, she was crying out, pressing her ass against my hips so that I was buried to my balls, her fingers scrabbling at the carpet and wordless grunts tearing from her throat.

I watched her come apart, the carefully coiffed and sculpted pieces of Poppy Danforth falling away like scaffolding, leaving behind a shuddering, incoherent creature of want, and then she ground out one word, and that was it, I was lost. Lost to my control, to my vows, to anything other than the need to mark this woman in the most primitive and the basest way possible.

One word.

Yours.

I went rough now, gripping her hips and slamming into her, grunting myself, chasing my release as she gasped her way through the aftershocks of hers, and her ass was so damn slick, so damn tight, everything squeezing me and gripping me, and then it took me like a tidal wave of darkness, the real frenzy, pounding and growling as it imploded up through my spine and my balls, and fuck, I was coming, coming, coming, and there was black crowding at the edges of my vision and I was going to pass out as I pulsed, pass out or just keep coming and coming like it had no end.

I'd pulled out at the very last moment so I could watch as my orgasm laced her ass and back with cum, drops and rivulets like some kind of rain, dripping down the pleated rose of her entrance and over the curves of her back and hips.

As my vision cleared and my senses returned, I could admire my handiwork, the panting, trembling woman in front of me, covered *with* me.

Poppy stretched back out on her stomach, somehow making the movement elegant, erotic. "Clean me up," she commanded like the little queen she was, and I rushed to obey. I washed her with a wet towel and then I kept her on the floor while I massaged her hips and thighs and back and arms, murmuring the sweetest things I could think of in Latin and Greek and quoting Song of Songs as I covered every inch of her skin in kisses.

And I could tell from the way she smiled to herself, the way she closed her eyes every now and again as if to push back tears, that this was something Sterling had never done. He'd never checked in with her after sex, he'd never petted her and praised her and rewarded her.

I didn't even try not to feel triumphant about that.

And then after she was cleaned up, she and I sat down and worked on our fundraiser. She helped me set up for the men's group and then she went to the women's group at Millie's house. And all the while I could smell the balsam on her skin and on mine, and nothing short of being with this woman every minute of every day would be enough to stop the yawning hunger low in my belly.

Or, even more dangerously, stop the hunger in my heart.

CHAPTER SIXTEEN

Something shifted for me that day, something that I realized had been shifting for a while. It was like the feeling I'd had as a child, when I'd taken off my roller skates after a few hours of skating and my feet would feel abnormally light and floaty. Or maybe like the feeling when I camped with my dad and Ryan, and we finally got to dump our gear on the ground after several hours of hiking, and I felt so light I could swear I was hovering a few inches above the ground.

I didn't have a name for it, but it was lightness and lifting, and it had something to do with Lizzy. Something to do with sharing her death and its aftermath with Poppy, something with Poppy's whispered words, *is Lizzy the reason you're afraid to let go with me?*

I realized now, as I cradled Lizzy's rosary in my palm, that Lizzy was the reason for a lot of things. She was the reason for everything. Her death was a weight I carried with me always, a wrong I had to avenge. But what if I could change that? What if I could trade vengeance for love? That was what Christians were called to do, after all, choose love above all else.

Love. The word was a bomb. An unexploded bomb living inside my chest.

That night, I texted Poppy. **Are you awake?**

A beat. **Yes.**

My response was immediate. **Can I come over? I have a gift for you.**

Well, I was going to say no, but now that I know there's a present...come on over ;)

I made my careful, quiet way across the park, wearing a dark T-shirt and jeans. It was late and the park was in a natural dell, sheltered from view, but I still felt nervous as I strode in quick steps down the path, cutting through the weed-choked grass to get to Poppy's gate. I let myself in, wincing at every creak of the rusted latch, and then walked up to her door, rapping once with my knuckle on the glass.

She opened the door and her face lit up with the most beautiful fucking smile I'd ever seen.

"Wow," she said. "You're here. Like a real person."

"Did you doubt that I was real before?"

She shook her head, standing aside so I could walk in and then closing the door after me. "I've never dated someone I couldn't actually date. I had half convinced myself that you only existed inside the church walls."

"Dating?" My voice came out too eager, too excited. I cleared my throat. "I mean, we're dating?"

"I don't know what *you* call it when you fuck someone's ass raw, Father Bell, but that's what I call it."

A sudden fear dropped into my stomach, and I stepped towards her, grabbing her hand and pulling her into me, so I could look down into her eyes. "Are you sore?" I asked, worried.

She beamed up at me. "Only in the best ways." She raised up to kiss my jaw and then moved into the kitchen. "Would you like a drink? Let me guess…a cosmo? No—a pomegranate martini."

"Ha. Whiskey—Irish or Scotch, I don't care. But neat."

She gestured toward the living room and I went, taking the opportunity to look around her house as I did. It was still mostly boxes and paint cans, and despite the attractive furniture and tasteful pictures and paintings resting against the wall, it was fairly plain that Poppy didn't find much interest in the domestic arts.

Stacks of books rested against the wall, waiting for a permanent home, and I ran my fingers down the ridged towers of their spines, both openly pleased and secretly jealous of how well-read this woman was. There were the usual suspects, of course—Austen and Brontë and Wharton—but names I would not have expected along with them—Joseph Campbell and David Hume and Michel Foucault. I was flipping through *Thus Spoke Zarathustra* (an old nemesis from both my mDiv and my history classes) when Poppy drifted over with our drinks.

Our fingers grazed against each other when I took my tumbler of Macallan, and then I set it down and set Poppy's drink down, because I wanted to kiss her. I wanted to slide my hands up that slender neck and cup her face as I explored her mouth, and I wanted to walk her back to the couch so I could lay her down and slowly peel every layer of clothing off her body.

But I had come here to do something, not to fuck her (well, not *only* to fuck her) so I contented myself with a kiss and then pulled back to get my drink again. She looked a little dazed from the kiss, a dreamy sort of smile hanging around her lips as she took a sip from her martini glass, and then she declared that she was going to get something for us to snack on.

I continued my slow perusal of her living room, feeling relaxed and peaceful. *I'm doing the right thing.* This could be a new beginning for us, for me. Something official to mark our relationship—that's how rituals worked, right? Something tangible to signal the intangible. A gift to show Poppy what she meant to me—what us meant to me—to show her the strange but also divine transformation happening in my life because of her.

The house was small, but it had been recently renovated, with sleek wooden floors and the original large fireplace and large, clean lines of trim. She had a wide wooden desk by a window, the only symbol of any true intent of unpacking and staying, with an iMac and a printer and a scanner, neat stacks of folders and a small wooden box filled with expensive-looking pens.

Next to the desk, in an open cardboard box, were her framed degrees, neglected and buried amongst other castoff office items—half-used pads of Post-its and open boxes of envelopes.

Dartmouth — Bachelor of Economics, summa cum laude.

Tuck School of Business at Dartmouth — Master of Business Administration, summa cum laude.

And then one I didn't expect, *University of Kansas* — Bachelor of Fine Arts, Dance. This one was dated from this past spring.

I held it up as Poppy returned with a cutting board loaded with cheese and sliced pears. "You got another degree?"

She actually blushed, busying herself with setting the tray down on the coffee table. "I had a lot of free time when I moved here, and once I started making so much money at the club, I thought I'd put it to good use. This time, my parents weren't around to tell me not to get a dance degree, so I just went for it. I managed to squeeze it into three years instead of four."

I came toward her. "Will you dance for me sometime?"

"I could do it now," she said, pressing her hand against

my sternum and pushing me down onto the sofa. She climbed over me, straddling me, and my cock immediately leapt with interest. But her thigh pressed against my slacks pocket and I remembered why I was there in the first place.

I trapped her with one arm around her waist, forcing her to hold still while I dug the small tissue-paper-wrapped packet out of my pocket.

She tilted her head as I handed it to her. "Is this my present?" she asked, looking delighted.

"It's…" I didn't know how to explain what it was. "It's not new," I finished lamely.

She unwrapped it, staring at the pile of jade beads nestled in the tissue paper. She pulled the rosary out slowly, the silver cross spinning in the low light. "It's beautiful," she whispered.

"Everyone should have a nice rosary. At least, that's what my grandmother always said." I slid my hands to rest on the outside of Poppy's thighs, mostly so I could look somewhere other than the rosary. "That one was Lizzy's."

I felt her body tense in my lap.

"Tyler," she said carefully. "I can't take this."

She tried to hand it back to me, but I caught her hand with my own, curling her fingers around it.

"After Lizzy died, no one wanted anything of hers that reminded them of what she had gone through at church. Her bible and holy cards and saint's candles—my dad threw them all away." I flinched, remembering his white-hot rage when he'd found out that I'd dug her rosary out of the trash. "But I wanted something of hers. I wanted to keep all the parts of her alive in my memory."

"Don't you still?"

"Of course, but after we talked the other night...I realized that I also need to let parts of her go too. And when I think about her—well, I know she would have loved you." I met her eyes. "She would have loved you like I do."

Poppy's lips parted, her eyes wide and hopeful and scared, but before she could respond to what I said, I took her fingers in mine and said, "Let me teach you how to use this."

Yes, I was a coward. I was afraid of her not telling me that she loved me, and I was afraid of her telling me that she *did* love me. I was afraid of the palpable tie between us, afraid of the ribbon that laced through my ribs and around my heart that was also laced and tied around hers.

Her eyes never left mine as I moved her hand from her forehead to her heart and then to each shoulder. "In the name of the Father and the Son and the Holy Spirit," I said for her. And then I put her fingers on the crucifix. "Now we pray the Apostle's Creed..."

We prayed the entire thing together with her on my lap, her echoing faintly after me, our fingers moving together through the beads, and it was somewhere near the last decade that I became aware of how hard I was, of how her nipples showed through her soft flowing tank top. Aware of those big hazel eyes and that long wavy hair and the watchful intelligence that peered through each and every expression of hers.

This is love, I thought dizzily, wondrously. *This is what laying down a cross feels like. This is what taking up a new life feels like…it feels like Poppy Danforth.* And as I intoned the final words of the rosary, I almost forgot whom I was praying to.

Hail holy queen…our sweetness and our hope.

Later that night, when I was moving over her and into her, those words tumbled around in my mind, words that were so indelibly Poppy, so indelibly attached to the brightness of her mind and the paradise of her body.

Holy. Queen. Sweetness.

Hope.

CHAPTER SEVENTEEN

"Jordan."

The priest kneeling in front of me didn't stop praying or even turn to face me. Instead, he kept murmuring to himself in the same measured voice with the same measured pace, and I knew Jordan well enough to know that this was a polite way of telling me to fuck off until he was done.

I sat in the pew behind him.

Jordan was the only priest I personally knew who still prayed the Liturgy of the Hours, a practice that was so monastic as to be almost obsolete, which was probably part of the reason it appealed to him. Like me, he loved old things, but his fascination went beyond mere books and the occasional spiritual encounter. He lived like a medieval monk, a life almost completely and totally devoted to prayer and ritual. It was this mystical, unearthly nature that had brought so many young people into his parish;

over the past three years, it had been his presence that had revitalized this old, inner-city church that had been so close to closing when he'd taken it over into something thriving and alive.

Jordan finished his prayers and made the sign of the cross, standing with a purposeful slowness to face me.

"Father Bell," he said formally.

I refrained from rolling my eyes. He'd always been like this—aloof and intense. Even the one time he'd accidentally drunk too much at the seminary barbecue and I'd had to babysit him as he puked all night. But what appeared to be haughtiness or coldness was actually just a symptom of his vibrant inner life, the constant atmosphere of holiness and inspiration that he lived in, an atmosphere so palpable to him that he didn't understand why other people didn't sense it as he did.

"Father Brady," I said.

"I imagine you are here for a confession?"

"Yes." I stood and he looked me up and down. There was a long pause, a long moment where his face went from confused to sad to unreadable.

"Not today," he finally said and then turned and started walking toward his office.

I was confused. "Not today? Like no confession today? Are you busy or something?"

"No, I'm not busy," he said, still walking away.

My brows knit together. Was denying someone

confession even legal according to ecclesiastical law? Pretty sure it wasn't.

"Hey, wait up," I said.

He didn't. He didn't even turn around to acknowledge that I had said something or that I was jogging after him.

We went into the small hallway lined with doors, and it was as I was following him into his office that I realized this was more than his usual reserved attitude. Father Jordan Brady was upset.

He definitely hadn't been upset when I'd arrived.

"Dude," I said, closing his office door behind me. "What the hell?"

He sat down behind his desk, the early afternoon light painting his blond hair gold. Jordan was a good-looking guy, with the kind of hair and healthy complexion that you usually only saw in Calvin Klein ads. He was fit too—we'd bonded in the first semester of our divinity program after we kept running into each other at the local gym. We'd ended up sharing an apartment for the next two years, and I was pretty sure I was the closest thing this guy had to a friend.

Which was why I refused to be blown off.

He kept his eyes down as he powered on his laptop. "Come back later, Father Bell. Not today."

"Canon law says you have to hear my confession."

"Canon law isn't everything."

That surprised me. Jordan was not a rule-breaker.

Jordan was like two steps away from being the creepy assassin in *The Da Vinci Code.*

I sat in a chair across his desk and folded my arms. "I'm not leaving until you divulge why exactly you won't hear my confession."

"I don't mind if you stay," he said calmly.

"*Jordan.*"

He pressed his lips together, as if debating with himself, and then he finally looked up, brown eyes concerned and penetrating.

"What's her name, Tyler?"

Fear and adrenaline spiked through me. Had someone seen us? Had someone figured out what was going on and told Jordan?

"Jordan, I—"

"Don't bother lying about it," he said, and he didn't say it with disgust, but rather with an intensity that unsettled me, put me more on edge than his anger ever could.

"Are you going to let me confess?" I demanded.

"No."

"Why the fuck not?"

"Because," Jordan said deliberately, bracing his elbows on his desk and leaning forward, "you aren't ready to stop. You're not ready to give her up, and until you are, there's no point in me absolving you."

I sank back in my chair. He was right. I wasn't ready to give Poppy up. I didn't want to stop. Why was I here, then?

Did I think that Jordan was going to say some special prayer over me that would solve all my problems? Did I think going through the motions would change what was in my heart?

"How did you know?" I asked, looking down at my legs and hoping to God it wasn't because someone had seen Poppy and me together.

"God told me. When you walked in." Jordan said it simply, the same way someone might share where they bought their clothes. "Just as He is telling me now that you are not at the end of this. You aren't ready to confess yet."

"God told you," I repeated.

"Yes," he said with a nod.

It sounded insane. But I believed him. If Jordan told me he knew exactly how many angels could fit on the head of a pin, I'd believe him. He was that kind of man—one foot in our world, one foot in the next—and I'd experienced enough with him over our years of friendship that I knew he really was able to see and feel things that others couldn't.

It had been a lot less frustrating when I hadn't been one of the others in question.

"You've broken your vows," he said now, softly.

"Did God tell you that too?" I asked, not bothering to keep the bitterness out of my voice.

"No. But I can see it in you. You carry equal burdens of guilt and joy."

Yep, that about summed it up.

I buried my face in my hands, not overcome with

emotion, but suddenly overwhelmed by it all, embarrassed by my weakness in front of a man who would never cave to any temptation.

"Do you hate me?" I mumbled into my hands.

"You know I don't. You know God doesn't either. And you know I won't tell the bishop."

"You won't?"

He shook his head. "I don't think that's what God wants right now."

I raised my head, still overwhelmed. "So what do I do?"

Jordan looked at me with something like pity.

"You come back when you're ready to confess," he said. "And until then, you be exceedingly careful."

Careful.

Exceedingly careful.

I thought about those words as I visited Mom and Dad, as I rinsed the dinner dishes in their sink, as I drove home in the dark. As I snuck across the park so I could fuck Poppy again.

Nothing about me was careful right now.

CHAPTER EIGHTEEN

Careful.

A week later, I stared up at Poppy's ceiling. She was pressed against me, her head nestled on my arm, her breathing slow and even. I had lain awake watching her after we'd made love, watching the soft lines of her face relax from ecstasy into peace, feeling nothing but mindless contentment. But now that she'd been asleep for several hours, the contentment had ebbed into an anxious doubt.

The last several days had been like something out of a dream or a fairy tale, where my days were chased by the structured benevolence that was my life as a priest, and where my nights were filled with gasps and sighs and skin sliding over skin.

At night, we could pretend. We could drink and watch Netflix, we could fuck and shower together afterwards (and then fuck again). We could drowse next to each other and fall softly into sleep. We could pretend we were just like any couple a few weeks into their relationship, that there wasn't anything keeping us from talking about normal couple things, like meeting each other's parents or where we would spend Thanksgiving.

But we were acutely and painfully aware of our own acting, of our own pretense. We were faking it because facing the truth was so much worse, the truth that this paradise would end one way or another.

What if it didn't have to end? What if I called the bishop tomorrow and told him I wanted to quit? That I wanted to be defrocked and made into a normal man again?

Laicized. That was the word for it. From the late Latin *laicus*, meaning layperson. To be made into a layperson.

What if a few months from now I could kneel in front of Poppy and do more than offer her an orgasm and offer her my hand in marriage instead?

I closed my eyes, shutting out the real world and letting my mind go where I hadn't let it go before—to the future. To a future where it was her and me and a house somewhere and little Bell children underfoot. I would follow her anywhere, and if she wanted to work in New York or London or Tokyo, or stay in Kansas City, I would go with her. I was like Ruth with Naomi, I was ready to make her life and her desires my own, and any place Poppy wanted to go, we would make a home together. Spend our hours together fucking and loving. Someday watching her stomach grow with my child.

But what would I do? I had two degrees, both equally useless in the real world, useless everywhere except temples of God and temples of learning. I could teach, I supposed, theology or maybe languages. I'd always wanted to be a scholar, sitting in some dusty library, poring over dusty books, excavating forgotten knowledge the way an archeologist excavates forgotten lives. The idea excited me, blowing like rain across my thoughts, drops and splashes of possibility. New cities, new universities…a list compiled itself in my head of places that had the best classics programs and the best theology programs—there had to be a way I could fuse the two together, maybe apply for a doctoral program or take a job as an adjunct…

I opened my eyes and that pleasant, fantastical rain stopped, and the weight of everything I would have to leave behind crushed against me. I'd be leaving this town—Millie, the youth group, the men's group, all the parishioners I'd so carefully courted back to God. I'd be leaving the pancake breakfast and clothes pantry and all the work on fighting predators in the clergy. I'd be leaving behind the gift of turning bread into flesh, wine into blood, of having one hand on the veil that separated this world from the next. I'd be leaving behind Father Bell, the man I'd become, and I'd have to molt him away like so much dead flesh and ruined feathers, and grow a new shape with painful new pink skin.

I had a life building treasures in heaven, beating myself like a runner for the race, and I was thinking of giving that up…for what? I tried to stop the verses I knew by heart crowding my mind, verses about sowing to the flesh and reaping corruption, verses about passions of the flesh waging war against my soul. *Put to death what is earthly in you.*

Put to death my love for Poppy.

My throat tightened and my mouth went dry; my anxiety spiked, as if someone was holding a knife to my throat and demanding that I choose, now, but how could I choose when both choices came at such cost?

Because if I stayed where I was, I lost the woman sleeping next to me, this woman who argued about racial and gender disparities on *The Walking Dead*, who pulled obscure literary quotes from the air, who drank like she was drowning, and who made me come harder than I ever had in my life.

That realization made the panic bite at me hard.

Turning to face her, I stroked a hand along her side, down the slope of her ribs and up the curve of her hip. She stirred a bit and snuggled in closer, still fast asleep, and my chest clenched.

I couldn't lose her.

And I couldn't keep her.

This kind of fear, this specific brand of panic, shouldn't have made me hard, but it did. Hard enough that I had to reach down and stroke myself. I was engulfed with the need to claim my girl once again, to bury myself inside of her, as if one more orgasm would make a difference in scaring away our doomed future.

I slipped a hand down between us as I turned my body towards hers, finding those soft lips below her legs, and I started teasing them apart, flicking my fingers across her clit and over the frilled pink skin around her entrance. She shifted and sighed a happy, sleepy sigh, her legs falling open to grant me better access, although her eyes remained closed and her face relaxed. She was still asleep.

I bent my head to take a nipple into my mouth, sucking gently, fluttering my tongue around the tightening peak, and she was squirming now, but still asleep and fuck it, I couldn't wait any longer. I lifted one of her legs and slung it over my hip as I positioned myself at her entrance. Holding her still, I pushed myself in, and like a curtain falling over a sunny window or a door closed against the noise of a party, the doubts were immediately muffled. They vanished in the face of our connection, the sensation of her tight cunt gripping me. God, I could stay like this forever, not even moving, just being inside of her, feeling her rouse and stretch like a languorous cat while I held her hips fast to mine.

Finally, her eyes opened, drowsy but pleased. "*Mmm*," she hummed, hooking her leg more securely around my waist. "I like waking up like this."

"I do too," I said huskily, reaching up to sweep a lock of hair off her cheek.

She put a hand on my shoulder and pushed me back, rolling with me so that I was laying flat with her on top of me; she began riding me with slow, dozy undulations. Sleep and sex had tousled her hair, and it hung in tangled, messy waves around her white shoulders and soft breasts, and the streetlight streaming in through the window painted her curves in shades of light and shadow.

Sometimes she was too beautiful to look at.

I laid back, lacing my arms behind my head, just watching as she ground her pleasure out of me, as she start moving faster and faster, her eyes falling closed and her hands braced against my stomach. From this angle I could see the needy bud being rubbed against my pelvis, the tiniest glimpse of where I was filling her and stretching her, and fuck, I could lose it right now if I wasn't careful.

"That's my girl," I whispered. "Use me to come. There you go. You're so fucking sexy right now. Come on, baby, get it. Get it."

Her mouth parted and I watched in fascination as the muscles in her stomach seized and tightened, as she moaned and quaked her way through her climax, eventually sliding forward to lay against my chest.

I held her tight to me and then rolled us back over, so that I was on top and she was on her back, and then I bent down and sucked on her neck. I reached under her and found what I wanted, the tight, little rim behind her cunt. She pressed herself into the mattress, as if trying to get away from my touch, but that wouldn't do, wouldn't do at all, because I had plans for that part of her that extended well beyond what one fingertip could do.

"Are you saying no?"

She bit her lip and then shook her head. "Not a *no*. Yes."

"Then give me your ass," I growled in her ear. "Give it to me and then I won't have to take it."

She gave a little gasp, a gasp that made me crazy, and then she stopped trying to fight my touch. "There's lube," she panted. "In the end table."

Not bothering to pull out, I simply stretched my weight over her as I reached for the end table drawer and grabbed the brand-new bottle of lube. "Looks like you've been preparing, little lamb."

"It was either that or get my own specially blessed oil," she said, half joking, half out of breath.

I withdrew from her, resting back on my knees and spreading her legs wider. I took my time warming her up, gradually working the lube into her while I rubbed her clit with my other hand, fingering both her holes until she was a twisting, slippery mess. Then I grabbed her thighs and pushed into her ass.

I should have stopped, given her a few moments to adjust, but I was so haunted by all the doubt and the dread, and the only things that would quiet my thoughts were the driving thrusts of my hips, her fingers digging into my back, the hot, hot heat of her like a vise around my dick.

"Tyler," she breathed.

"Lamb," I said, rising up to my knees and curling my hands around her hips.

"I'm going to come again."

"Good." My own climax was almost there as well, a barbed throb in my pelvis, driven on by the sight of the goose bumps rippling up her skin and the flush creeping up her stomach as she played with her clit.

"Oh, that's so good, baby," I grunted. "You're such a good girl. Show me how much you like it."

Her eyes locked on mine. "Fuck me like you want me to be yours."

Her words tugged at that ribbon, jerking against my heart, and I pressed my eyes closed. I could so easily fuck her like that, because I did want her to be mine—forever. We'd only known each other six weeks, and I wanted her for the rest of my life.

I was such a fool.

I pulled her closer, stabbing into her narrow opening over and over again, watching her crest and peak as she continued to beg me to make her mine, and how could she not see that she already was? That I was already hers? We belonged to each other, and as I watched her cunt pulse with her orgasm, as I sank up to the hilt and shot my load inside of her, I realized that there was no undoing that, no untangling what had become so tangled over the past month and a half.

As we both came down, we stared at each other, and whatever solace I had managed to eke out vanished in an instant. I got up to get a warm washcloth, and when I came back, Poppy was watching me thoughtfully.

"Tyler."

"Yes?" I sat on the bed and started cleaning her.

"I don't know how long I can do this."

I froze. "What do you mean?"

"You know what I mean," she said, and there was a quaver in her words. "I want to be with you. I want to claim you. I'm in love with you, Tyler, and the fact that there's no future for us is killing me."

I finished cleaning her as I thought of a reply, tossing the used towel onto a nearby chair. "I don't know what the future looks like," I finally said. "I know that I love you…but I also love my job and my life. Poppy, what I have here…it's more than just charity or prayer. It's a way of life. I get to live my entire life for my god, every minute of every day, and I don't know if I can live without that."

We both avoided the fact that these past few minutes had hardly been lived for God, that they'd been for us and us alone.

"Don't you think I know that?" she said, sitting up. She didn't bother to cover herself with the sheet, and I forced myself to look away from those perky tits so I could focus on what she was saying. "It's all I think about. I can't make you give this up—I can see that you love it. Hell, it's what I love about you. That you are passionate and giving and spiritual, that you've devoted your life to God. But then I worry"—and there were real tears now—"that you're going to give me up instead."

"No," I whispered. "Don't do that to yourself."

But I didn't tell her what she wanted to hear. I didn't know if I would give her up or not, because while it would kill me, being discovered and losing everything I'd fought for would kill me too.

I could see the moment she realized it, that I wasn't going to tell her that we would stay together, and before I could say something else—I don't know what, but *something*—she laid back down, turning on her side so that her back was to me.

"I want you so badly that I can taste blood when I think about it. But I won't be the reason you lose your life," she said, her voice reverberating like a bell in my mind. "I won't be the reason for any regret. I don't think I could bear it…looking at you and wondering if there was a part of you that hated me just a little bit for being the reason you laicized."

She even knew the right word for it…she'd done her research. That heartened me at the same time it saddened me.

"I could never hate you."

"Really? Even if I made you choose between me and your god?"

Fuck, that was stark. "That's not all there is, Poppy. Don't do that."

She took a breath, the kind of breath that usually presaged a sharp retort, but then she seemed to freeze. Instead she said, "You should go home. It's getting close to morning."

Her tight voice killed me. I wanted to comfort her, hug her, fuck her. Why did we have to talk about these awful things when we could keep pretending? "Poppy…"

"I'll see you later, Tyler."

Her tone was as definitive as any safeword. I was dismissed.

I walked across the foggy park, hands in my pockets and shoulders hunched against the September-night chill, trying to pray but only finding snippets of thoughts to send up instead.

She wants a full life, I told God silently. She wanted a life with marriage and kids, a life where love could be just as present as work and family and friends, a life where she didn't have to hide. And who could blame her?

What am I supposed to do?

God didn't answer. Probably because I'd broken my sacred vow to serve Him, desecrated His church in all manner of ways, and repeatedly committed a litany of sins that I barely regretted because I was so infatuated. I'd made an idol out of Poppy Danforth, and now I would reap the consequences of finding myself isolated from God.

Repent. I have to repent.

But not seeing Poppy anymore…even the mere idea tore a hole right through my chest.

I climbed up the stairs and walked to the back door of the rectory, navigating through my kitchen in the bluish light of early dawn. I still had a couple hours to sleep before I had to get up for morning Mass, and I hoped that something would be different in the morning, that the way forward would be clear, but I knew it wouldn't, and that knowledge was so very, very depressing.

"Late night?"

I nearly had a heart attack.

Millie was sitting in my living room in the half dark, wearing a matching sweat suit.

"Millie," I said, trying to pretend that I hadn't almost pissed myself. "What are you doing here?"

"I take walks every morning," she said. "Very early. I don't think you would have ever noticed, given that you seem to sleep in until the latest possible moment."

"I haven't noticed, you're right." Was she inviting me on a walk now?

She sighed. "Father Bell, I know."

"Pardon?"

"I *know*. About you and Poppy. I've seen you skulking through the park during the mornings."

Oh shit.

Oh shit oh shit oh shit.

"Millie—"

She held up a hand. "Don't."

I sat heavily in a chair, despair and panic coiled together in my stomach. Someone knew, someone knew, someone knew. Of course it was always going to be like this. I was never going to have the luxury of choosing for myself how this all played out, and I was a fucking idiot for ever thinking otherwise.

I looked up with wide eyes, and what came out was not gracious or kind or selfless, but pure lizard brain survival. "Millie, please, you can't tell anyone." I slid to my knees in front of her. "Please, please don't tell the bishop, I don't know how I could live with myself…"

But then I trailed off because I was doing nothing less than begging an honorable woman to abandon her honor, all for the sake of an unrepentant sinner.

"I'm so sorry," I said instead. "You must think I'm such a terrible, awful person…I'm so ashamed. I don't even know what to say."

She stood. "You can say that you'll be careful."

I looked up at her. "What?"

"Father, I came here to warn you, and there's a reason I did that instead of going to the bishop. This town *needs* you, and it definitely doesn't need another scandal about a priest." She shook her head with a small smile. "Especially when it's about something as innocuous as falling in love with a grown woman who would be perfect for you…if you weren't a priest."

"Millie," I said, and my voice was broken, desperate. "What do I do?"

"I don't have that answer for you," she said, walking toward the door. "All I know is that you better make a decision soon. These things never stay hidden, Father, no matter how hard you try. And there's no way a woman like her would be willing to be your secret mistress for the rest of her years. She is worth far more than that."

"She is," I echoed, a cold, iron weight crushing me as I realized that I was no better than Sterling. I was making her do essentially the same thing, except I wasn't even doing her the service of being upfront about it…or offering her anything in return.

"Goodbye," Millie said, and I nodded a goodbye in return, miserable and agitated, too miserable and agitated to even think about sleeping.

Had it just been a couple weeks ago that I'd given Poppy Lizzy's rosary? And now everything felt like it was falling apart, like broken rosary beads scattering wildly across the floor, too numerous and fast for me to chase.

Millie knew. Jordan knew. Poppy maybe didn't even want to be with me…

I went for a long run, and then got to the church early to unlock it and prepare for Mass, distracted throughout the whole service by my encounter with Millie, by my earlier non-fight with Poppy, by the fact that now two people knew about my affair and that was two people too many.

Secret mistress.

Be careful.

I'm in love with you, Tyler.

In fact, I was so distracted that I almost spilled the wine and then I accidentally said the closing prayer twice in a row, my mind miles away from the sacred invocation of the divine and only in the swirling maelstrom of how much was going fucking wrong right the fuck now.

After Mass, I emerged from the sacristy with my head down, checking my phone (Poppy hadn't been at Mass and she hadn't messaged me either) and wondering if she was still angry with me. So I didn't notice that there was someone standing in the center aisle at first, not until they shifted and the noise caught my attention.

It was a man—tall, black-haired, my age. He wore a khaki suit with a blue tie and silver tie bar, far too dressy for a September Friday in Weston, but somehow he made it work without looking ridiculous. He took off a pair of sunglasses and eyed me with an icy blue gaze.

"You must be Tyler Bell."

"I am," I confirmed, sliding my phone into my slacks pocket. I had removed my chasuble and stole and all the other trappings of my office other than my collar, and I was feeling suddenly underdressed, like I needed some kind of extra armor, extra authority, with this man.

Which was stupid. He was a visitor to my church. All I needed was to be friendly.

I strode forward and shook his hand, which he seemed to welcome, a small, appraising smile on his lips.

"Can I help you with anything?" I asked. "Unfortunately, you missed our morning service, but we will have another service tomorrow."

"No, I think you've already helped," he said as he stepped past me, his head swiveling to take in every corner of the church. "I just wanted to meet you and see for myself what this Father Tyler Bell was like."

Uh…

Uneasiness knotted in my gut. Even though I knew it wasn't possible, I couldn't help but worry that somehow he was a result of Millie and Jordan knowing the truth, that he was here to finally tug on the thread that would unravel my life.

The man turned on his heel and faced me. "I like to know the size and shape of my competition."

"Competition?"

"For Poppy, of course."

It only took the barest instant for my mind to catch up, to reassess this encounter, and calculate that I was talking to Sterling Haverford III. To size up his body (in good shape, fuck that guy) and his clothes (expensive, fuck that guy again) and his bearing, which was almost absurdly confident, confident to the point of hubris, and there was the chink in this man's armor. He had no doubt that he would be successful, he had no doubt that he would leave here with what he wanted (and yes, I suspected that Poppy was a *what* to him and not a *who*). In that bare instant, I knew exactly where we stood, exactly what weapons he'd be fighting with, and I also knew that one of those weapons was the emotional hold he had on Poppy, and that I could very well lose this battle…this battle I had no right to fight.

And that bare instant was all Sterling needed to feel like he had the upper hand. His mouth curled into a sneer, subtle enough to be ignored, but present enough to demonstrate in exactly what light he held his *competition.*

However, I wasn't an idiot, whatever Sterling might think, and I certainly wasn't going to conform to his expectations of how he thought I would behave.

"I'm afraid you are mistaken," I said, giving him an easy smile. "There's no competition. Ms. Danforth has been attending my church and she's interested in pursuing the path to conversion, but that's as far as our friendship extends." I almost hated how easily the lie rolled off my tongue—lying was something I used to pride myself on not doing, but there was a lot I couldn't be proud of anymore. And this moment wasn't about morality, this moment was about survival.

Sterling raised an eyebrow. "So this is how it's going to be." He put his hands in his pockets, everything about his posture screaming boardrooms and yachts and arrogance.

Good Guy Tyler, be Good Guy Tyler, I told myself. *Better yet, be Father Bell.* Father Bell wasn't jealous of this man, jealous of his good looks and expensive clothes and the claim he had on Poppy. Father Bell didn't care about a pissing match with a stranger, and he certainly wouldn't engage in something as barbaric as competing for a grown woman, who was capable of making her own choices and exercising her own agency.

I leaned against a pew and gave him another smile, knowing my posture conveyed an easy control and a casual friendliness, while also reminding him that I was just as tall and built as he was.

"I'm sorry. I don't think I understand you," I finally said. "Like I just told you, there's no competition."

He took my words in a different way than I'd meant them. "You would like to think that, wouldn't you?" He looked me over once again, and then seemed to change tack, leaning against a pew himself and crossing his arms.

"Has she talked about me?" he asked. "I'm sure she has. Confession—that's a Catholic thing, right? Did she mention me in her confessions?"

"I'm not at liberty to—"

He waved a hand and his wedding ring glinted against his skin. "Right. Of course. Well, maybe she wouldn't want to confess things about me after all. How many times I can make her come. How loudly she cries my name. All the places I've fucked her. You know I once fucked her mere feet away from a U.S. Senator? During an art opening at The Met? She was always good to go. For me, at least."

It was only years of cultivated compassion and self-discipline that kept me from driving my fist right into this guy's classically square jaw. Not only from jealousy, but from the equally macho urge to protect Poppy's dignity and stop her choices from being reframed by this asshole.

She doesn't need you to defend her honor, Feminist Ally Tyler told me. But regular Tyler, the Irish-American one who enjoyed fucking and whiskey and roaring obscenities at soccer games, didn't care. It didn't matter if she needed me to and it didn't matter that I didn't have a right to—the universe had been knocked off-balance by this guy's assholery and my fist itched to correct that.

"Did that strike a nerve?" Sterling asked, amused.

"I consider Poppy one of my flock," I said, inclining my head in admission. Luckily, my voice betrayed nothing but mild disapprobation. "It pains me to hear any of them spoken of disrespectfully."

"Oh, certainly," Sterling said. "And I admire how committed you are to your story. I'm a man of appearances myself." He pulled a manila envelope from the inside of his suit jacket and handed it to me. "However, I'm also a man of means, and so we can move past this initial posturing and right into the heart of the matter."

I stared at him as I unwound the string at the top of the envelope and pulled out the large glossy pictures inside. Part of me worried that they would be pictures of Poppy and him, more evidence of their past to unsettle me, but no. No, it was much, much worse.

A broad-shouldered man crossing a small park at night. That same man at a darkened garden gate. A shot through a kitchen window of a man and a woman kissing.

I exhaled.

There was no nudity, thank Jesus, and nothing more sinful than a kiss, but it didn't matter, because it was clearly my face in all of them and that was enough. In fact, they were more than enough—they were damning.

"And be reassured that I have all the digital files of these," Sterling said cheerfully. "So feel free to keep those. As mementos."

"You had us followed," I said.

"I told you that I was a man of means. When Poppy kept refusing to answer my calls, even after I told her I was coming for her, I started to wonder if she'd met someone else. So I looked into it. Since she hasn't agreed to my arrangement—yet—I wouldn't have minded if she'd been fucking someone. But falling in love with another man...well, I know Poppy and I know what kind of obstacle that would present."

"You had us followed," I repeated. "Do you even hear yourself? That is insane."

Sterling seemed baffled. "Why?"

"Because," I said, my anger getting the better of me and making my words tight and forced, "people don't have other people followed. *Especially* their ex-girlfriends. That's stalking—that's actually the legal definition of stalking. I don't care that you're wealthy and can pay for someone else to do it for you—it's the same damn thing."

He still looked confused. "That's what you're upset about? Not that I have evidence that can ruin your life? Not that I'm going to inevitably walk away from this town with Poppy at my side?"

"You are so assured of this outcome," I said, forcing myself to move past him having Poppy followed. "But you forget, it has nothing to do with you or me—it's her choice."

Sterling shrugged one shoulder, as if I were being either deliberately obtuse or deliberately precious, and he didn't have time for it anymore.

"So what's the heart of the matter?" I asked, sliding the photos back into the envelope.

"Pardon?"

"You said you wanted to move past the posturing." I tossed the pictures on the pew next to me and stood up straight, crossing my arms. I was happy to see that Sterling also straightened up, as if unhappy with the extra inch I had on him. (In height, I mean. [Although a really awful, crass part of me was ridiculously pleased to know that I was the biggest Poppy had ever had.])

"Yes. Well, here it is, Father." He said the word *father* as if it had quotation marks. (I allowed myself another brief fantasy where I slammed my fist into his eye socket.) "I want Poppy to come home with me to New York. I want her to be mine."

"Even though you're married."

He gave me that look again, that slightly incredulous *are you an idiot* look, and it would have bothered me if I didn't have the moral high ground in this competition. Except...I couldn't really claim any part of any moral ground now, high or low, could I? That thought depressed me immensely.

Luckily, Sterling didn't notice and continued on. "Yes, even though I'm married. Marriage isn't a sacrament in my family—it's a tax write-off. And I have no intention of holding a legal arrangement above what I want out of my life. I've never loved my wife and she feels the same way about me."

"But you love Poppy?"

Sterling pressed his lips together. "Love and want are essentially the same thing," he elided. "Not that a man like you would know that."

"I respect your honesty, at least," I said. "You're not lying to yourself, and I assume you won't lie to her."

This unexpected compliment seemed to surprise him, but he quickly recovered. "Poppy doesn't care about that as much as she thinks she does," he told me. "You may labor under the illusion that she won't come back with me unless I love her, but she's not like you. She knows numbers, sense, mortgages. I'm offering her the currency she knows—money and lust and security—and that is why I will win."

I thought of her crying in the confessional booth, of the

moment we'd stood together in the sanctuary, bathing in God's presence. She wasn't merely a spreadsheet with spread legs, and Sterling was an idiot if he'd grown up with her and managed to miss all the deeply spiritual, deeply emotional facets of Poppy Danforth.

"She's so much more than that."

"That's sweet. That really is." Sterling put his sunglasses back on. "And just so you know, you are so much *less* than I expected. Here I was, expecting Alexander Borgia, and instead I find Arthur Dimmesdale. I was so prepared to fight dirty, and yet I suspect I won't have to fight at all."

"It's not a fight," I said. "It's a person."

"It's a woman, Father." Sterling flashed me a white, wide grin. "Soon to be *my* woman."

I didn't respond, even though every neuron was firing *you're wrong, you're wrong, you're wrong.* Instead, I simply watched as he tossed me a wave and strode easily down the aisle to the door, his hands in his pockets as if he didn't have a care in the world.

CHAPTER NINETEEN

The difference between envy and jealousy is subtle but distinct, once you know the flavors and contours of both. Jealousy is wanting what someone else has, like for example, wanting the same kind of car or house as a neighbor. (Or wanting to be the man who owns your girlfriend's heart rather than some WASP-y asshole who probably has a drawer just for all of his cuff links.)

Envy is hating the fact that someone else has something you don't, and hating *them* for having it, like wanting to slash your neighbor's tires because he doesn't fucking deserve a BMW and everyone fucking knows it, and if you can't have it, then it's no fucking fair that he gets to have one either.

Sterling fell into this last category. It's not that he wanted Poppy necessarily, not beyond the way he probably wanted other things in his life—a new vacation home, a new yacht, a new tie bar. But the idea of someone else having her chewed away at the inside of him, an insatiable parasite of possession worming away in his gut.

I had a lot of time to think about this today because Poppy was apparently MIA. At first, after Sterling had left, I'd tried to play it cool, pacing in my office and calling her and then texting her, the manila envelope like a scarlet letter burning a hole on my desk. What would I say if she picked up? I would simply tell her that Sterling paid me a visit, and oh, also he's been stalking us, and oh, also he's blackmailing me into letting you go, totally normal Friday, want to watch Netflix tonight?

But she didn't answer my calls or my texts, and answering promptly was something she normally did, and I spent a long hour walking tight circles around my office. I should just go over to her house. This was really important, and we needed to talk about it right now, but with Millie's confrontation still front and center in my brain—not to mention this fucking black-hole-burning-pyre-beating-guilty-heart of an envelope inches away from me—I was too frightened to walk over to her house lest we be caught...*again.*

And then I wanted to yell at myself for being such a pussy. We needed to figure this out and that was more important than anything else. And I would just go on another run, that was all. Everybody was used to seeing me running at all hours of the day and night, and if I happened to run past the old Anderson house, nobody would think it odd at all.

I quickly changed into my running clothes and strapped my phone to my arm, and I was at Poppy's house in less than two minutes. Her Fiat was in the driveway, but when I slipped into the garden (grateful once more for the overgrown shrubs that provided such great cover) and knocked on her door, there was no answer. Where the fuck was she? This was pretty important shit and she was unavailable? Was she taking a nap? In the shower?

I knocked and waited. Texted, knocked, and waited. Paced and waited and knocked some more and then growled *fuck it* and unlocked the door with the key under the bamboo plant pot.

But I could tell the moment I walked in that she wasn't napping or in the shower. There was the kind of silence filling the corners that only came with emptiness, with absence, and sure enough, I saw that her phone and purse were gone from the place she usually kept them on her desk, although her keys were still there. So she'd gone somewhere without her keys. Had she walked into downtown? To the coffee shop or maybe the library?

I turned to leave, and then a thought formed and stabbed me in the chest like an icy blade.

What if she was with Sterling?

I actually sagged against the wall. It made sense. What, I had thought he'd come all the way up here just to warn me? That he'd declare battle and then wait a few more days to fire his opening salvo? No, he'd probably gone straight to Poppy after leaving the church, and while I had been pacing the worn carpet in my office like an idiot, he'd been here persuading Poppy to go somewhere with him. To dinner. To drinks. To some sleek hotel in Kansas City where he'd fuck her against a floor-to-ceiling window.

That icy blade stabbed me over and over again, in my throat, in my back, in my heart. I didn't even bother to fight the twin dragons of jealousy and suspicion as they coiled around my feet, because I knew beyond a shadow of a doubt that I was right. There's no other reason she would be ignoring my calls and texts.

She was with Sterling. She was with Sterling and not with me and I was utterly powerless to make it otherwise.

After realizing that Poppy wasn't at home that afternoon, I'd run by the coffee shop and the library and the wine garden, just to double-check that she hadn't stepped out to work someplace other than her desk. But no, she hadn't been any of those places, and when I'd gotten home and unstrapped my iPhone, she still hadn't texted or called.

Bishop Bove had.

I didn't call him back.

That night at youth group, I was a mess. An angry, distracted mess, but luckily it was Xbox game night, and my frustration and tension blended in with those of the rowdy teenagers also playing with me. And at the end of the night, I made our prayer brief and to the point.

"God, the psalmist tells us that your word is like a lamp to our feet—that even though we don't always know where you are leading us, you promise that you will show us the next step. Please keep your lamp burning for us, so that our next step, our next hour and our next day, is clear. Amen."

"Amen," the teens mumbled, and then went home to their concerns that (to them) were as troubling and stressful as mine. Homework and crushes and unsympathetic parents and a graduation date that seemed too far away. I remembered those problems acutely, even though they'd been so massively overshadowed by Lizzy's death. Teenagers felt differently than adults—they felt keenly and powerfully, without the frame of experience to remind them that they wouldn't be broken by a bad grade or an unrequited love.

But I had that frame of experience. So why did I still feel like I could be broken?

After youth group, I sat in my living room with my phone in my hands, wondering if I should call the bishop back, if he'd called because Millie or Jordan had told him about my shattered vows, wondering if I could even keep up my own pretense if he *didn't* know. And that's when I saw it—the picture message.

It came from an unknown number, but I knew who it

was the second I opened the message and saw the picture, a shot of Poppy in a car, her face turned away toward the window. The light was low, as if the person taking the picture hadn't used a flash, and it appeared to be taken in a back seat, which made me think that they had a driver. I could just barely make out the wisps of hair around her neck and ears, the glimmer of the small diamond studs she sometimes wore, the pearlescent sheen of her tie-neck blouse.

Sterling wanted me to know that he was with her. And I knew it could be something as innocent as dinner and conversation, but honestly, when was dinner with an ex ever completely innocent?

I tried to swallow down my feelings of betrayal. What claims did I have on her time, when I could only give her stolen slices of mine? I was not the kind of boyfriend—or whatever I was—to want her to account for every one of her minutes, every one of her thoughts, in the jealous hope that this would keep her faithful. Even if I had the right to demand her fidelity—which I didn't, given that I was unfaithful in my own way, cheating on her with the Church—I still wouldn't. Love is freely and unconditionally given, and even I knew that much.

Besides, this was exactly what Sterling wanted. He wanted me to stew and fume, he wanted me to brood over his victory, but I would not grant him that satisfaction and I would not do Poppy the disservice of lobbing accusations via text or voicemail.

We would wait to talk about it until she came back. That was the reasonable thing to do.

But strangely, having a plan of action (or a plan of inaction, as it were) didn't help. I tried to watch TV and read, I tried to sleep, and in every pause of dialogue, in every paragraph break, was that picture of Poppy and all the unbidden, awful images of her and Sterling talking and touching and fucking. Finally I gave up on it all and went downstairs to the rectory basement where I lifted weights and did sit-ups until the moon started to sink, and then I drained four fingers of Macallan 12 and went to bed.

I woke up that morning with sore muscles and an even sorer conscience and a phone still devoid of missed calls or messages. I indulged in the quiet fantasy of dropping it into a boiling pot of water and walking away or maybe microwaving it—punishing it for everything that had gone so terribly wrong in the last twenty-four hours—but I settled instead for leaving it behind as I went to prepare for Mass and then for the pancake breakfast.

The morning went by in a robotic blur—especially after Millie told me that Poppy had called in sick to volunteer (this was followed by a look that was not exactly scathing but was certainly grumpy and I must have looked fairly pitiful, because she relented and gave me a dry kiss on the cheek before she left).

And then I found myself with a Saturday afternoon with nothing to do but try to avoid feeling my feelings, and you know what? I decided that I was going to work out some more.

And drink. That too.

When I finally finished cleaning the church basement and went home, I saw that Bishop Bove had called again and sent me a badly garbled text message that also included several what I assume were accidental emojis.

I should call him back.

But instead, I changed into my gym shorts, grabbed the half-empty bottle of scotch and trotted downstairs, where I turned up the Britney as loud as the speakers would go, and brutalized my screaming muscles with more weights, more sit-ups, more squats, chugging whisky straight from the bottle in between each set.

I would drink and sweat until I forgot that Sterling existed. Hell, I would drink until I forgot Poppy existed.

And I was getting close. The drunk push-ups were beginning to drive home how much my body did not appreciate the concurrent intoxication and exertion, and my arms were about to give out when the music stopped abruptly, and I heard my name called by the only voice I wanted to hear.

Startled, I got to my knees as Poppy walked over to me, wearing the same pale tie-neck blouse that she was wearing in the picture last night. Did that mean she spent the night with Sterling? The Macallan and exhaustion destabilized me enough that I wanted to ask—no, *accuse*—just that.

But then she got to her knees too, and without hesitation, wove her fingers into my sweaty hair and pulled her face to mine.

The moment her lips touched me, everything else flared up and burned away, like so much flash paper thrown into the air. I forgot why I was punishing my body, why I was drinking, why I hadn't been able to sleep last night.

She slid her arms around my waist and parted her lips, beckoning me inside her mouth, and I went where I was summoned, finding her tongue with mine and kissing her with everything I had. I seized the back of her neck with my hand, gripping her in the way that I couldn't grip her commitment or her time, and my other hand reached under the wrinkled pencil skirt she was wearing and found the lace of her thong, pushing it aside to find the soft skin between her legs. Without preamble or prologue, I pushed a finger inside of her pussy, which was tight and not entirely ready for me, although I could tell that she was getting there.

She moaned into my mouth at my intrusion, breaking our kiss with a gasp as I started rubbing her clit with my thumb while I crooked my finger inside of her.

She leaned against me as I worked her cunt, and God forgive me, I was so jealous that Sterling might have touched it the night before that I couldn't discern whether I was touching her for her benefit or mine—as if I could reclaim her if I made her come.

Watching her pant into my shoulder with her day-after

hair and day-after makeup, her creased clothes, that general walk-of-shame look, was so fucking hot and so goddamn infuriating at the same time, and it was no wonder she flinched at my voice when I said, "On your hands and knees. Facing away from me."

She swallowed and slowly obeyed. "Tyler…" she said, as if realizing for the first time that maybe she owed me an explanation.

"No. You don't get to talk." My voice was raspy from the workout and the scotch. "Not a fucking word."

My dick had been stiff the instant I heard her voice, but by the time I moved her skirt over her hips and pulled her thong down to her knees, I was so hard it hurt.

I should warn her that I've been drinking. I should warn her that I'm angry.

Instead, I pulled my shorts down to expose my cock, nothing in my mind but fucking that pussy, but the moment I notched my head against her cleft, my jealousy got the better of me. My jealousy and perhaps my conscience, which was beaten and gagged, but still not ready to let me fuck a woman drunk and in anger.

So I withdrew and instead of having sex with her, I fisted my cock, staring at her ass as I stroked myself. It was not quiet—I grunted every time my hand slid back up over my glans, and my hand and my dick made the distinctive sound of jacking off—and Poppy cried out, starting to turn back to me.

"That's not fair!" she protested. "Don't do this, Tyler—fuck me. I want you to fuck me!"

"Turn around."

"You're not even going to let me watch?" she said, and she sounded hurt, shut out.

Well, boo fucking hoo, Macallan Tyler thought and Good Guy Tyler winced. But no. No, she should atone. Somehow.

I smacked her ass and she jerked against my hand, letting out a low groan that told me she wanted more, and I wanted to give it to her, but part of me also didn't want to give her anything, not until I knew that she wasn't back together with Sterling, but then fuck it, it could be part of her atonement, and I spanked her again and again, the flat of my palm landing on her ass, alternating cheeks, until it glowed pink.

I could see her getting wetter, her cunt practically weeping for me, and I didn't care, let it weep, and then it was there like a vicious riptide, and I shot all over her day-old clothes, a climax that was powerful, but harsh and nasty and short, because she wasn't there with me. She wasn't satisfied, and so I wasn't either, although it hadn't been about satisfaction, it had been about some kind of revenge, and God, I was a fucking asshole.

I sat back on my heels, my cheeks flushed with shame. I should touch her; I should spread her legs and lick her until she came. What kind of bastard did this to a woman—while drunk and jealous—and didn't return the favor? But how could I touch her now, when I felt so disgusting with all of my sins and failures, when I was still so suspicious and upset that I couldn't trust myself to be in control of her body?

I couldn't. It was a dick move, but it was even worse to touch her with the kind of feelings I had inside of me.

After stuffing myself in my shorts, I grabbed her a towel and wiped my semen off her clothes as best as I could.

"Are you...are we not..." She turned around and faced me, not bothering to fix her clothes, and the sight of her bare cunt sent a jolt straight to my dick. I'd be hard again in a minute.

I forced myself to look away. "Let me help you up. And then I think you should go home."

She stood and pressed herself against me. "You've been drinking," she said, looking up into my face. "You look like shit."

She reached up to caress my cheek and I caught her hand, holding it in the air as I wrestled back the thousands of dark temptations, the feeling that if I fucked her hard enough, I'd pound the memory of Sterling right out of her.

I let go of her hand.

"Go home," I said tiredly. "Please, Poppy."

Her eyes hardened, huge agate stones of determination. "No," she said, and there was that senatorial voice, that Chairwoman of the Fed voice. "Upstairs. Now."

I wasn't going to argue, because of the voice and also

because upstairs was the way she needed to go if she was going to leave, but once we got to my living room, she put her hands on my shoulders and guided me to the bathroom instead of going to the door, and I was way drunker than I'd originally thought because I could barely make it without weaving into the wall, and crap, it was still daylight outside. I'd managed to get shit-faced and fuck over the world's most perfect woman all before four p.m.

Tyler Bell: American Hero.

I let Poppy guide me to the edge of the bathtub, where I sat.

"Why won't you go home?" I asked plaintively. "Please go home."

She knelt and unlaced my sneakers, tugging impatiently on the strings. "I'm not leaving you like this."

"I don't need to be taken care of, dammit."

"Why? Because you feel too vulnerable? Is that why you wouldn't fuck me? Or touch me? Or even look me in the eye?"

"No," I spluttered, even though it was the truth and we both knew it.

"Stand up," she ordered, again in her Madame Secretary voice, and I obeyed, not enjoying the submission, but enjoying the interaction, the way she was fussing over me like she cared about me. Like she loved me.

She tugged off my shorts so that I was naked and then she reached past me to turn on the shower. "In."

I made to protest until I saw that she was unbuttoning her blouse and slipping out of her heels. She was going to join me.

The warm spray felt like heaven on my sore muscles, and then Poppy was there, and there was something clean-smelling and a washcloth, and for a while it was just the fresh smell of soap and the massage of the washcloth and the soft rain of the water, warm and comforting. When she had me kneel so she could knead shampoo into my hair, I dropped to my knees without question, pressing my face against her stomach, wondering if there was a word for the skin there that meant more than supple, meant more than soft and sexy, that meant all of those things combined.

I closed my eyes and groaned as she massaged my scalp, her fingers applying the kind of pressure that relaxed and stimulated at the same time. I turned my face and kissed her navel, a supplicating kiss. Supplicating for what, though, I didn't know.

What I did know was that for the first time in twenty-four hours, I was not roiling with hot-tempered emotions, I was not brooding with guilt, I was not punishing myself. I was with Poppy and her pussy was so close to my mouth, and I bent down and kissed the top of her clit, feeling her quiver.

But then she put her hands on my shoulders, pushing me away from her. "Not until I finish taking care of you," she said firmly and rinsed the shampoo out of my hair. Then she had me stay there while she quickly washed her own body and shampooed her own hair. She wasn't putting on a show, she wasn't trying to be sexy, but it was still one of the sexiest things I had ever seen, the way her nipples slipped between her fingers as she soaped up her breasts, the way the suds funneled down her stomach to stream over her cunt and thighs, the way water poured over the smooth globes of her ass as she held her head back and stood under the spray.

By the time she shut off the water, I was as hard as a fucking rock, and I caught her staring at my erection out of the corner of my eye, staring in a hungry way that made me want to tackle her right there on the bathroom floor.

But I was also sobering up (not very much) and coming to terms with what a jerk I'd been to her down in the basement and also realizing how much I didn't deserve this sweet treatment she was giving me now. So I didn't tackle, I merely toweled off and let myself be meekly towed to the bed.

"Lie down," she said. "And go to sleep."

She wasn't staying with me? Fuck. "Poppy, I'm so sorry. I don't know—"

"What came over you?" she finished for me. "By the looks of it, half a bottle of scotch. But"—and here she lowered her eyes—"I guess I deserved that."

"No," I said firmly, but not very firmly because now that I'd settled into the pillow, I'd realized the room was spinning around me. "You didn't deserve anything of the sort. I feel so ashamed of myself right now, and I don't deserve you even being here. You should go."

"I'm not going," she said with the same firmness I hadn't been able to muster. "You are going to take a nap and I'm going to read a book, and when you wake up, I have a way for you to make it up to me. Okay?"

"Okay," I whispered, not sure if I deserved a chance to make it up to her or not. But also I wanted her to know *why* I'd been such an ass, *why* I'd acted like such a phenomenal bastard. It was that stupid human desire to justify one's actions, as if I could erase the wrong of it all if only she saw my reasons.

As someone who heard people's wrongdoings and the reasons for said wrongdoings on a professional basis, I should've known better. But I was desperate for her not to hate my guts, and yes, maybe there was a tiny part of me that also wanted to shift the blame, because let's face it, she'd spent the night with Sterling and then showed up in her day-after state, and how the fuck was I supposed to react?

"I know that you were with him last night," I blurted and then held my breath, terrified that she'd confirm it and even more terrified that she'd try to deny it.

But she didn't really do either. Instead, she sighed and drew the blanket up to my chest. "I know you know," she said. "Sterling told me that he sent that picture."

And then she looked away. "I fucking hate him so much."

That heartened me a bit. Maybe last night had been sex-free after all. Maybe this wasn't all an elaborate prelude to her telling me that she was leaving me for Sterling.

"I didn't screw him, Tyler," she said, noticing my look.

And I believed her. Maybe it was the clear, open way she said it. Maybe it was her eyes, wide and innocent. Or maybe it was something more ephemeral than that, some spiritual connection that knew her words to be true.

Either way, I chose to believe that she was telling me the truth.

She took a deep breath. "We'll talk more when you wake up. But I didn't—nothing happened. I didn't touch him…he didn't touch me." She found my hand and squeezed it, and that squeeze was the axis on which the room drunkenly tilted. "I only want *you*, Father Bell."

CHAPTER TWENTY

"Wake up, sleepyhead."

The voice pierced through the smoky, smudgy veil of heavy sleep, sound waves and nerve receptors working together to rouse my brain, to coax me awake and back into the world of the sober living.

My brain wasn't having it. I rolled over, but rather than finding one of my ancient, flattened pillows, my face found bare flesh. Bare thighs. I wrapped an arm around them in an automatic gesture, burying my face in the smooth, sweet-smelling skin.

Fingers twined through my hair. "It's time to wake up."

It was the thighs more than the request, but I finally managed to force my eyes open, and once I did, I regretted it.

"Ugh," I groaned. "I feel like shit."

"Because of the booze or because of the way you acted?"

I kept my face against Poppy's thigh. "Both," I mumbled.

"That's what I thought. Well, time to feel better. I've laid out some clothes for you on the bed."

The thighs moved away, which made me sad. She swung her legs over the edge of the bed and stood up, stretching her arms as if she'd been in the same position for a long time, but she wasn't naked any longer, she was wearing a short tunic belted at the waist and gladiator sandals.

"You left," I accused.

She nodded. "I couldn't go where we're going in one of your undershirts and I certainly wasn't going to go in my dirty clothes. I was only gone for a few minutes, I promise."

I sat up slowly and took the water and Advil she offered. "Now get dressed," she said. "We have a date."

* * *

Thirty minutes later and we were pulling on the interstate in the Fiat. I was wearing dark jeans and a soft pullover sweater Sean had given me last Christmas in his continuing quest to improve my closet. It was a casual outfit—despite the sweater's ridiculous price tag—and I wondered why we were driving down to the city if not to go to someplace dressy and expensive.

"Where are we going?" I asked.

Poppy didn't answer at first, checking her mirrors and craning her neck as she water-bugged through the dense

Saturday night traffic. I decided not to push her, even though the curiosity was killing me, as well as the faint, nervous worry that someone would see us out together.

Finally she said, "Someplace I've wanted to take you for a while. But first: yesterday. We need to talk about yesterday."

Yes, we did, but now that I knew she hadn't slept with Sterling, I half wanted to avoid the painful dialogue altogether. This last day and a half had shoved us roughly past the pretending phase, past the place where we could just imagine the world outside as an irrelevant storm beating ineffectively at our window, and I hated it. Because beyond that place were all the decisions and discussions that would slowly break my life apart, one piece at a time.

"So, Sterling came to my house yesterday," she said. "After he saw you."

She knew about that?

As if reading my mind, she followed up with, "Sterling loves to brag about his conquests. Business, romantic, vengeful, any kind of victory. I think he thought I'd be impressed that he's so thoroughly boxed us in with the photographic evidence of our relationship."

God. He's such a tool.

"You have to understand, I knew he'd come here eventually, and I knew that I would tell him I didn't want to be with him. But I also knew that he wouldn't accept anything less than a full, face-to-face rejection, and also I felt like I at least owed him dinner, a chance to talk everything over. I mean, we dated for *years*...."

"Years that he cheated on you," I muttered.

She looked over at me. The look wasn't entirely pleasant. "Anyway," she continued, her voice edged with agitation, "I agreed to drive down to the city and get dinner with him. We ended up talking so late that I fell asleep in his hotel room."

I didn't like that detail.

I didn't like that detail at all.

"But like I said," she said, "nothing happened. I dozed on his couch until morning and then his driver brought me back home. To you."

"So he knows now that you're done with him? He's leaving?"

She hesitated. "Yes?"

"Is that a question? Are you saying you don't know for sure?"

Her eyes stayed on the road. "When I left this morning, he said he understood my decision completely. He said he didn't want me to be with him unwillingly—that it mattered to him how I felt. And so he'd be stepping back."

I thought of the man I'd met yesterday, of those icy blue eyes and that calculating voice. He didn't seem like the kind of man who'd step back. He did, however, seem like the kind of man who would lie about stepping back.

"So the pictures he's taken of us...he went to all that

effort to set up a potential blackmailing scheme and he's just going to give that up?"

She bit her lip, checking over her shoulder and changing lanes again. I liked the way she drove—fast, capable, with a flavor of aggression that never actually translated into anything unsafe. "I don't know," she said a bit helplessly. "He seemed so determined and so yeah—it's hard to imagine him going to all that effort just to leave, but I also don't think he'd lie about it either."

"I do," I said under my breath.

She heard. "Look, Sterling is not a saint, but it's not fair to demonize him just because he is my ex. Yes, he did bad things, but it's not like he's a psychopath. He's just a spoiled boy who's never had anyone say no to him. And I honestly don't think he'll do anything with those pictures."

Is she defending him? It felt like she was defending him, and that pissed me off a little.

"Did he offer to return the files to you? Or even to delete them?"

"What? No. But—"

"Then I don't think he's planning on going anywhere," I said, keeping my gaze on the window, where the dusk-covered fields were slowly turning into the sprawl of the city. "He said what he knew you wanted to hear, but this isn't over, Poppy. It won't be over for him until he gets what he wants. Which is you."

Her hand slid over mine, and for a minute, I petulantly

thought about ignoring it, about not lacing my fingers through hers, whether to hurt her or to show my disagreement, I wasn't sure.

God, I was being such a tool.

When I grabbed her hand, I grabbed it tight. "I'm sorry," I said. "It's just—it's like this trident pointed right at my heart. That I might lose you or lose my job—or both."

"You're not losing me," she insisted, glancing over. "And you won't lose your job. Unless you want to."

I rested my head against the cool glass of the window. And there it was…the choice. Black and white, night and day, one or the other. Poppy or God.

"Millie knows," I said out of nowhere.

I felt her hand tense in mine, and there it was again, that weird anger, because why would Millie—awesome, dependable Millie—be more worrisome than Sterling? But I took a breath and then eased it out. I refused to let this latest cascade of events drive a wedge between us.

I wouldn't allow it.

"She's not going to tell anyone," I reassured Poppy. And then I told her about what had happened to me yesterday, ultimately choosing to tell her every single thing, even my ugly, stupid thoughts, because I owed her that. I wanted to owe her that. And really, what did I have to lose? I was this close to losing everything anyway. Might as well be honest.

She listened as I told her everything, about Millie, and about Sterling's blackmail, and about how I had guessed she was with him even before he texted me, and about all the nasty, jealous feelings currently corkscrewed into my chest, and when I finished, her lips were pressed together in a red line, hiding those teeth I found so strangely sexy, pulling her features into a serious expression that was somehow just as attractive.

"I know we haven't known each other long," she said. "But you never have to worry about me cheating on you. It won't happen. Period. I don't cheat."

"I didn't mean…" I struggled for the right words. "I know *you*, the real you, and I know you wouldn't do anything to hurt me. But I also know that Sterling is more than just an ex-boyfriend to you. I know that there's something between you two that's old and powerful, and I guess that's what had me worried, not some imagined weakness in your character."

"It doesn't matter how much history is between Sterling and me. I'll never cheat on you. It's not in my nature."

I hoped that was true. I hoped it so much. But it occurred to me that there was no way I could ever be sure that she wouldn't cheat, there was no warranty for trusting someone you loved and no court where you could sue them if they ended up betraying you. Loving her, choosing to trust her with Sterling, it would make me vulnerable.

But she was already vulnerable, loving a man who wasn't actually allowed to love her back, so maybe this made us even.

To lighten the mood, I said, "I guess I understand that. Sean and Aiden even have a name for why people are the way you are; they call it the monogamy gene."

"The monogamy gene," she repeated. "I suppose that's about right."

I sat back. Downtown Kansas City came into view, glass and brick monoliths scraping against a lavender sky, the river a steel-gray snake below.

"They also used to joke I had the celibacy gene," I said. "Although now I'm not so sure." Streetlights and stoplights flashed across through car, and Poppy deftly maneuvered through the traffic to pull into the heart of the city.

"Maybe it wasn't the celibacy gene," I said, more to myself than to her. "Maybe it's just that I was always waiting for you."

She sucked in a breath and jerked the car into an alley between two buildings. Before I could ask her what she was doing, she'd put the car in park and was crawling onto my lap, which made my dick perk up with interest.

Her lips met mine with urgency, a hot, determined hunger, and her hands were everywhere—in my hair, on my chest, pulling impatiently at the fly of my jeans.

"I love you," she breathed, over and over again, and the tension of the drive melted away. "I love you, I love you, I love you. And I'm so sorry for everything today."

I found her ass under her dress and squeezed, sliding my fingers beneath her thighs to run my fingertips along the crotch of her thong, which was damp.

But before I could delve any further into this interesting new development, she pulled back, breathing hard.

"We have a big night ahead, so I don't want to ruin it by getting started early," she said with a smile. "But you don't know what you do to me when you say things like that."

"They're all true," I whispered to her. "I care about you so fucking much and I just wish—" I pulled her tight to me, her chest in my face, her pussy flat against my denim-clad erection. "I just wish it was like this all the time. You and me. No decisions. No problems. Just…us."

She kissed the top of my head. "Well, if it's escape you're looking for, then you'll like tonight."

At first, I thought maybe Poppy had lost her mind, because instead of going to a restaurant or a movie theater or anything remotely date-like, she pulled into an office parking garage (and I only knew it was an office because the Business Brothers worked two skyscrapers down and Aiden used to date a girl who worked here).

We walked over to the glassed-in elevator vestibule and Poppy ran a keycard over the secured door. When it clicked open, she led me to the far elevator, ran the keycard again, and we shot up to the 30th floor.

Finally, I ventured to ask. "Where are we going?"

She gave me a small smile, one of those smiles that left

me transfixed by her mouth. "To my job."

I barely had time to process this before we were walking inside, before Poppy was nodding at the woman at the front desk (who was dressed in a tailored suit, as if she was working at an investment firm and not at a strip club). Poppy pushed at the smoked glass doors, and I followed, and then we were inside the most exclusive club in this city, the place that had lured a Dartmouth MBA to stay when Wall Street couldn't.

Walls had been constructed along the perimeter of the space, blocking the windows, presumably so the flashing lights wouldn't shine out during the night (and so that daylight wouldn't shine *in* during the day). But there was a sizable gap between the walls and the windows, meaning any guest could take his drink and roam in between the two, gazing out at the cityscape, as several men were doing now, some of them fielding what sounded like business calls as Poppy led me past.

Here and there, the walls broke, giving me a glimpse inside the main room. Two or three women danced alone in glassed-in boxes, but several were out on the floor, and I instinctively turned my eyes away from all the exposed female flesh. Maybe I was still a priest at heart.

But then my eyes were drawn back to Poppy's short tunic and where I could see the shape of her ass through the fabric.

Yeah, right.

We ducked through one of the openings and then Poppy led me inside a room.

"What are we doing?"

"My boss said I can use these rooms whenever I want. And I want to right now."

"For me?"

"For you. Now wait here," she said with a grin, and then left, closing the heavy wood door with a *snick*.

So these were the private rooms she'd told me about, like the one she'd fucked Sterling in. That thought sent the now-familiar corkscrew of jealousy spiraling deeper, but then I remembered the car, her desperate I love yous. She was here…with me. Not with him.

But why did this snake of anger still slither in my belly? I hated myself for feeling it, but I couldn't chase it out, couldn't dig it out. It slunk through my veins, tickling the inside of my fingertips with the urge to—to what? Spank her ass for spending time with her ex without my permission? Fuck her until she grunted, until my cock was the only thing she knew?

God, I was such a fucking Philistine.

To distract myself, I examined my surroundings. I'd never been to a strip club before, but this was admittedly much nicer than what I'd expected. There was a chair and a sofa, both leather (*easily cleaned*, a bitter voice thought) and a dais in the middle of the room, wide enough to host a pole and also wide enough for a dancer to dance without it.

The light was low—shades of blue and purple—and the music was loud but not loud enough to be annoying. The kind of volume where it sank into your blood with a thrumming, demanding beat, where it fused with your own thoughts and set your pulse higher, set your adrenaline on a slow, steady drip.

I sat on the leather sofa and leaned forward, looking at my hands. What was I doing here? Why had she brought me? Of all the places—

But then the door opened and I stopped wondering anything except when I could push my cock inside her because *fuck.*

She wore a wig the color of blue cotton candy, and eye makeup so heavy that all I could picture were those kohl-rimmed eyes peering up at me as she sucked my dick. And I immediately saw what she'd meant when she said the club liked to hire girls who looked expensive. Because while I knew fuck all about lingerie, I did know that the delicately embroidered fabric of her sheer panties was probably not the usual stripper garb. Nor the matching silk shelf bra or the lace pasties covering her nipples—all in a soft champagne. A strip of the same champagne-colored silk was tied around her neck in a bow, and I wanted to unwrap her like a present, right then and there. She always looked amazing—in clothes and naked—but she was transformed right now, a Poppy I had only seen glimpses of even in our most intimate moments.

She strode over to me, just as graceful in six-inch heels as she was in ballet flats, and held out her hand. "Your wallet."

Confused, I dug it out of my (suddenly very tight) jeans and handed it to her. She dug a roll of crisp fifties and hundreds out of her bra and slid them neatly inside my wallet, handing it back to me. "I want to play a game," she said.

"Okay," I said, my mouth suddenly dry. "Let's play a game."

She licked her lips, and I realized that I wasn't the only one crazy fucking turned on right now. "You're just a client, and I'm just a dancer, okay?"

"Okay," I echoed.

"And you know there're certain rules about private rooms, don't you?"

I shook my head, unable to keep my gaze from raking over her form, over her expensive lingerie, over that strip of silk tied around her neck that could so easily be turned into a leash…

"Well, first you have to pay me for being here." And then she put a hand on her hip, looking so impatient and so hot, and any philosophical arguments Good Guy Tyler might have had about pretending something so degrading—about being in a strip club in the first place—vanished. And the moment I placed the bills in her hand, the air instantly changed. The game vanished and this was our reality—no matter that we loved each other, that this wasn't even my money—I was paying her and she was taking it and now she was on the stage, one hand on the pole, her eyes on me.

She started dancing, and I leaned back, wanting to memorize every detail of this, of the way her legs wrapped around the pole as she swung, the way her blue hair brushed against her shoulders, the way the muscles in her arms and shoulders pulled and strained against each other.

The low light, the loud music, the anonymity of the sex on display in front of me…all combined with the heated blaze in her eyes, like she wanted *me* and me specifically and me right now—I now understood why Herod had offered Salome anything she'd wanted after she danced for him. There was something so delicious in the tug of power between us; I presumably held all the control and dignity in this situation, but the reverse was actually true. She was captivating me, she was putting me under her thrall, until I wanted to offer her everything, not just the money she'd put in my wallet, but my house, my life, my soul.

Poppy and her dance of seven veils.

And then she bent over, and I was distracted by the fact that her ass was now front and center, that I could see the shadow of her folds through the fabric, and I would've sworn any oath right then to caress her there.

I shifted, trying to make more room for myself in my jeans, but it was useless. And then she was in front of me, a hand on each of my knees, and she spread them wide so she could step between them. She turned so that her ass was in front of my face, so close that I could make out the individual flowers embroidered on her lingerie, and I ran a finger across them.

She caught my hand. "You have to pay more if you want to touch," she purred, and I followed Herod down the path to spiritual perdition, because no price was too high for her.

I handed over the money without question, which she tucked in her bra. Then she guided my hands to her hips and moved them down to her flanks and then back up to her tits. I toyed with the pasties a moment, both loving and hating the unfamiliar feeling of having her nipples blocked from me.

She sat in my lap, pressing her ass against my erection and laying her head back against my shoulder as I fondled her tits. I nuzzled her neck. "I bet you do this with all the guys who come in here."

"Just you," she said in a velvet voice, wriggling against me, the friction against my dick making me groan quietly. She flipped over, so she was straddling me.

"You know," she said, in that same low, kitten voice, "I never let guys do this, but if you want, I'll let you see my pussy."

Yes, please.

"I would like that." I am very proud that I managed to not squeak like a teenage boy.

She extended her hand, and I fished out the wallet again. It was just as well that this was a game; I'd never be able to afford Poppy on a priest's salary.

After she was paid, she hopped on the dais and spread her legs wide again, pulling the crotch of her panties aside to show me what I wanted to see. It was wet and an enticing rose color in the dim blue light of the room—the color Renaissance painters should've used to paint the light of Heaven.

I stared, hypnotized, as she slowly let her hand drift from her neck, down past her breasts to the gentle rise of her pubic bone. From there she traced wide, light circles around her pussy, a loose spiral across her lower stomach and inner thighs, drawing closer and closer, and when she finally grazed her clit, I let out a shaky breath I didn't know I'd been holding.

She too sighed at her touch, her hips rocking tiny little rocks into her hand, as if she was unconsciously trying to fuck the air, and I was beginning to lose track of everything that wasn't her cunt. Didn't she know I could fill it for her? Didn't she know I could make her feel good, if only she'd let me?

I stood up and walked to the dais. Our eyes were at the same level, and I kept her gaze as I slid my hands from her knees up to her inner thighs, my thumbs coming teasingly close to her pussy. I did it again, this time daring to go closer, wondering if she would let me, if her lust would overtake her rules about money. My thumbs ran over her folds and she shuddered, and so did I, because holy shit, she was wet. So wet that I knew I'd be able to push my dick right in with no resistance.

"You want to stick your fingers inside me?" she asked.

I nodded, taking my thumbs and spreading her folds apart, moving that smooth pink flesh aside so that her entrance was completely exposed, begging for fingers or a cock.

"It's going to cost you," she said mischievously, placing her hands over mine.

"You drive a hard bargain," I breathed. Hard was the right word for how I felt too. I was about three seconds away from unzipping my jeans and taking matters into my own hands (as it were).

I found the bill, folded it lengthwise to make it easier for her to stow away, but this time she didn't take it with her fingers, she took it with her mouth, her lips grazing my fingers, and it was so degrading, so wonderfully degrading, and the Herod in me was exultant on his throne, delighted with a king's delight to see her with that money in between her teeth, knowing that now her pussy was mine to touch as I wanted.

She raised up on her knees as if to stand, but I was getting what I paid for, and right *now*, and I wrapped one arm around her waist and yanked her down, onto the two fingers I had waiting for her. She cried out and I smiled grimly, planning on taking full advantage of this particular service tier. With the arm around her waist, I pushed her down even farther, so that her pussy was grinding against my hand (which was currently smashed against the dais, but I didn't mind), and so the hot locus of nerves at her front rubbed relentlessly on my palm. My fingers crooked forward, finding the soft textured spot that would send her over the edge.

I moved my fingers while I crooned in her ear. "If I make you come, do you have to pay me?"

She laughed but the laugh immediately faded into a ragged sigh as I pressed her harder against my hand. I bit at her collarbone and at the soft skin around her pasties, her wetness quivering against my hand and that silk bow just begging to be wrapped around her wrists, and then she came with a sharp noise, bucking fruitlessly against me as I held her tighter, worked her harder, wrung every last drop of pleasure from her climax.

As she came down, her body relaxed against mine, but I was nowhere near relaxed. I slid my hand out from underneath her and put my fingers to her lips, making her suck her own taste off of them, my other hand unbuttoning my jeans.

Poppy glanced down and back up to my face. "You want me to put it in my mouth?" she asked, looking at me from under her lashes in a way that was utterly fucking debilitating to my ability to form coherent thoughts.

I grabbed a few bills and tucked them into her bra myself. Then I took that silk bow in hand and slowly untied it, baring that lovely neck for me to suck and nip at, as I slid the silk through my hands—reverently, like I would hold my stole or my cincture.

I pulled back and wrapped one end of the length around her neck, tying it to itself in a secure knot—the kind of knot that meant I'd be able to yank on it without worrying about it tightening around her neck.

Leash secured, I wrapped the loose end once around my hand and gave an experimental tug. She jerked forward a bit, making a surprised noise, but her pupils dilated and her pulse thrummed in her neck, so I felt free to pull again, forcing her to slide carefully off the dais and to her knees. I sat in the chair and made her crawl to me, watching the way her tits swung as she did.

Once she was in between my knees, I yanked up, perhaps a bit harder than I should have, but I was almost lost with lust at this point, lost to my inner caveman and my inner Herod, and all he wanted was that pretty red mouth on his dick right the fuck now.

She curled her fingers around the waistband of my black boxer briefs and pulled down, and my dick sprang free, jutting up between the V of my zipper. I wound the end of the leash around my hand a few more times until the silk was taut, and then I pulled her head to my cock, but she didn't open her mouth right away, those red lips sealed. But the hint of a smile was at the corners of her mouth, a delighted defiance in her eyes, and I remembered my kitchen counter all those weeks ago, when she'd asked me to steal her kisses—no, not even steal. She'd wanted me to *force* them from her.

So I wound the leash tighter and jerked, her mouth now pressed against the underside of my penis, the sensation of her breath against my skin enough to make me wild.

Play the game, Tyler.

"I paid you to suck," I hissed. "You can either suck me on your own or I can make you do it. So unless you want that, you better open that pretty little mouth and do your fucking job."

She was covered in goose bumps, and I didn't miss the way she tried to rub her thighs together. Impatiently, I stuck a finger between her lips and forced them apart.

"Put me in your mouth," I warned, "or there will be hell to pay."

It didn't take an astute observer to notice the extra flare of interest in her eyes at that idea; she *wanted* there to be hell to pay, but I also think she wanted to suck me, because she finally perched her candy apple lips at my tip, and—meeting my eyes as she did so—slid her mouth down and over me, her tongue flat and scorching against my shaft.

Keeping my hand tight on the leash, I leaned back to watch the show, watch her breasts move as she worked me, watch those hazel eyes gaze up at me with a look that would get me hard in the shower for years to come. And those lips like a gorgeous red halo around my dick…it was the only halo I ever wanted again, a circle of wicked wants and devilish delights.

Up and down she went, sometimes fluttering her tongue, sometimes running it in a hot, wide line down my shaft. I thrust up to meet her, hitting the back of her throat and—losing all semblance of patience—grabbed the back of her head to keep her from pulling away. I held her head with both hands and pumped that way for several long seconds, fucking her throat like I fucked her pussy—hard and without apology, and she deserved it for being such a brazen, shameless tease.

"You like that?" I asked. She was breathing carefully through her nose, and she couldn't speak, so I talked for her. "I know you do. You like it when a paying customer treats you roughly. It makes you wet to be treated like the slut you are, doesn't it?"

She made a noise that could have been a *yes* or a *no* or simply a moan of pure pleasure. Whatever it was, it made my stomach clench and my hands dig into her scalp and my balls tighten with the need to release. But I didn't want to come in her mouth.

"Off," I ordered, pulling on the leash. She obeyed, coming off my dick with watery, smudged eyes and one of the biggest smiles I'd ever seen on her face.

I used the leash to bring her face to mine as I leaned

toward her. "How much to fuck?"

Her smile faded into a darker expression, an expression that promised me everything I wanted. "We—we aren't supposed to do that," she said faintly.

"I don't care," I growled. "I want to fuck you. How much?"

"The rest of what you have," she said, with a defiant arch of her eyebrow, and I silently commended her for her dedication to our game. I took out my wallet and the remaining cash—about $700 (fuck, Poppy had a lot of money)—and then tossed the bills in the air. They floated slowly down to the floor.

"Pick them up with your mouth."

"No."

"No?" I tugged on the leash, just enough that she remembered it was there. "I want to get what I paid for. Now. Pick. Them. Up."

I saw the moment she gave in by the set of her shoulders, but as she started to bend down to reach for the bill closest to her, I put my shoe on the money. "Panties off first."

She worried her lower lip between her teeth, and I don't know what my face looked like, but whatever expression was there must have convinced her that she didn't want to test me. She stood up, hooked her thumbs at the sides of her panties and slipped them down, one gold heel coming off the floor and then the other as she stepped out of them.

Then she bent over and began collecting the money.

I kept a loose grip on the leash as she did, spooling it out so she'd have plenty of slack, licking my lips at the swollen perfection exposed between her legs. When we got home, I wanted to worship her with my mouth, I wanted her coming on my tongue again and again. She deserved it, my little lamb, for going to such lengths for me, creating this little game where I could take and take from her. Yes, after this, I was going to reward her.

But as for right now…

I got on the floor behind her, also on my knees, and because the music was so loud, I don't think she heard. She was bent completely over, her face to the floor, her ass high in the air, and I took my dick and shoved into her with one rough thrust, all the way in, slapping her hard on one ass cheek as I did.

She squealed—a happy noise—and that was enough to keep my conscience at bay as I fucked her harder than was purely gentlemanly, not fast necessarily, just *hard* and *deep*, the kind of deep that made her toes curl and my balls swing against her clit.

And then the snake slithered again, that angry, bitter snake, as I remembered that I was not the first man to do this to Poppy here, that she'd been fucked before like this, in this very place, and then that anger was itching at my palms and coiling in my pelvis.

I wanted to punish her. I wanted to hurt her the way she

hurt me with making me care so much, but instead of hurting her, I pulled out and stood up, my cock wet and as hard as fucking steel, throbbing with the need to screw the pussy still raised up in offering to me.

I didn't want to be Herod. Not really.

I sat down on the chair. "Come here." I jerked my head towards my cock so that she knew what I wanted, and she didn't hesitate to climb up my lap and then impale herself on me, sinking down with her tight, hot cunt, her tits right in my face.

And here, now that I could see her face, now that I couldn't be brutal, I confessed. "I can't, like that. It makes me want to…"

But I couldn't get the words out. They were too awful. Instead, I buried my face in her breasts, smelling the lavender smell of her, the clean fabric of her bra.

She tugged at my hair so that my head was pulled back. "Want to hurt me?"

I closed my eyes. I couldn't look at her. She must hate me, but she was still fucking me, rocking back and forth like women do instead of up and down, using my dick to get her off as if the rest of me was irrelevant.

God, that was hot.

"I guessed as much today," she said. "That's why I brought us here."

My eyes flew open. "What?"

"You're a man, Tyler. It doesn't matter what I tell you

or even what you choose to believe…there's always going to be this Neanderthal inside you that wants to claim me. Reclaim me, if necessary, and I thought here…" She slowed her movements, looking uncertain for the first time. "I thought if we played like this, it would be easier for you to let go. To satisfy that part of you that you don't want to acknowledge. That part that you hide from. Because it's a bigger slice of you than you think."

As if to underscore her point, she scratched her fingernails down my stomach—hard—and my hand spanked her ass so fast that I barely knew what I was doing. She gave a little moan and ground herself down on me.

"See? You need this. And I need this. I'll take you to every place I've ever been and let you fuck me there, so you can rewrite my history as your history, if you want," she promised. "Let me give that to you."

I looked at her in amazement. In gratitude. She was so astute and so giving and of course I hadn't needed to watch out for her well-being. As always, she had both of us under control when she surrendered her control to me.

"I don't know what to say," I admitted.

"Say yes. Say that you'll finish the game."

I'd been wrong. She wasn't Salome right now. She was Esther, using her body to save her kingdom—our kingdom of two. And how could I act out my primal need to claim her knowing that? Knowing how generous and brave she was?

"It doesn't feel right, to treat you like this…to claim you like some sort of property. And more importantly, I don't want to hurt you."

"I *want* you to claim me like property," she said, leaning to whisper in my ear. The change in position squeezed her cunt around my length and I sucked in a breath. "And if you hurt me, I'll tell you. You trust me to say stop, and I'll trust you to stop if I say it. Sound good?"

Fuck yes, it sounded good. It sounded too good to be true, but then again, that was my Poppy, a woman made like God himself had designed her for me. And maybe He had.

I decided to trust her. Trust Him.

Mind made up, I grabbed her thighs and stood, keeping her pelvis pinned to mine as I stepped over to the sofa. I kissed her—a soft, searing kiss—a reminder of how much I loved her before the rough part of me took over, which it did right after our mouths broke apart. I set Poppy down and flipped her over the arm of the sofa, so that her ass was higher than her head, and then notched the head of my dick in her entrance.

"Press your legs together," I commanded. "Make it tighter."

She obeyed, and I sank in with a groan. "So tight like this," I managed. "You make it so good for me."

I shoved in again, hard enough that her feet came off the floor, and I kept going like that, her beautiful ass filling my hands and her satin cunt around my cock and her moans as she ground her clit against the firm arm of the sofa.

And in this moment of her Esther-like love for us and a future that was so ephemeral as to be nonexistent, it came to me that there was no sin here. This was love, this was sacrifice, the opposite of sin, and maybe it was fucked up to feel like God was here with us in the back room of a strip club, but I did, like He was bearing witness to this moment where Poppy opened herself to the worst of me and erased it with her love, just like God did for us sinners every moment of every day.

That feeling that Poppy and I had felt in the sanctuary, that God-feeling of presence and promise, it was here right now, making my chest tight and my head swim with the potency of the air itself, and once again I felt like a bridegroom, the man shouting his joy for all his friends and family to hear, and this room was our chuppah, our marriage tent, the faint blue lights the lamps of the ten virgins, our bodies echoing the joining God had already forged between our immortal souls.

How was this not marriage? How was this not more binding and more intimate, us bare with each other in the presence of God? At the very least, this was a betrothal, a promise, an oath.

I spanked my betrothed, wishing I could drink her squeals like scotch and eat her moans afterward. I fucked her hard, taking in the blue hair tumbling over her back, the delicate lines of her small waist as they swelled into her perfect hips and ass, her wet cunt gripping me, and the pink aperture of her asshole—all of it mine. I was the monarch of all I surveyed—no, I was the master of all I surveyed, and I spanked and scratched and stabbed her over and over again with my cock until finally, finally, she made a noise that was half gasp, half wail, pulsing around me, her hands scrabbling at the leather as she was lost to everything but her body's response to me.

I was lost to it too—this moment where I had rewritten history, her body's history—where I had made this room belong to *me* and the orgasms that *I'd* given her. Where I'd made her *mine* and no other man's, where I had taken an oath of marriage in my heart, and it was that *mine* that made me pull out and force her on her knees. I wanted her to witness my orgasm, I wanted her to see what she had given me.

The leash in one hand, the other hand with its rough grip and brutal pressure on my cock, using the wetness she'd left on me as lubrication, and it only took a few rough tugs before I shot streams of semen on her waiting lips, on her swan's neck, on the fringes of her long eyelashes.

The tip of her tongue, pointed and pink, licked a drop off her upper lip, and then she gave me a soft, happy look that sent one more jet of cum out to land on her collarbone.

We both breathed heavily for a moment, pleasure still thick in the air, but it was the only thing thick in the air now:

the tension and bitterness and anger from earlier were gone. It had worked—Poppy's game had worked. I had burned away the jealousy and primal urges, and in the interim, also burned away something else. My guilt maybe, or the feeling of sin. Something had shifted, like it had for me those moments on the altar, where the line between sacred and profane blurred completely, and I felt like I'd just participated in something holy, just pressed my naked hands to the mercy seat in a cloud of incense and sweat.

I knelt in front of her and untied the silk leash, using the material to carefully dab my climax off her face. "Game over," I said gently, running the tip of my nose along her jaw.

"Who do you think won?" she murmured.

I wrapped her in my arms and pulled her into me, kissing the top of her head. "Do you even have to ask? It's you, little lamb." She nestled into me, and I rocked her back and forth, my precious one, my sweet woman. "It's always you."

CHAPTER TWENTY-ONE

The autumn night pressed against the outside of the car as we drove home, and I kept my eyes on Poppy's profile, which was lit by the lights on the dash and silhouetted against the velvet night outside.

What had happened in the club…it had been dirty and cathartic and galvanizing, although I couldn't articulate to myself exactly why. The answer hovered just out of reach, shimmered beyond a veil that I could only graze with the fingertips of my thoughts, and as we passed out of the city and into the countryside, I stopped trying and just let myself take in the majesty that was my Esther, my queen.

I wanted her to be my bride.

I wanted her to be my bride.

The thought came with the clarity of cold steel, certain and true and no longer something I felt in the moment of sex and God, but something I felt sober and calm. I loved

Poppy. I wanted to marry her.

And then the veil finally fluttered down and I *understood.* I understood what God had been trying to tell me these past two months. I understood why the Church was called the Bride of Christ, I understood why Song of Songs was in the Bible, I understood why Revelation likened the salvation of the world to a wedding feast.

Why had I ever felt like the choice was between Poppy and God? It had never been that way, it had never been one or the other, because God dwelled in sex and marriage just as much as He dwelled in celibacy and service, and there could be just as much holiness in a life as a husband and a father as there was in a life as a priest. Was Aaron not married? King David? Saint Peter?

Why had I convinced myself that the only way a man could be useful to God was in the clergy?

Poppy was humming along with the radio now, a sound barely audible over the dull roar of the Fiat on the highway, and I closed my eyes and listened to the sound as I prayed.

Is this Your will for me? Am I giving in to lust? Or am I finally realizing Your plan for my life?

I kept my mind quiet and my body still, waiting for the guilt to rush in or for the booming voice from Heaven to tell me I was damned. But there was nothing but silence. Not the empty silence I'd felt before all this, like God had abandoned me, but a peaceful silence, free of guilt and shame, the quiet that one had when one was truly with God.

It was the feeling I'd had in front of the tabernacle, in the sanctuary with Poppy, on the altar as I'd finally claimed her for my own.

And as we were in her bed later, my face between her thighs, it was 29th chapter of Jeremiah that finally surfaced as the answer to my prayers.

Take wives and have sons and daughters...for surely I have plans for you, plans for your happiness and not for your harm, to give you a future full of hope...

I didn't tell Poppy about my epiphany. Instead, after making her come time after time, I left for my own bed, wanting to sleep alone with this new knowledge, this new certainty.

And when I woke up early that morning to prepare for Mass, that certainty was still there, glowing clear and weightless in my chest, and I made my decision.

This Mass would be the last Mass I ever said.

"If your hand causes you to stumble, cut it off; it is better for you to enter life maimed than to have two hands and go to hell...and if your eye causes you to stumble, tear it out; it is better for you to enter the Kingdom of God with one eye than have two eyes and to be thrown into hell..."

I looked up at my congregation standing before me, at the sanctuary that was full because of me, because of three years of unceasing toil and labor. I looked back down to the lectionary and continued reading the Gospel selection for today.

"Salt is good; but if salt has lost its saltiness, how can you re-season it? Have salt in yourselves and be at peace with one another." I took a breath. "The Gospel of the Lord."

"Praise be to you, Lord Jesus Christ," the congregation recited and then sat down. I caught sight of Poppy sitting near the back, wearing a fitted dress of mint green linen, bisected by a wide leather belt. The sun came through the windows perfectly to frame her, as if God were reminding me of my decision, of why I was doing this.

I let myself stare for one beat longer, at my lamb in those shimmering, tessellated beams of light, and then I leaned forward to kiss the text I had just read, murmuring the quiet prayer I was supposed to pray at this point and then another silent one asking for courage.

I closed the lectionary gently, revealing my phone with my homily notes. I'd reluctantly written the kind of homily you'd expect with this gospel reading, about the nature of sacrificing ourselves to avoid sin, about the importance of self-denial and discipline. About keeping ourselves holy for the work of the Lord.

Hypocrisy had haunted me as I'd typed every word, hypocrisy and shame, and as I stared at the notes now, I could barely remember the agony that man had been in, torn between two choices that were ultimately false. The way forward was now clear. All I had to do was take the first step.

I flipped my phone over so that the screen faced down and raised my eyes to the people who trusted me, who cared for me, the people who made up the living body of Christ.

"I spent the week writing a homily about this passage. And then when I woke up this morning, I decided to throw the whole thing in the trash." I paused. "Figuratively speaking, I mean. Since it's on my phone, and even I'm not holy enough to give up my iPhone."

The people chuckled, and the sound filled me with courage.

"This passage has been used by many clergy as a platform for condemnation, the ultimate declaration by Jesus that we are to abandon any and all temptations lest we lose our chance of salvation. And my old homily was not far away from this idea. That self-denial and the constant shunning of temptation is the path to heaven, our way to the small and narrow gate."

I glanced down at my hands resting on top of the lectern, at the lectionary in front of me.

"But then I realized that the danger of preaching this was that you might walk out of this building today with an image of God as a small and narrow god—a god as small and narrow as that gate. I realized that you could walk out of here and believe—really and truly believe—that if you fail once, if you slip and act like the messy, flawed human that you are, that God doesn't want you."

The congregation was silent. I was treading outside of

normal Catholic territory here and they knew it, but I wasn't afraid. In fact, I felt more at peace than I ever had delivering a homily.

"The Jesus of Mark's Gospel is a strange god. He is terse, enigmatic, inscrutable. His teachings are stark and relentlessly demanding. He talks about things we would consider either miraculous or insane—speaking in tongues, handling snakes, drinking poisons. And yet, he is also the same god we encounter in Matthew 22, who tells us that the greatest commandments—the only rules we need to abide by—are loving God with all of our hearts and all of our souls and all of our minds, and loving our neighbors as ourselves.

"So which Jesus is right? What rubric should we use when we're confronted by challenge and change? Do we focus on pruning out all evil, or do we focus on growing love?"

I stepped out behind the lectern, needing to move as I talked, as I thought my way through what I wanted to say.

"I think the answer is that we follow this call from Mark to live righteously, but the caveat being that we have to redefine righteousness for ourselves. What is a righteous life? It is a life where you love God and love your neighbor. Jesus tells us how to love in the Gospel of St. John—*there is no greater love than to lay your life for your friends.* And Jesus showed us that love when He laid down His own life. For us. His friends."

I looked up and met Poppy's eyes, and I couldn't help

the small smile that tugged on my mouth. She was so beautiful, even now when her forehead was wrinkled and she was biting her lip in what looked like worry.

"God is bigger than our sins. God wants you as you are—stumbling, sinning, confused. All He asks of us is love—love for Him, love for others, and love for ourselves. He asks us to lay down our lives—not to live like ascetics, devoid of any pleasure or joy, but to give Him our lives so that He may increase our joy and increase our love."

I stared out at their upturned faces, reading their faces, which ranged from pensive to inspired to downright doubtful.

That was okay—I was going to model this sermon for them. This afternoon, I was going to call Bishop Bove and lay down my own life. I would resign from the clergy. And then I would find Poppy and I would ask her to marry me.

I would live my life awash with love, just as God had intended.

"This won't come easy to us Catholics. In a way, it's easier to dwell on sin and guilt than it is to dwell on love and forgiveness—especially love and forgiveness for yourself. But that's what's been promised to us, and I for one, will not refuse God's promise of a full, love-filled life. Will you?"

I stepped back behind the lectern, exhaling with relief. I'd said what I needed to say.

And now it was time to lay down my life.

CHAPTER TWENTY-TWO

I couldn't find Poppy after Mass, but that was okay. I wanted to call the bishop right away, while my mind and spirit were certain. I wanted to move forward, I wanted to explore this new life, and I wanted to start exploring it right the hell now.

It wasn't until I was actually dialing Bishop Bove's number that the full, complex reality of what I was doing sank in.

I would be leaving the congregation in a lurch—they would need visiting priests until they could find a new one to stay at St. Margaret's. Worse, I was echoing the departure of my predecessor. Yes, I was leaving to marry, not because I was being arrested, but still. Would it feel the same to my parishioners?

No more work at panels and conventions, crusading for purity in the clergy. No more work in Lizzy's name, on

Lizzy's behalf. No more youth groups and men's groups, no more pancake breakfasts.

Was I really ready to give all that up for a life with Poppy?

For the first time, the answer was a definitive *yes.* Because I wouldn't really be giving all that up. I would find ways to serve as a layperson; I would do God's work in other ways and other places.

Bishop Bove didn't answer—it was still early in the afternoon, and he could be wrapped up with his congregation after Mass. Part of me knew that I should wait, should speak with him personally, rather than leave a message, but I couldn't wait, couldn't even think about waiting; even though there would be more conversations involved than just this voicemail, I still wanted to start the process before I went to Poppy. I wanted to come to her as a free man, able to offer my heart completely and without reservation.

As soon as I heard the tone, I started speaking. I tried to keep my message brief, direct, because it was impossible to explain everything clearly without also delving into my sins and broken vows, and *that* at least, I really would rather not do on a voicemail.

After I finished leaving my thirty-second resignation, I hung up and stared at the wall of my bedroom for a minute. I'd done it. It was really happening.

I was done being a priest.

I didn't have a ring, and on my salary, I couldn't go out and buy one, but I did go to the rectory garden to pick a bouquet of anemones, all snow-white petals and jet-black middles, and tied the stems together with yarn from the Sunday School room. The flowers were elegant without being flashy, just like her, and I stared at them as I crossed the park to her house, my heart in my throat.

What would I say? How would I say it? Should I get down on one knee or is that something they only did in the movies? Should I wait until I could afford a ring? Or at least had more than unemployment on my horizon?

I knew that she loved me, that she wanted a future with me, but what if I was moving too fast? What if instead of an ecstatic yes, I got a *no*? Or—almost worse—an I don't know?

I took a deep breath. Surely, this is what all men dealt with when they prepared to propose. It was just that I hadn't ever thought a proposal was in my future, at least not for the last six years, and so I hadn't even considered how I would do it or what I would say.

Please let her say yes, I prayed. *Please, please, please.*

And then I shook my head and smiled. This was the woman I had been with last night, in our own chuppah, God all around us. This was the woman who had been my own personal communion on the church altar. The woman God had made for me and brought to me…why did I have doubts? She loved me and I loved her, and of course she was going to say yes.

I realized too late that I was still in my collar, something that I had already officially (sort of) quit, but I was already halfway across the park and I had these flowers in my hand and I didn't want to turn back for a detail that was now so trivial. Actually, the irony of it made me grin a little bit. A priest proposing in his collar. It sounded like the setup for a bad joke.

Poppy would think it was funny too; I could picture the small smile she got when she was trying not to laugh, her lips pressed together and her cheeks trying not to dimple, her hazel eyes bright. Fuck, she was beautiful, especially when she laughed. She laughed the way I'd always imagined princesses laughed when I was boy—sunnily, airily, the fate of kingdoms ringing in their voice.

I opened the gate into her garden, my stomach flipping backwards and sideways, my cheeks hurting from smiling so much, my hand shaking around my fresh bouquet, which was still wet from the morning's drizzle.

I walked through the flowers and plants, thinking of Song of Songs, of the bridegroom going to his bride, singing as he goes. I know exactly how he must have felt.

As a lily among brambles, so is my love among women.

I climbed the porch, clutching the flowers tight as I walked towards the back door.

You have captivated my heart, my bride. You have

captivated my heart with one glance of your eyes…

I murmured the other verses to myself as I got ready to open the door. Maybe I would murmur them to her later, maybe I would trace them with my fingers on her naked back.

The door was unlocked, and I stepped inside her house, smelling the lavender smell that was all hers but not seeing her in the kitchen or the living room. She must be in her bedroom or the shower, although I hoped she was still in that pretty mint dress. I wanted to peel it off of her later, expose inches and inches of ivory flesh as she murmured yes to me over and over again. I wanted to kick it away from our feet as I took her in my arms and finally made love to her as a free man.

I took a deep breath as I rounded the corner into the hallway, about to announce my presence, and then something made me freeze—instinct maybe, or God himself—but whatever it was, I hesitated, my breath catching in my throat, and that's when I heard it.

A laugh.

Poppy's laugh.

It wasn't just any laugh either. It was low and breathy and a little nervous.

And then a man said, "Poppy, come on. You know you want to."

I knew that man's voice. I'd only heard it once before, but I knew it immediately, as if I'd heard it every day of my life, and when I took another step into the hallway, I could finally see into her bedroom, and the entire scene was laid bare.

Sterling. Sterling was here, here in Poppy's house, here in her *bedroom*, his suit jacket thrown carelessly over the bed and his tie loosened.

And Poppy was there too, still in that mint dress, but with her shoes off and two spots of color high in her cheeks.

Sterling and Poppy.

Sterling and Poppy together; and now he was gathering Poppy in his arms, his face bending to hers, her hands on his chest.

Push him away, a desperate voice pleaded inside me. *Push him away.*

And there was a moment where I thought she would, where her face tilted away and she took a single step back. But then something passed over her face—determination maybe or resignation—I couldn't tell because then the back of his perfectly groomed head was in the way.

And he kissed her. He kissed and she let him. She not only let him, but she kissed him back, parting those sweet vermillion lips, and I was Jonah swallowed by the whale, I was Jonah after the worm had eaten his shade plant—

No, I was Job, Job after he had lost everything and everyone, and there was nothing left for me ever again, because then her hand slid behind his neck, and she sighed into his mouth, and he chuckled a victory chuckle, pressing her into the wall behind them.

And I could taste ashes in my mouth.

The flowers must have fallen from my hand, because when I made it back to the rectory, I didn't have them, and I didn't know whether they had fallen inside her house or in her garden or on my way back through the park, I didn't know because I couldn't remember a single goddamned detail about how I got back home, whether I was loud when I left, whether they noticed me, whether my lifeblood was actually bleeding out of my chest or whether it only felt that way.

What I did remember was that it had started raining again, a steady sweeping rain, October rain, and I was only able to recall this because I was wet and chilled when I came to myself, standing numbly in my dim kitchen.

I should have been furious in that moment. I should have been devastated. I've read the novels, I've seen the movies, and this is the moment where the camera would zoom in on my tortured expression, where a two-minute montage would have stood in for months of heartbreak. But I felt nothing. Absolutely nothing, except wet and cold.

I was on the highway.

I wasn't precisely sure what constellation of decisions had led to this, except the storm had grown stronger and there had been thunder, and all of sudden my kitchen had felt so much like my parents' garage, which was the first and only other place my life had crumbled into ash.

Except Lizzy's death had made me angry at God, and I wasn't angry at God now, I was only desolate and alone, because I had given up everything—my vows, my vocation, my mission in my sister's name—and it had been repaid with the worst faithlessness, and you know what? I deserved it. If I was being punished, I had deserved it. I had earned every hollow second of blank pain, had earned it with all those stolen seconds of sharp, sweaty pleasure…

Is this how Adam felt? Driven from the garden to the cold, stony soil of an uncaring world, and all because he couldn't resist following Eve until the last?

I drove down to Kansas City, and once there, I drove around for hours. Going nowhere, looking at nothing. Feeling the full weight of Poppy's betrayal of me, the full weight of my betrayal of my vows, and worst of all, feeling the end of something that had meant everything to me, even if it was only for a short amount of time.

I didn't have my phone, and I couldn't remember if that was an intentional decision or not, whether I'd decided to trade radio silence on her terms for radio silence on my terms—because I knew, deep down, that she wouldn't text me or call me, she never had when we'd fought, and I also knew I would make myself miserable with the constant checking, the disappointment when there was nothing on my screen but the time.

And when I pounded at Jordan's door at midnight, and he opened the door to me and the relentless rain, he didn't turn me away like he had done last time. He gave me long look—piercing, but not ungentle—and then nodded.

"Come in."

I confessed right there in Jordan's living room. It was fucking miserable.

Unsure of where to start or how to explain it all, I simply told him about the first day I'd met Poppy. The day I'd only heard her voice. How breathy it was, how layered with uncertainty and pain. And then the story unspooled from there—all the lust, all the guilt, all the thousands of tiny ways I'd fallen in love, and all the thousands of tiny ways I'd crept away from being a priest. I told him about calling Bishop Bove, about my handmade bouquet. And then I told him about Sterling and the kiss, and how it was as if every fear and paranoia I'd ever had about them had been birthed into something monstrous and snarling. Infidelity was terrible, but how much worse was infidelity when you'd suspected all along that there was something between the two parties? My brain wouldn't stop screaming at me that I should have known better, *I should have known*, and what had I expected to happen? Had I really expected a happy ending? No relationship with such a sinful start could lead to happiness. That much I knew now.

Jordan listened patiently the entire time, his face devoid of any judgment or disgust. Sometimes his eyes were closed, and I wondered what else he was hearing besides my voice—who else, rather—but I found I no longer had the energy to care about anything, even my own story, which ground to a slow, painful halt after I got to the part where I found Sterling and Poppy. What else was there for me to say? What else was there for me to feel?

I buried my head in my hands, but not to cry—anger and grief still hovered elusively out of reach—there was only shock and emptiness, the blank stunned feeling one might have after stumbling out of a war zone.

I breathed in and out through my palms, and Jordan's voice drifted in, like it was coming from someplace remote, even though we were sitting close enough that our knees touched.

"Do you truly love her?" he asked.

"Yes," I said into my hands.

"And do you think it's over between you?"

I took a moment to answer, not because I didn't know, but because the words were so hard to speak. "I don't see how it can't be. She wants to be with Sterling. She's made that abundantly clear." Of course, if she showed up on Jordan's doorstep, I'd take her into my arms without a single word.

Less the unconditional love of God than the keening need of an addict.

"Without her..." Jordan met my eyes. "Do you think you still want to leave the priesthood?"

Jordan's question hit me with the force of a cannon. I honestly didn't know what I wanted now. I mean, I'd never wanted to be with a woman rather than be a priest, I'd wanted to be with *Poppy* rather than be a priest. I didn't want the freedom to fuck, I wanted the freedom to fuck *her*. I didn't want a family, I wanted a family *with her*.

And if I couldn't have her, then I didn't want this other life. I wanted God, and I wanted things the way they were.

I supposed I could call the bishop and explain and hope that he would allow me to stay in the clergy. It would be hard to stay in Weston, knowing Poppy was there too, seeing all the places we'd been together, but then again, at least I'd have my parish and my missions to fill my time. The more I thought about it, the better it sounded—at least I could keep a sliver of my life the way it was. I could keep my vocation, even if I lost my heart.

"I don't think I still want to leave," I answered.

Jordan was quiet for a minute. "Are you ready for your penance?"

I nodded, still not bothering to lift my head.

"You will offer God one day in its entirety, a day of complete and utter companionship with him. He wants to talk with you, Tyler. He wants to be with you in this time of suffering and confusion, and you should not shut Him out in your grief."

"No," I mumbled. "That penance isn't enough. I need something more—I deserve something harder, something worse..."

"Like what? A hair shirt? Walking barefoot for three months? A thorough self-scourging?"

I looked up, so I could glare at him. "I'm not being funny."

"Neither am I. You came to me for absolution and I'm giving it—along with God's message for you. In fact, this day of penance should be tomorrow. Stay here with me tonight, and no matter what happens, you spend tomorrow here. You'll have the church to yourself after the morning Mass, so plenty of time and space to pray."

Jordan's face was as it always was—calm and beatific at the same time—and I knew without a doubt that he was right. A day of reflection after the heady exhilaration of the past three months was no small thing for me to muster, and it was also the exact thing I needed. It would be painful, to spend hours examining myself honestly and conversing openly with God, but necessary things are often painful.

"You're right," I conceded. "Okay."

Jordan nodded, and he said a quiet prayer of absolution, and then we sat in silence for a few minutes. Most people were uncomfortable with silence, but Jordan wasn't—he was at home in it. At home with himself. And that made it slightly easier to be with *myself*, even with all the unfelt feelings still looming above me.

At least until the phone rang.

Jarred out of our reverie, we both stared at Jordan's phone on his kitchen counter. By this point, it was almost two in the morning, and Jordan stood quickly, because phone calls at this time of night were generally of the bad kind—car crashes, unexpected turns for the worse, hospice patients finally gasping their last breaths. The kinds of things where people needed their priest by their side.

I watched him answer the phone, silently saying a prayer that nobody was seriously hurt—a prayer purely out of habit, words spoken from rote—and then watched as his eyes flicked over to me.

"Yes, he's with me," Jordan said quietly, and my heart started beating in erratic staccato thumps, because it couldn't be Poppy, it couldn't be, but what if it was?

Oh God, what I would give if it were.

"Of course, just a moment," Jordan said and handed the phone to me. "It's the bishop," he whispered.

My heart stopped beating then, plummeting down into my stomach. The bishop at two in the morning?

"Hello?" I said into the phone.

"Tyler," and all it took was that one word for me to know that something was deeply, troublingly wrong, because I had never heard my mentor sound this upset. Could it simply be about me quitting?

"About that voicemail," I said, "I'm so sorry for not waiting to speak to you properly. And now that I've had some time to think, I'm not sure that I do want to leave the clergy. I understand that I have a lot to explain and a lot to atone for, but things have changed for me today, and—"

The bishop's voice was heavy as he interrupted me. "Unfortunately, I'm afraid that some other things have come to light…rather publicly, I'm afraid."

Shit. "What things?"

"I tried calling you all day, and I called your parents and some of your parishioners, but no one knew where you were, and it wasn't until tonight that I thought you might have gone to your confessor."

It felt like he was stalling, like he was hesitant to tell me about whatever happened, but I had to know. "Bishop, please."

He sighed. "Some pictures were released. On social media. You and a woman—your parishioner, I believe, Poppy Danforth."

The pictures. The ones Sterling had blackmailed me with.

I knew that I was in serious trouble, that Sterling had made good on his promise and burned my life down, but at the moment, the chief thing that stuck out was the sound of Poppy's name on someone else's lips, as if her name spoken aloud was an incantation, and it was that incantation that finally ripped me open, punched a hole in my chest like a bullet going through a pop can.

Tears started rolling down my face, hot and fast, but I

managed to keep my voice steady. "Okay."

"Okay, as in you already know about these pictures?"

"Yes," I managed.

"Dammit, Tyler," the bishop swore. "Just—*dammit*."

"I know." I was actively crying now and then something was nudged into my hand. A tumbler of scotch, amber-colored and with a single spherical ice cube in the middle. Jordan was standing over me, and he nodded his head at the glass.

Things were bad indeed if Jordan Brady was giving me a drink. I wouldn't have even guessed he owned a single bottle of liquor to begin with.

"Tyler…" the bishop said "…I don't want to have to fire you."

His meaning was clear. He wanted me to quit. *It will be that much cleaner for the press releases*, I thought. The repentant priest who had already turned himself in made a much better byline than the sexually rapacious priest who had to be fired.

"Are those my only two choices? Quit or be fired?"

"I suppose…if the relationship were over—"

"It is."

"—there would have to be discipline and definitely relocation—"

I'd expected this, but the confirmation gutted me. I'd have to move. A new parish, new faces, all while the old parish had to sort through a rumor-cloud of my sins. No matter what, no matter if everything else went perfectly, I'd still lost this. My parish. My people.

My fault.

"—and even then, I don't know how the cardinal would feel about this, Tyler." The bishop sounded tired, but also something else—loving. It was deep in the timber of his voice. He loved me, and that made me feel even more deeply, unhappily ashamed to be having this conversation with him. "If you are truly committed to staying in the clergy, then we will figure out the next steps."

I didn't feel relieved by this, possibly because I was still so unsure of what I wanted, but I said, "Thank you," anyway, because I knew what a giant clusterfuck I'd created for the archdiocese, and I knew even thinking of staying in the clergy would make it worse.

"Let's talk tomorrow evening," the bishop said. "Until then, please don't talk to the press or even go online—there's no sense in complicating things until we know for sure where we're headed."

We said good night and clicked off the phone, and then I drained my scotch and fell into a dreamless sleep on Jordan's hard, unwelcoming couch.

CHAPTER TWENTY-THREE

I went to Jordan's Mass early the next morning, which was substantially better attended than my own morning Masses back home. I had called Millie the moment I woke up, to tell her where I was and how to get a hold of me. Millie—who surfed Reddit and Tumblr even more than I did—already knew about the pictures, but she didn't say *I told you so*, she didn't sound hateful, and so I had hope that she'd forgiven me in her own cranky way. She'd also volunteered to post a sign on the door, saying that office hours and weekday Masses were temporarily suspended, and so, with my church matters taken care of for the moment, I could focus on the here and now.

Although I couldn't help but ask, "Have you seen Poppy?" before we hung up, hating myself as I did.

Millie seemed to understand. "No. In fact, her car hasn't been in her driveway since last night."

"Okay," I said, heavily and tiredly, not sure how I felt about this news. What I did know was that it did not improve the feeling that there was a giant crater where my heart should be.

"Father, please take care of yourself. No matter what, the parish loves you," she said, and I wanted so much for those words to be true, but how could they be after I'd ruined everything?

After Mass, I had the sanctuary to myself. Jordan's church was old—more than a hundred years old—and made almost purely of stone and stained glass. No old red carpet here, no faux-wood siding. It felt like a real church, ancient and echoing, the kind of place where the Holy Spirit would hover, like an invisible mist, sparkling among the rafters.

Poppy would love it here.

I was shaky and empty-feeling from crying last night, like my soul had been poured out of me along with my tears. I should kneel, I knew, I should kneel and close my eyes and bow my head, but instead, I laid down on one of the pews. It was made of unforgiving wood, hard and cold, but I didn't have the energy to support myself for a moment longer, and so I stayed there, blinking sightlessly at the back of the pew in front of me with its missals and attendance cards and tiny, dull golf pencils.

Tell me what to do, God.

I guessed that a part of me had hoped that I would wake up and it would all be some terrible nightmare, some hallucination brought forth to test my faith, but no, it wasn't. I really had caught Poppy and Sterling together yesterday. I really had fallen in love just to have the shit kicked out of me (by the very woman I'd wanted to marry).

Do I leave the clergy and hope Poppy will take me back? Do I try to find her? Talk to her? And what's the best thing for the Church—for me to stay? Is the Church more important than Poppy?

There was nothing. The distant roar of city traffic outside, the dim light glinting dully off the wood of the pew.

I don't even get an air conditioner now? Now? Of all the times, now is when I get nothing?

I was quite aware I was being petulant, but I didn't care. Even Jacob had to wrestle his blessing out of God, so if I had to pout my way into one, I would.

Except I was tired. And empty. I couldn't keep whining, even if I wanted to, so instead my thoughts wandered, my prayers becoming aimless—wordless even—as I simply just contemplated where I found myself. Here in a church that wasn't my own, alone and wounded. I'd brought harm to my parish through my actions and had betrayed the trust of my bishop and my parishioners—the thing I had tried the hardest not to do since becoming a priest.

I'd failed.

I'd failed as a priest and as a man and as a friend.

I stared at the stone floor, blinking slowly in the silence. So would I stay? Would remaining a priest be the best way to atone? Would that be the best for the church? For my soul? Quitting now, not on my own terms, felt like a petulant act of self-hatred, an *I screw everything up, so I quit* kind of act, and whatever decision I made about my future, it had to come from someplace other than that.

It had to come from God.

Unfortunately, He didn't seem to be in a talkative mood today.

Maybe the real question was, could I still imagine life without the priesthood and without Poppy? I'd decided to quit because of my love for her, but once I had made the decision, I had felt all these other potential futures rolling out in front of me—inspiring, intoxicating, invigorating futures. There were so many ways I could serve God, and what if that was what all of this was about? Not about bringing me and Poppy together, but about nudging me out of the comfortable bubble I'd created for myself? A bubble where I could only do so much, and I would always have an excuse for not dreaming bigger and better, a bubble where it was easy to cultivate stasis and stagnation in the name of humble service.

So many of the things I'd wanted to do when I was younger—things like Poppy had done, such as extended mission trips—had become impossible once I'd settled into a parish. But if I were free, I could go fight famine in Ethiopia or spend a summer teaching English in Belarus or dig wells in Kenya. I could go anywhere, anytime.

With anyone.

Well, not *anyone*. Because when I closed my eyes and summoned the dusty plains of Pokot or the forests of Belarus and lost myself into wordless fantasies of the future, there was only one person I imagined beside me. Someone short and slender, with dark hair and red lips. Carrying water with me, or maybe it was fresh notebooks for the children, or maybe it was just her sunglasses as we laced fingers to walk to a community meeting together. Maybe she was in the hammock above me, where I could see the diamond-shaped imprints the hammock had made on her skin, or maybe we were sharing a stark, unheated dorm together, curled like twin commas on a hard bed.

But wherever we were, we were helping people. In the kind of direct, physical—sometimes intimate—ways that Jesus had helped people. Healing the sick with his hands, curing the blind with mud and saliva. Getting his hands dirty, his sandals dusty. That was one of the real differences between Jesus and the Pharisees, wasn't it? One went out among the people and the others stayed indoors, arguing over yellowing scrolls while their people were casually brutalized by an indifferent empire.

I remembered the moment I'd chosen to be a priest, the excitement, the burning anticipation I'd felt. And I felt it now, like the brushing of dove's wings and a baptism of fire all at the same time, because it was becoming clear. Not just clear, but obvious.

I sat up.

God wanted me in the real world and in the midst of the ordinary lives of His people. Maybe the plans He had for Tyler Bell were so much more exciting and wonderful than I'd ever counted on.

Is this what You want? I asked. *For me to leave—not for Poppy, not for the bishop, but for me? For You?*

And the word came into my mind with a calm, resonant authority.

Yes.

Yes.

It was time for me to stop. Time for me to leave my life as a priest.

Here was the answer I'd wanted, the path I had asked for, except it wasn't really what I had asked for, because before, I'd been asking the wrong question.

This time there was nothing showy—no burning bushes, no tingly feelings, no beams of sunlight. There was only a quiet, contemplative peace, and the knowledge that my feet were now pointed to the path. I only had to take the first step.

And when I called the bishop later that night to tell him my decision, my newfound peace remained. We both knew that it was the right decision—for me and for the church—

and just like that, my life as a priest, as Father Tyler Bell, came to a subdued and solemn end.

That next weekend was Irish Fest, and I'd already said goodbye to my parishioners and cleared out the rectory, so there was no reason for me to drive up there, even though I hated missing out on the kickoff for the church's fundraiser.

"Afraid they'll stone you?" Sean said when I mentioned I wasn't going. (I was staying with him until I found a place of my own.)

I shook my head. Actually, despite the national splash on social media, where I was simultaneously demonized and turned into something of a celebrity because of my looks, my own parishioners had reacted so much better than I deserved. They told me they wanted me to stay—some actually begged me to stay—others thanked me for talking openly about abuse—some simply hugged me and wished me well. And I gave them honest answers to whatever questions they asked; they deserved that from me at least, a complete and open accounting of my sins, so that there would be no shadow of doubt, no circulating rumors. I didn't want my sin to stain the community any further than it absolutely had to.

But at the same time, despite their warmth and love, it wouldn't be healthy for me to go back. Even as I'd packed up my things last week, I'd been haunted by Poppy, and after Dad and I had loaded everything into the moving van,

I made some excuses about saying goodbye to a few extra people, and went to her house. I had no plan for what I would say, and even then I wasn't sure if I was furious with her or desperate for her or both—the kind of betrayed where only her body would be able to heal me, even though it was the thing that had hurt me.

But it didn't matter. She was gone, and so were all of her things—her iMac, her booze, her books. I peered through the windows into the empty house, my face pressed to the glass like a child at a shop window. I had the ridiculous feeling that if I could only go inside, I would feel better. I would be happy, just for a minute.

Using this addict's reasoning as rationale, I went to go get the spare key on her back porch, but of course it was gone, and all the doors were locked. I even tried one of the windows before I finally got a grip on myself. She'd gone to go live with Sterling, and I was here, about to get arrested for breaking and entering.

At least fucking keep it together until you can go home and get a drink, I scolded myself, and I managed to accomplish this. Dad and I unloaded the contents of the van into his basement, and then we shared several glasses of whiskey without sharing a single word. More Irish grieving.

Even though Weston only held painful memories for me now, I was still happy to see that, after the festival, the Kickstarter was working exactly like Poppy had planned: by the beginning of November, St. Margaret's had raised almost ten thousand dollars for its renovation.

It hurt a little to think of this project that I had poured so much time and energy into falling into the lap of some other priest, and it was also a little galling that so many of those online donations had come in from the "Tylerettes," an internet fan group that had popped up not long after the pictures had. The Tylerettes seemed more interested in speculating about my relationship status or digging up shirtless pictures of me from college than charity. But I supposed if it was all for the greater good, then it was okay.

"At least you know you can get pussy whenever you want," Sean said as we ate takeout in his penthouse living room one night a couple weeks later.

"Fuck you," I replied, without any heat. It didn't really matter. There was only one woman I wanted, and she was gone, and no number of internet fangirls (and fanboys) was going to change that.

"Please tell me that you're not going to do the celibate thing even now that you've been lateralized."

"*Laicized*, and it's none of your fucking business."

Sean threw a soy sauce packet at my head and seemed to enjoy the effect quite a bit, so he threw several more, the asshole, and then pouted when I winged a container of sweet and sour sauce into his chest and spilled pink goop all over his latest Hugo Boss dress shirt.

"Uncalled for, *dickweed*," he muttered, scrubbing futilely at the fabric.

And that was mostly my life—arguing with my brother, eating shitty food, generally having no idea what to do next. I thought about Poppy constantly, whether I was researching graduate programs or whether I was with my parents, who were supportive but tentative, as if afraid that saying the wrong word would make me have a Vietnam flashback and start crawling on the floor with a knife between my teeth.

"They're afraid you're going to hulk out, because of all that stuff on the internet and they think maybe you're repressing your feelings about it or something," Ryan had helpfully explained when he'd overheard me mention it to Aiden and Sean. "So, you know. Don't hulk out."

Don't hulk out. How funny. If anything, I was hulking in, shrinking and folding into a smaller man, a weaker man. Without Poppy, it was as if I had forgotten all the things that made me into Tyler Bell. I pined for her like a person would pine for air, incessantly, gaspingly, and it left so little room to think about anything else. I couldn't even watch *The Walking Dead* because it reminded me too much of her.

"I'm lost," I admitted to Jordan one day after Thanksgiving. "I know I did the right thing by leaving the clergy, but now there're so many choices—so many places I could go, so many things I could do. How am I supposed to know which one is the right one?"

"Is it because they all feel wrong without her?"

I hadn't mentioned Poppy to him at all, so his acuity

unnerved me, even though I should know better by now. "Yes," I said honestly. "I miss her so much it hurts."

"Has she tried to contact you?"

I looked down at the table. "No."

No messages. No emails. No phone calls. Nothing. She was done with me. I supposed this meant she'd seen me that day in her house, that she knew I knew about Sterling, and that almost made it worse. No explanation? No apology? Not even the charade of feeble excuses and well wishes for the future?

I knew she'd moved away from Weston—Millie called to give me weekly updates on the church and my former parishioners—but I had no idea where she'd gone, although I assumed it was to New York City with Sterling.

"I think you should try to find her," Jordan said. "Get some closure."

Which was how I ended up at the strip club with Sean that December. He'd practically imploded with excitement when I had asked him to bring me, talking about getting me laid, getting *him* laid, and also about how we should bring Aiden, but not tonight because he wanted to focus on my game.

"I don't want to hook up with a stripper," I protested for the ten thousandth time as we rode the elevator up.

"What, they're too good for you now? You were fucking one just a couple months ago."

God, had it been two months already? It felt so much

shorter than that, except the times when it felt longer, the times when I was sure it had been years since I'd last tasted the sweetness of Poppy's body, since I'd felt her cunt so warm and wet around my dick, and those were the times I'd found myself so painfully erect I could barely breathe. Luckily, Sean was desperate to climb the ladder at his job and worked lots of late nights, and so I had the penthouse to myself most of the time. Not that jacking off ever helped—no matter how often I came into my hand thinking of her, it never dulled the ache of losing her, it never softened the blow of her betrayal. But betrayal or not, my body still wanted her.

I still wanted her.

"That was different," I told Sean now in the elevator, and he shrugged. I knew I'd never be able to explain it to him, because he'd never been in love. *Pussy is pussy*, he would say whenever I tried to make him understand why I didn't want to be set up with some random girl he knew, why I didn't want to date at all. What was so special about hers?

The club was busy—it was a Saturday night—and it only took a couple vodka and tonics to convince Sean to go do his own thing. I stayed near the bar, sipping a Bombay Sapphire martini and watching the dancers out on the floor, remembering what it was like to have Poppy dance for me and me alone.

What I wouldn't give just to have a few of those

moments back—her and me and that goddamn silk thing around her neck. With a sigh, I set my drink down. I hadn't come here to reminisce. I came here to find out where Poppy went.

The bartender came down my way, wiping down the bar. "Another?" she asked, gesturing to my martini.

"No, thanks. Actually, I'm looking for someone."

She raised an eyebrow. "A dancer? We usually don't give out schedule information." *For safety reasons*, I could see she wanted to say, but she didn't.

I couldn't even be offended, because I knew how it looked to her. "Actually, I'm not looking for schedule information per se. I'm looking for Poppy Danforth…I think she used to work here?"

The bartender's eyes widened in recognition. "Oh my God, you're that priest, aren't you?"

I cleared my throat. "Um, yeah. I mean, I'm not technically a priest anymore, but I was."

The bartender grinned. "That picture of you playing Frisbee in college—it's the background on my sister's work computer. And have you seen the Hot Priest memes?"

I had indeed—for better or for worse—seen the Hot Priest memes. They were made using the picture that used to be on St. Margaret's website, the one that Poppy admitted to looking up all those months ago.

I thought maybe it would be easier if I knew what you looked like.

And is it easier?

Not really.

Now that we had established I wasn't just some random guy harassing dancers, I tried again. "Do you know where Poppy went?"

The bartender turned pitying. "No. She gave her notice so fast, and she didn't tell anybody why she was quitting or where she was going, although we all knew about the pictures, so we guessed it had something to do with those. She didn't tell you?"

"No," I said, and I picked up my martini again. Some truths went better with gin.

She hung her towel off a nearby rack and then spun toward me again. "You know, now that I think about it, I think she left something here when she came to pack up her things. Let me go grab it."

I tapped my fingers against the stainless-steel bar, not letting myself believe that it was something as important as a letter left specifically for me, but still craving it all the same. How could she just have left? Without a word?

Had it all meant that little to her?

Not for the first time, my chest went concave, crumpling inward with the pain of it. The pain of one-sided love, of knowing that I had loved her more than she had loved me.

Is this how God feels all the time?

What a sobering thought.

The bartender came back with a thick white envelope. It had my name on it, Sharpied in hasty, thick strokes. When I took it, I knew immediately what it was, but I opened it anyway, more pain slashing through my gut as I pulled out Lizzy's rosary and felt its weight in my hand.

I held it up for just a minute, watching the cross spin wildly in the low light of the dance floor, and then I thanked the bartender, slung back the rest of my martini, and left, leaving Sean to have his strip-adventures on his own.

It was over. Really, it had been over the moment I'd seen Sterling and Poppy kiss, but somehow I knew that this was her definitive signal that there was nothing left between us. Even though I'd given the rosary freely, as a gift, had never thought once about wanting it back, she had seen it as some sort of bond, some sort of debt, and she was rejecting that bond, just as she'd rejected me.

Yes. It was time I accepted it.

It was over.

CHAPTER TWENTY-FOUR

I'd love to say that I walked out the club and used this newfound closure to get my life together. I'd love to tell you that a white dove came fluttering down and the heavens opened and God told me exactly where to go and what to do.

Most of all, I'd love to tell you that the rosary—and the implicit message it sent—healed my broken heart, and I spent no more nights thinking of Poppy, no more days scouring the internet for mentions of her name.

But it took longer than that. I spent the next two weeks much like I'd spent the two weeks before I got the rosary back: listening to sad indie movie soundtracks and apathetically filling out applications for different degree programs, imagining in vivid detail what Poppy was doing right then (and whom she was doing it with). I went to Jordan's church and mumbled my way through Masses, I exercised constantly, and I immediately undid all that exercise once I finished by eating shitty food and drinking even more than my Irish bachelor brothers.

Christmas came. At our big family meal, we had this Bell family tradition of saying what our perfect present would be—a promotion, a new car, a vacation, that sort of thing. And when we went around the table, I realized what I wanted the most.

"I want to be *doing* something," I said, remembering lying on Jordan's pew and fantasizing about distant shores and dusty hills.

"So do it," Aiden said. "You can do anything you want. You've got, like, a million college degrees."

Two. I had two.

"I am going to do it," I decided.

"And what is *it*?" Mom asked.

"I have no idea. But it's not here."

And two weeks later, I was on a plane to Kenya on an open-ended mission trip to dig wells in Pokot, for the first time running *to* something, rather than away.

SEVEN MONTHS LATER

"So you're a lumbersexual now?"

"Fuck you." I shoved my bag into Sean's chest so I could dig out some money for the airport vending machine. Dr. Pepper, the Fountain of Youth. I almost wept after taking the first sip, the first cold, sweet, carbonated thing I'd had since the Nairobi airport.

"So no pop in Africa, eh?" Aiden asked as I took my bag back and we started walking out of the airport.

"And no razors apparently," Sean said, reaching over and giving my beard a fierce yank.

I punched him in the bicep. He yelped like a girl.

It was true that I had a fairly extensive beard, along with a deep tan and dramatically leaner body. "No more pretty boy muscles," Dad had remarked after I'd walked in the door and he'd hugged me. "Those are real-work muscles."

Mom had just pursed her lips. "You look like Charlton Heston in *The Ten Commandments.*"

I felt a bit like Moses, a stranger both in Egypt and in Midian, a stranger everywhere. Later that night, after the longest shower I could ever remember taking (months of one-minute, tepid showers had instilled a deep love of running hot water in me), I laid down on my bed and thought about everything. The faces of the people—workers and villagers alike—that I'd come to know on such an intimate level. I knew why their children were named what they were, and I knew that they loved soccer and *Top Gear*, and I knew which of the boys I'd wanted on my team when we played impromptu rugby games in the evening. The work had been hard—they were building a high school along with better water infrastructure—and the days were long, and there had been times when I'd felt unwanted or wanted too much or like the work was pointless, bailing out the *Titanic* with a coffee tin, as Dad would have said. And then I would go to sleep with prayers circling in my head and wake up the next day, refreshed and determined to do better.

I wouldn't have left, honestly, if during my monthly satellite call, Mom hadn't told me about the pile of acceptance letters waiting for me at home. I could literally have my pick of universities, and after a lot of thought, I'd decided to come home and pursue my PhD at Princeton—not a Catholic seminary, but I was okay with that. Presbyterians weren't so bad.

I pulled Lizzy's rosary out of my pocket and watched the cross spin in the low city lights filtering in through the window. I'd taken it with me to Pokot, and there'd been many nights when I'd fallen asleep with it clutched in my hand, like by holding on to it, I could hold on to someone, except I didn't know who I was trying to feel close to. Lizzy maybe, or God. Or Poppy.

The dreams had started my second night there, slow, predictable dreams at first. Dreams of sighs and flesh, dreams so real that I would wake up with her scent in my nostrils and her taste lingering on my tongue. And then they'd changed into strange ciphered visions of tabernacles and chuppahs, dancing shoes and tumbling stacks of books.

Hazel eyes bright with tears, red lips curved downward in perpetual unhappiness.

Old Testament dreams, Jordan had said when I called him one month. *Your old men will dream dreams and your young men will see visions*, he'd quoted.

("Which kind of man am I?" I'd wondered aloud.)

No amount of prayer, no amount of hard, exhausting work during the day, made the dreams go away. And I had no idea what they meant, except that Poppy was still very much inside my heart, no matter how much I distracted myself during my waking hours.

I wanted to see her again. And it was no longer the wounded lover who wanted it, no longer the anger and the lust both demanding to be satisfied. I just wanted to know she was doing okay, and I wanted to give her the rosary back. It had been a gift, she should keep it.

Even if she was with—*fuck*—Sterling.

Once I had that thought, it was impossible to shake, and so the idea became completely embedded into my plans. I was moving to New Jersey, and New York City wasn't far away. I would find Poppy and I would give her the rosary.

Along with your forgiveness, came a quiet thought out of nowhere. A God-thought. *She needs to know that you've forgiven her.*

Have I? Forgiven her? I nudged one arm of the crucifix to set it spinning again. I suppose I had. It hurt—deeply—to think of her and Sterling together, but my anger had been poured into the African dust—poured away and sprinkled down, sprinkled as sweat and tears and blood onto the soil.

Yes. It would be good for both of us. Closure. And maybe once I handed off the rosary, the dreams would stop and I could move on with the rest of my life.

The next day, my last day home, Mom took scissors to my beard with an almost creepy glee.

"It didn't look that bad," I mumbled as she worked.

Ryan was hitched up on the counter, for once without his phone. He had a bag of Cheetos in his hand instead. "No, dude, it really did. Unless you were trying to look like Rick Grimes."

"Why wouldn't I? He's my hero."

Mom clucked. "Princeton students don't look like Paul Bunyan, Tyler. Hold still—no, Ryan, he can't have Cheetos while I'm doing this."

Ryan had shoved the bag in my outstretched hand after hopping down to find his phone ("This is so sick. I have to stream it.")

I sighed and set the Cheetos down.

"I'm going to miss you," Mom said, out of nowhere.

"It's just school. I'll be back to visit all the time."

She finished with the scissors and set them down. "I know. It's just, all you boys have stayed so close to home. I've been spoiled by having you all here."

And then she burst into tears, because we weren't all here, hadn't been all here since Lizzy.

"Mom..." I stood up and hugged her tightly. "I love you. And this isn't permanent. It's just for a few years."

She nodded into my chest, and then sniffed and pulled away. "I'm sad because I'll miss you, but I'm not crying because I want you to stay." She met my eyes with her matching green ones. "You boys need to live your lives without being chained down by obligation or grief. I'm glad you're doing something scary, something new. Go and make new memories, and don't worry about your silly mother here in Kansas City. I'm going to be just fine, plus, I still have Sean and Aiden and Ryan."

As much as I wanted to scoff, I couldn't. Sean and Aiden were attentive in their own ways, never missing a family dinner, carving out time to call and text during the rest of the week, and Dad was here. Still, though. I worried. "Okay."

"Sit down, so I can finish up on this monstrosity of a beard."

I sat, thinking about leaving home behind. I'd seen enough grief as a priest to know that people never really moved on, at least not in the linear, segmented way our culture expected people to. Instead, Mom was going to have good days and bad days, days where she circled back to her pain and days where she was able to smile and fuss over things like beards and the cost of Ryan's car insurance.

Mostly, I knew that I wouldn't be able to carry her pain for her, even if I stayed here. We'd each have to find our own ways of living with Lizzy's ghost, and we'd have to find them in our own time. I felt like I'd already started, and maybe Mom had too.

"Now, go shave," she ordered me now, brushing at my face with a dry towel and dropping a light kiss on my forehead. "Unless you've forgotten how."

Moving wasn't so hard. I found an inexpensive apartment not too far away from campus and used my dwindling savings to put in a deposit. I'd be a teaching assistant as well as a student, and the stipend was enough to cover room and board, even if I would have to take out a few loans for tuition. I didn't have much to move, really, all of my furniture having belonged to the rectory and my weights being left in Kansas City. Clothes and books, and then a futon and a table I scrounged from Craigslist.

After settling in, I spent a long day or two trying to hunt down a new address for Poppy on the internet, even just a place of work, but there was nothing. She was either very careful or very quiet or both—the last mentions of her that I could find were around the time of her graduation from Dartmouth, and a handful of campus dance performances from her time at the University of Kansas a few years ago.

I could find no trace of her, and I even went as far as calling her parents, using numbers I found online for her father's company and for her mother's nonprofit. But they were well-guarded by rings of assistants and receptionists, none of whom seemed inclined to give up any information about Poppy or forward me on to her parents. Not that I could blame them; I probably wouldn't give out information to a strange man either, but it was still frustrating as hell.

Why did she have to leave Weston? Why did she have to leave the rosary? Maybe if she hadn't, I wouldn't be consumed with the idea of giving it back…

There was one person who I knew would almost certainly be willing to talk to me about Poppy, and the thought of seeing him again filled me with immense distaste, but I was running out of options. The semester would start soon and I wouldn't have time to gallivant about the eastern seaboard looking for my ex…girlfriend? Ex-lover? And I couldn't imagine having this kind of idealistic, ultimately hopeless quest on my plate until Christmas.

After two hours on buses and trains in various states of overcrowdedness, I was in Manhattan's Financial District, staring up at the large steel and glass structure that belonged to the Haverford family. I wandered inside, surrounded immediately by marble and busy-looking people and an overall air of industry, and this persisted even when an elevator took me to the central office sixty floors up. *No wonder Poppy chose Sterling.* I'd never be able to offer her anything like this. I didn't have fleets of black cars and portfolios of investments, I didn't have a marble-floored empire. All I'd had was a collar and a home that didn't legally belong to me—and now I no longer even had those.

God, I'd been such a fool to think I could have kept Poppy Danforth for my own. This was the world she'd come from—of course this was where she would return.

The receptionist inside was a pretty blonde girl, and asshole that I was, I wondered if Sterling had slept with her too, if his life was just a parade of money and infidelity, a parade without any consequences, a parade without a single concern other than how to get what he wanted.

"Um, hi," I said as I approached her desk. "I was wondering if I could see Mr. Haverford?"

She didn't even look up from her computer screen. "Do you have an appointment?"

"I'm afraid not," I said.

"No one without an appointment can get in…" her voice trailed off as she looked up at me and then her eyes widened. "Oh my God! You're the guy from the Hot Priest meme!"

Sigh. "Yeah, that's me."

She lowered her voice conspiratorially. "I follow a bunch of the Tylerette fan accounts. Is it true you went to go live in Africa? Were you hiding? *Entertainment Tonight* said you were hiding."

"I was on a mission trip," I said. "Digging wells." Although the lack of internet in Pokot had definitely been its own perk.

She made a high-pitched *aww* noise, peering up at me with her big brown eyes, suddenly looking very young. "You went to go help people? That's so sweet!"

She bit her lip and glanced around the empty waiting room. "You know, Mr. Haverford never keeps track of his own appointments. He wouldn't know if you were on the books or not." A few keystrokes. "And now you're officially on the books."

"Wow, thank you," I said, feeling grateful—that is, until she handed me a business card with a number scrawled on the back.

"That's my phone number," she said a bit coyly. "In case you ever feel like breaking your vows again."

Sigh. "Thank you," I said as politely as I could manage. There didn't seem to be much point in explaining my current non-clerical position to her, or that there was only one reason I'd ever broken my vows, and that reason was why I was here in my enemy's stronghold in the first place.

"Can we take a selfie?" And before I could answer, she was up and on the other side of her desk, standing next to me with her phone extended in front of us.

"Smile," she said, pressing herself against me, her blonde head against my shoulder, and I dutifully smiled, at the same time realizing how deep Poppy remained in my system. I had a slender blonde smashed against me, warm and willing, and all I wanted was to peel myself away. I'd rather be in the next room fighting with Sterling than enduring this girl's flirtatious advances. Sean would be ashamed of me.

"You can go in now if you'd like—he's between appointments," the receptionist said, still conspiratorially, thumbs working fast and nimble over her screen as she posted her selfie everywhere on the internet.

Sterling's office was as impressive as the rest of the building—dizzying views, a massive desk, a low bar filled with expensive scotch. And then Sterling himself, sitting like a king on his throne, signing reams of paper covered with dense type.

He glanced up, clearly expecting one of his employees, and then seeing me instead, his mouth fell open. I expected him to be angry or triumphant—ask me to leave, maybe—but I didn't expect him to stand up, walk over to me, and then extend his hand for a shake, like we were old business partners.

I ignored the proffered hand. I may have been a priest, but even I have my limits.

However, my rudeness didn't seem to bother him in the least. "Tyler Bell—sorry, *Father* Bell," he exclaimed, pulling back to look me in the face. "How the fuck are you?"

I rubbed the back of my neck, uncomfortable. I'd prepared for every possible shade of Sterling's assholery on the train ride here, but not once had I considered the possibility that he could be, well, *friendly*. "It's actually not Father anymore. I left the clergy."

Sterling grinned. "I hope it wasn't because of those pictures. I did feel a bit bad after I released them, I'll be honest. Do you want something to drink? I've got this amazing Lagavulin 21."

Um… "Sure."

Sterling went over to the bar, and I hated to admit it to myself, but right now, now that he no longer considered me his enemy, I could see what Poppy once saw in him. There was a specific kind of charisma in his manner, coupled with the kind of sophistication that made you feel like you were sophisticated too, just by being around it.

"So I imagine you came to gloat, which I deserve, I admit. I'll be a man about it." He unstoppered the Lagavulin and poured us both a healthy glass. He walked over and handed it to me. "I'm surprised you didn't come sooner."

I literally had no idea what the hell he was talking about. I took a sip of the scotch to hide my confusion.

Sterling leaned against the edge of his desk, swirling the scotch with a practiced hand. "How is she?"

Was he talking about Poppy? He couldn't be, he was with Poppy, but yet she was the only she that we both shared. "I came here to ask you the same question, actually."

Sterling raised his eyebrows. "So you two"—he used his glass to gesture at me—"you guys aren't together?"

I narrowed my eyes at him. "I thought *you* were together with her."

A shot of pain—real pain, not disappointment or

anger—flashed through his face. "No. We aren't…we weren't. We weren't what I thought."

I found myself—ridiculously—feeling sorry for him. And then his words began to really sink in, and a small flower of hope bloomed in my chest…

"But I saw you two kiss."

His brow crinkled. "You did? Oh, that must have been in her house."

"The day you released those pictures."

"I am sorry about that, you know."

Yeah, yeah, yeah. It wasn't water under the bridge exactly, but I was much more interested in how they'd gone from kissing in her bedroom to not being together. I should tamp down this hope now, before it truly blossomed, but I couldn't bring myself to—although if she wasn't with Sterling, then why hadn't she tried to contact me?

One question at a time, I coached myself.

Sterling must have read the meaning behind my expression, because he took a sip and then set his glass down and explained. "That day, I had finally gotten tired of waiting, so I drove up to that craphole town—no offense—and told her I'd release those pictures if she didn't promise to be with me. She was standing by the window, and then all of a sudden she shuffled me into her bedroom and tore my jacket off. I kissed her, thinking that's what she wanted. But no. After one kiss, she shoved me away and kicked me out." The way he rubbed his jaw just then made me wonder if *kicked me out* had involved a punch to his jaw. I really hoped it had. "I went ahead and released the pictures because I was pissed—understandably, I think, given the circumstances."

I sat down in the nearest chair, staring at the scotch in my hand, trying to sort out what this all meant. "You only kissed that once? She didn't leave Missouri to be with you?"

"Obviously not," he said. "I assumed she'd gone running back to you."

"No. No, she didn't."

"Oh, rough luck, old sport," he said sympathetically.

I digested this. Poppy had kissed Sterling once and then demanded that he leave. Sterling was either a terrible kisser or she didn't want to be with him at all—but if she didn't want to be with him, then why hadn't she stayed with me? And after those pictures, after I'd left the clergy, she hadn't once reached out. I'd assumed it was because she was with Sterling, but now that I knew differently, that stung a bit more. She could have at least said goodbye or sorry or something, anything.

My heart twisted some more, a tired washcloth still being wrung out. *Rosary*, I reminded myself. *This is about returning the rosary and giving her your forgiveness. And you can't forgive her if you're bitter about what happened.*

Besides, at least she wasn't with Sterling. And that was some small comfort.

"Do you know where she is now?" I asked. "I want to talk to her."

Of course he did. He went back around his desk, found his phone, and within a few seconds, I was holding a scrap of paper with his neat block handwriting. An address.

"I stopped keeping track of her last year, but this was a property that the Danforth Foundation for the Arts purchased not long after I came back home. It's a dance studio here in New York."

I studied the address, then looked up at him. "Thank you." I meant it.

He shrugged and then drained the last of his glass. "No problem."

For some reason, I extended my hand, feeling a bit bad about ignoring his gesture earlier. He took it, and we had a brief but courteous handshake. Here was the man who'd ruined my career, who I thought had taken my Poppy away from me, but I was able to walk away without any hatred or ill will, and it wasn't just because of the $1500 scotch.

It was because I forgave him. And because I was going to walk out of this door and find Poppy and return this rosary and finally, finally move on with my life.

CHAPTER TWENTY-FIVE

The dance studio was in Queens, in a colorful but run-down neighborhood, the kind of neighborhood that seemed like it was on the cusp of gentrification, but no developers had moved in yet, only scores of artists and hipsters.

The Little Flower Studio, from what I could tell from the internet search on my phone on the subway there, was a nonprofit studio dedicated to giving free dance lessons to the youth in the community, and seemed particularly aimed at young women. There was nothing about Poppy on its website, but the studio had opened only two months after she'd left Weston, and the entire project was funded by her family's foundation.

It was a tall brick building, three stories, and the front seemed very recently renovated, with tall windows looking into the main dance studio, a view of blond wood and gleaming mirrors.

Unfortunately, since it was the middle of the day, there didn't seem to be anybody at the studio itself. The lights were off and the door was locked, and no one answered the bell when I rang it. I tried the studio's phone number too, and then watched the phone on the front desk light up again and again. No one was here to answer it.

I could hang around until someone came back—someone who I hoped desperately would be Poppy—or I could go home, try again some other day. It was bakingly hot, the kind of hot where I worried my shoes might melt if I stood on the sidewalk too long, and there was no shade outside the studio. Was it really the best idea to stay here and turn into a sweaty sunstroke victim?

But the thought of leaving New York without seeing Poppy, without talking to her, was a thought I couldn't stomach for longer than a few seconds. I'd spent the last ten months in this misery. I couldn't spend another day more.

God must have heard me.

I turned back toward the subway station—I'd seen a bodega nearby, and I wanted a bottle of water—and I caught a glimpse of a spire between two rows of houses—a church. And my feet turned there without me even thinking about it; I suppose I was hoping there would be air-conditioning inside and maybe a place to pray until the dance studio reopened, but I was also wishing (hard) that I'd find something else inside.

I did.

The front doors opened into wide foyer studded with stoups full of holy water, and the doors to the sanctuary were propped open, wafting blessedly cool air into the entryway, but that's not the first thing I noticed.

The first thing I noticed was the woman near the front of the sanctuary, kneeling with her head bowed. Her dark hair was spun up in a tight bun—a dancer's bun—and her long neck and slender shoulders were exposed by the black camisole she wore. Dance clothes, I realized as I got closer, trying to be quiet, but it didn't seem to matter. She was so absorbed in her prayer that she didn't even move as I slid into the pew behind her row.

I could trace every inch of her back from memory, even after all these months. Each freckle, each line of muscle, each curve of her shoulder blade. And the shade of her hair—dark as coffee and just as rich—I'd remembered that perfectly too. And now that she was so close, all of my good intentions and pure thoughts were being subsumed by much, much darker ones. I wanted to unpin that bun and then wrap that silky hair around my hand. I wanted to pull down the front of her top and fondle her tits. I wanted to rub the softness between her legs through the fabric of her stretchy dance pants until it was soaking wet.

No, even now, I wasn't being honest with myself, because what I really wanted was so much worse. I wanted to hear the sound of my palm against her ass. I wanted to make her crawl, make her beg, I wanted to scrape the skin of her inner thighs raw with my stubble. I wanted to make her erase every minute of pain I'd felt because of her—erase those minutes with her mouth and her fingers and her sweet, hot cunt.

I was tempted to do just that, scoop her up and throw her over my shoulder and find someplace quiet—her studio, a motel, an alley, I didn't really care—and show her exactly what ten months apart had done to me.

Just because she isn't with Sterling doesn't mean she wants to be with you, I reminded myself. *You're here to give her the rosary, and that's it.*

But maybe just one touch, one touch before you give the rosary and say goodbye forever...

I got down on my own kneeler and reached forward, extended one finger, and then, when I was only an inch away from her skin, I murmured my name for her. "Lamb," I said. "Little lamb."

She stiffened right as my finger grazed the creamy skin of her neck, and she turned around, her mouth parted in an unbelieving *o*.

"Tyler," she whispered.

"Poppy," I said.

And then her eyes filled with tears.

I should have waited to see how she felt about me, I should have asked for consent to touch her, I know all these things. But she was crying now, crying so hard, and the only place she belonged was in my arms, and so I moved to her pew and pulled her into me.

She slid her arms around my waist, burying her face in my chest, her whole body trembling.

"How did you find me?" she managed.

"Sterling."

"You talked to Sterling?" she asked, pulling away, swiping at her eyes.

I ducked down to meet her gaze. "Yes. And he told me what happened that day. The day you kissed—" and my own resolve failed here, because despite job changes and living on a different continent, seeing her now and remembering the hole carved in my chest the moment I saw her kiss Sterling was too much for me to speak out loud.

She cried harder now. "You must hate me."

"No. In fact, I came to find you to tell you that I don't."

"I thought I had to, Tyler," she mumbled, looking down at the floor.

"Had to what?"

"I thought I had to make you leave me," she whispered.

Even my pulse paused to listen. "What?"

Her eyes were raw with pain and guilt. "I knew we could make it through anything Sterling threw at us, but I couldn't handle the thought of you leaving the clergy…leaving *for me.*" She looked at me, face pleading. "I couldn't live with myself if you had. Knowing that I had taken your vocation from you—your entire life—all because I couldn't control my feelings for you…"

"No, Poppy, it wasn't like that. I was there too, remember? I was choosing the same things you were; that mantle of guilt wasn't yours to bear alone, if at all."

She shook her head, tears still falling. "But if you'd never met me, you wouldn't have ever thought about leaving."

"If I'd never met you, I would never have really lived."

"Oh God, Tyler." She buried her face in her hands. "Knowing what you must have thought about me all these months. I hated it. I hated myself. The moment Sterling's lips touched mine, I wanted to die, because I saw you coming through the park, I knew you were there, and I knew you were hurting, but I had to. I wanted you to forget all about me and keep living your life the way God wanted you to."

"It hurt," I admitted. "It hurt a lot."

"I hated Sterling so much," she said into her hands. "I hated him as much as I loved you. I never wanted him, Tyler, I wanted you, but how could I have you without you losing everything? I told myself it was better to push you away than watch you wither."

I peeled her fingers away from her face. "Am I withered now? Because I did leave, Poppy, and not because of you and not because of the pictures Sterling released, but because I realized that God wanted me elsewhere, living a different life."

"You left?" she whispered. "I thought they made you leave when the pictures came out."

"I did. I thought...I guess I thought that you would know that."

"But the rumors...everyone said..." She took a deep breath, her eyes on me. "I just figured the pictures had ruined you. And it killed me knowing that it was partially my fault, because if it hadn't been for me, Sterling never would have targeted you. Knowing that split my heart in two, and I couldn't take it. I had no heart left to split. I missed you so much."

"I missed you." I pulled out the rosary and poured the beads into a clinking pile in her palm. "I brought this back for you," I said, curling her fingers around the rosary. "I want you to have it. Because I forgive you."

That's not the whole truth, Tyler.

I took a deep breath. "And there's more. I was so hurt—gutted—by what you did. And I'm angry with you now, for doing something that only brought both of us pain. You should have talked to me, Poppy, you should have told me how you felt."

"I tried," she said. "I tried so many times, but it was like you didn't hear me, like you didn't understand. I needed you to forget about me so that I didn't ruin your life."

I sighed. She was right. She had tried to tell me. And I had been so caught up in our love, so caught up in my own struggles and my own choices, that I hadn't really listened to her. "I'm sorry," I said, meaning those two words more than any person ever has before. "I'm so sorry. I should have listened. I should have told you that it didn't matter what happened with my job, with us, because in the end, I believe God is looking out for you and me. I believe God has a plan for us. And wherever I go—wherever we go—and no matter what awful things happen, we'll be comforted by His love."

She nodded, tears streaming down her cheeks. And something happened then, an infusion or an awakening, because I realized something.

I still want her.

I still love her.

I still need to be with her for the rest of my life.

And even though it made no sense, even though it was only a few minutes ago that I'd found out she and Sterling weren't together, had never been together, I still did it. I still lowered myself to one knee on the floor.

"That day, I was on my way to propose to you. And if you'll have me, I still want to marry you, Poppy. I don't have a ring. I don't have money. I don't even have a real job right now. But all I know is that you are the single most amazing person God has ever put in my path, and the thought of a life without you breaks my heart."

"Tyler…" she breathed.

"Marry me, lamb. Say yes."

She glanced down at the rosary and then looked back up to me. And her clear, tearful *yes* reached my ears about the same time her lips reached mine, her mouth greedy and jubilant and desperate, and I didn't care where we were or who might see us, I unzipped my jeans, yanked her pants down to her knees, and brought her wet heat against my cock, grinding against her, half wrestling and half tumbling to the narrow space of floor between the pews until I could knee her legs apart and push my way inside.

It was short and rough and loud, but it was perfect, just me and Poppy and God in his tabernacle standing watch over us both. I wanted this woman for all eternity, and I wanted eternity to start as soon as fucking possible.

EPILOGUE

POPPY

Your hand is clapped over my mouth as your other hand digs under layers of lace and tulle to find my pussy—bare at your request. Bare precisely for this moment.

Outside, the guests are beginning to filter into the church, a Catholic church despite my parents' playful protests, and in exchange for having a Catholic wedding, they extracted from us a grudging acceptance to let them throw the lavish affair they wanted to throw for their princess—fireworks and gallons of champagne and strings of lights under a starry Rhode Island sky.

But I'm nobody's princess right now. I'm a panting lamb, squirming as your fingers find my clit—already ripe and swollen—and pinch it, gently. There are thousands of dollars of designer lace and silk pooled around my waist and I want you to rip it all off, expose my garter and stockings and naked cunt to the air. But you don't.

Instead, you murmur in my ear, "You did as you were told. Good lamb." You drop your hand from my mouth to cup my breast.

I lean back against you. "Isn't there something about not seeing the bride before the wedding?"

"It's bad luck, they say, but I think starting married life with a fuck is nothing but lucky, don't you?"

We're in a small chapel off the main room, with a screened window that opens onto the sanctuary. It's difficult to see inside and we've locked the thin wooden door, but it does nothing to muffle the sounds, and as quiet as I am, there's no mistaking the rustle of my dress and my frantic breathing as your fingers move past my clit to the wet folds of my cunt.

Then you spin me around, drinking me in with hungry green eyes. You shaved this morning, your square jaw smooth and stubble-free, and even though I know your mother fussed over your hair earlier, a few stray locks have fallen over your forehead. I reach to tug on them but you catch my wrist in your hand before I do. Not necessarily to stop me, but so you can yank me closer to you, making the delicate skin of my pussy rub against your tuxedo pants. I feel your erection there–a hot, rigid length–and I moan.

The hand comes over my mouth again, and your

normally smiling face is serious. "One more noise, Mrs. Bell," you hiss in my ear, "and it will be your ass I'm fucking instead."

Is that supposed to be a punishment? "I'm not Mrs. Bell yet," I tease.

"But you still belong to me."

There's no arguing that. I've belonged to you since the first time I sat down in your confession booth.

The dress–a v-necked affair belted at the waist and skirted with a layer of fine, gauzy tulle–is a cloud around my hips, and it blocks my view of your hand reaching down to free your cock. Then your arm is sliding past my waist to my legs and I'm being half lifted, half shoved into the wall.

I feel the wide head of your cock notching into my folds, and you don't give me a moment to catch my breath, you simply pierce me without preamble, and I'm trying so hard not to moan, but it's so delicious, you in your tux and my wedding dress hiked up like a teenager's dress in a prom hotel and your hand so firm and insistent against my mouth as you pound into me with rough, uncaring strokes.

"All those people out there," you breathe, "they have no idea you're so close to them, getting fucked so hard. Fucked in your wedding dress, like a little whore who can't help herself."

My heart is pounding like a bird in a cage–fast and fluttery–and my inner thighs are tensing against the abrasive fabric of your tuxedo pants. I've long since stopped trying to figure out why I like it so much when you call me these names, especially since outside of the bedroom you are so unfailingly respectful and adoring. Maybe it's the naughty-priest-vibe that your new academic career hasn't been able to strip away from you, or maybe it's that you're such a **good** person and it's thrilling to see you lose control and act more like a sinner than a saint. Whatever it is, it drives me crazy, and you know it, and you whisper all sorts of awful things in my ear, *take it* and *dirty fucking girl* and *come for me, you better fucking come for me*.

I do, my moans swallowed by your hand, as you continue to pump into me, each thrust pinning me harder against the wall, and each thrust drawing my climax further and further out, and then you look up and meet my eyes. You're so close, and I think of all the times we've screwed, of all the times I've woken to your mouth flickering hot and wet between my legs, all the times where it felt like we'd fucked each other right out of the real, ordinary world and into someplace new and shimmering and magical. I feel like that now, actually, as I search your gaze, and watch you bite your lip as you fight to hold it back.

"Si vis amari, ama," you tell me. If you wish to be loved, love.

Words we'd exchanged what feels like a million years ago.

It was your love that had brought us back together, your unflagging love that lasted through my deception and my seclusion. I'd thought I was making the right sacrifices for you to be with God, but I'd been wrong the whole time. Now we are both with God and we are together, giving up our individual lives today to fuse into one eternal soul.

No greater love than this... I think dreamily as you lose all control now, your hand moving from my mouth to my other leg so you can hold me up and open as you chase your release, your dark head nestled into my neck, kissing and biting.

"Te amo," you're saying in my ear. Latin for I love you. *"Te amo, te amo, te amo."*

Fuck, I love you too, and then you're coming so hard, your whole body is shuddering and your hands digging into my stockinged thighs, and your climax sends another orgasm chasing through me. Together we pulse, like a shared heartbeat, like the powerful waves of a single ocean, until we come down together with a sigh.

Somewhere in the church, an organ starts to play something pretty and light, walking-in-and-finding-a-seat music. My bridesmaids and mother are probably panicking.

You set me down and use the silk handkerchief in your tuxedo pocket to clean the traces of you from my legs. Then you fold it back up and replace it in your pocket–from the outside, perfectly clean and tidy, but we both know what's hidden inside. "Just a little reminder," you tell me with a dimpled smile, patting the pocket.

"A trophy, you mean."

You don't refute this, still grinning your adorable Irish grin as you help me rearrange my dress and straighten the cathedral-length veil.

You look down at your palm, stained with my lipstick, and your lips part and your eyes darken. I swear I can see you get hard again. "You might want to check on your makeup," you say, and your eyes linger around my mouth. I have to push you away though, because if you kiss me again, I won't be able to say no, and then we'll be late for our own wedding.

"What should we tell them we were doing?"

You are now all zipped up and rearranged too, looking totally composed save for the possessive glint in your eyes. "It's a chapel. We'll say that we were praying."

"Think they'll believe us?"

Irish grin again. "Well, I was a priest once, you know."

I think about this as the rest of the day unfolds, as my lipstick is freshened and then my father walks me down the aisle, and as I see you blinking back tears when Dad places my hand in yours. As we take communion, both of us remembering a very different kind of communion shared between us. And then as you kiss me, deep and long and searchingly, a kiss that make my cunt wet and nipples hard, even in the house of God.

You were a priest once.

I still mourn that sometimes, but I realize now that what we have together is just as holy, just as profound. Someday, we will start a family. We will be creating life together, which is perhaps the most God-like thing any human can do, and I wonder, as we dance together under the gentle May sky, if we will have a son.

Maybe he'll become a priest too.

THE END.

ACKNOWLEDGMENTS

Priest is a bit of a special book for me. It's my first contemporary romance, my first standalone, and definitely my first time writing about a holy man! I couldn't have done it without the incredible support of my readers and my favorite bloggers—chiefly the Dirty Laundry and Literary Gossip crew. You girls are so patient with me juggling multiple personalities while also being a hermit crab. I love you.

Priest would also not be here without my early readers and critique partners, Laurelin Paige (my sometimes bedmate and always soulmate), Melanie Harlow (Father Bell's biggest fan), and Kayti McGee (who kept me encouraged with her dimpled enthusiasm.)

It would also not be here without the bleeping fantastic editing of Tamara Mataya and the sage advice of Geneva Lee, not to mention the ladies who Order me around.

And finally, this book would not be here without the sexy, patient man I'm married to, who perfected every type of Hamburger Helper to feed our kids while I wrote this book.

ALSO BY SIERRA SIMONE

The Priest Series:

Priest

Midnight Mass: A Priest Novella

Sinner

Saint

Thornchapel:

A Lesson in Thorns

Feast of Sparks

Harvest of Sighs

Door of Bruises

Misadventures:

Misadventures with a Professor

Misadventures of a Curvy Girl

Misadventures in Blue

The New Camelot Trilogy:

American Queen

American Prince

American King

The Moon (Merlin's Novella)

American Squire (A *Thornchapel* and *New Camelot* Crossover)

Co-Written with Laurelin Paige

Porn Star

Hot Cop

The Markham Hall Series:

The Awakening of Ivy Leavold

The Education of Ivy Leavold

The Punishment of Ivy Leavold (now including the novella *The Reclaiming of Ivy Leavold)*

The London Lovers:

The Seduction of Molly O'Flaherty (now bundled with the novella *The Persuasion of Molly O'Flaherty)*

The Wedding of Molly O'Flaherty

ABOUT THE AUTHOR

Sierra Simone is a USA Today bestselling former librarian who spent too much time reading romance novels at the information desk. She lives with her husband and family in Kansas City.

Sign up for her newsletter to be notified of releases, books going on sale, events, and other news!

www.thesierrasimone.com
thesierrasimone@gmail.com

CPSIA information can be obtained
at www.ICGtesting.com
Printed in the USA
LVHW040313180122
708312LV00004B/4